CORNELIUS

Book One: Germania

By

Richard C. Peele

ISBN: 1-4140-0553-9 (e-book)
ISBN: 1-4140-0554-7 (Paperback)

This book is printed on acid free paper.

1stBooks - rev. 11/18/03

Book One: Germania

I will send an Angel before you to keep you in the way and to bring you into the place, which I have prepared.
   Exodus 23:20

The battle raged all across the countryside and more men died because of the forest than were killed by the sword.
   2 Samuel 18:8

Dedication

For my brother Brian; Your help and encouragement means more to me than you will ever know.

For Beth whose enthusiasm and excitement for the story of Cornelius gave me the confidence and endurance to finish it.

And to my wife Anne whose presence and love is tangible in every page.

Table of Contents

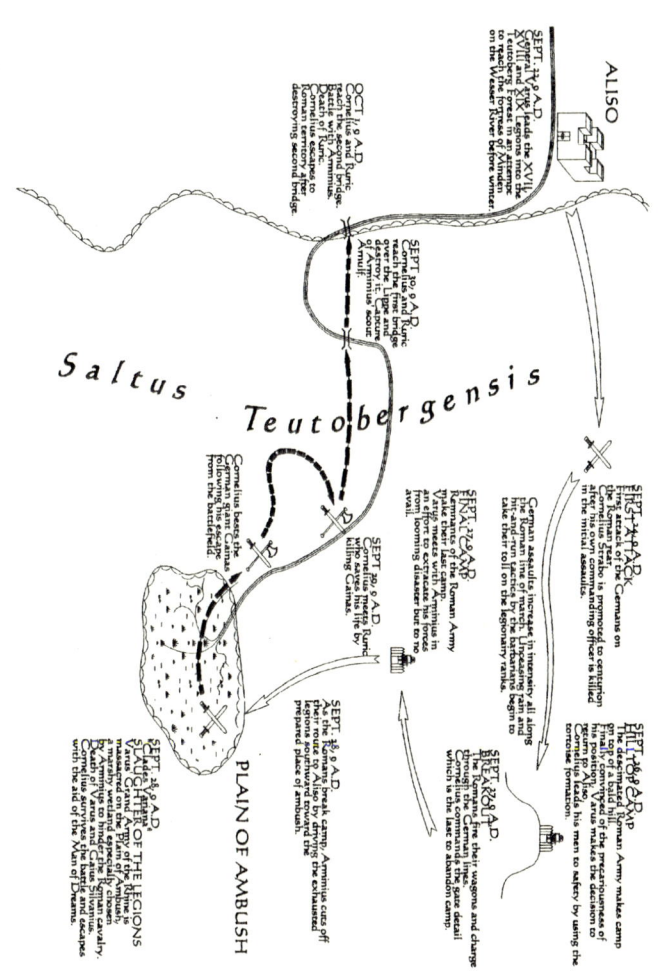

ALISO

SEPT. 11, 9 A.D. General Varus leads the XVIIth, XVIIIth, and XIXth Legions into the Teutoberg Forest in an attempt to reach the fortress of Minden on the Weser River before winter.

OCT. 11, 9 A.D. Cornelius and Runic reach the second bridge. Battle with Arminius. Death of Runic. Cornelius escapes to Roman territory after destroying second bridge.

SEPT. 19, 9 A.D. Cornelius and Runic reach the first bridge over the Lippe and destroy it. Capture of Arminius' scout, Arnulf.

Saltus Teutobergensis

FIRST ATTACK First attack of the Germans on the Roman rear. Cornelius Scipio is promoted to centurion after his own commanding officer is killed in the initial assaults.

German assaults increase in intensity all along the Roman line of march. Unceasing rain and hit-and-run tactics by the barbarians begin to take their toll on the legionary ranks.

SECOND CAMP The decimated Roman Army makes camp on top of a bald hill. Finally convinced of the precariousness of his position, Varus makes the decision to turn. Cornelius leads his men to safety by using the tortoise formation.

FINAL CAMP Remnants of the Roman Army make their last camp. Varus meets with Arminius in an effort to extricate his forces from looming disaster but to no avail.

SEPT. 20, 9 A.D. Cornelius meets Runic who saves his life by killing Cainas.

SEPT. 9 A.D. As the Romans break camp, they take their wagons and charge through the German lines. Cornelius commands the gate detail which is the last to abandon camp.

BREAKOUT As the Romans break camp, Arminius cuts off their route to Aliso by driving the exhausted legions southward toward the prepared place of ambush.

SEPT. 9 A.D. Cornelius battles the German giant Cainas following his escape from the battlefield.

SEPT. 9 A.D. SLAUGHTER OF THE LEGIONS On the Plain of Ambush, the legions are massacred by Arminius and especially chosen cavalry. Death of Varus and Caius Silvanius. Cornelius survives the battle and escapes with the aid of the Man of Dreams.

PLAIN OF AMBUSH

I

The sound was like that of distant thunder.

The primordial woodlands of the quasi-Roman territory of Germania Inferior in late August of this the thirty-fifth year of the principate of Gaius Julius Augustus Caesar lay prostrate beneath a blanket of suffocating heat. No breeze stirred the roof of the great forest stretching like a living wall from horizon to horizon. Nor did it lift the drooping crowns of thistle and golden rod that ran in a sundering band along the rim of the ancient wood. Above the sweltering landscape the silhouette of a wheeling hawk pressed itself against the breathless height of the summer sky. Gliding past the edge of the forest wall, the great bird of prey caught the lip of a funnel of warm air pushing up from the sun-baked fields below and using it as leverage, began to drift back toward the forest rooftop. No sooner had its shadow begun to skim back across the leafy denseness of the forest canopy when the hawk suddenly pulled up shrieking. From somewhere inside the recesses of the forest its keen ears had picked out the tell-tale jangling of bit and bridle. *Men! Blundering through the forest on their great slathering beasts!! There would be no likelihood of food as long as such creatures were about!* Petulantly, the hawk angled its long powerful wings against the rising thermal and banked away from the clamor in the wood flying toward the far line of tall trees that marked the boundary of the Great River. Before long the rumble of hooves grew louder and more insistent until it threatened to overwhelm even the ubiquitous drone of the day's dying katydids.

Suddenly, a column of armored horsemen burst through the face of the forest wall with such force that their passage threw a cloud of dust and underbrush up into the stultified air. The riders, twenty in all, rode in single file under a discipline learned from the legionary camps of Rome. Grim faces stared out from beneath the heavy rims of their distinctive brass helmets, each cunningly fashioned with embossed brow plates and cheek pieces. Upon their crowns, mounted in molded boxes of the Greek style, grew plumes of scarlet-dyed horsehair, proclaiming their membership to the cavalry cohorts of the Praetorian Guard, personal bodyguard to the Emperor himself. Heavy red military cloaks billowed out behind them as they rode, revealing bodies sheathed in the gorgeous lines of muscled cuirasses and tight-fitting greaves. They carried neither shield nor javelin, preferring to sacrifice power for the economy of speed. They were armed with only short sword and dagger, oiled and ready in scabbards of red leather and brass and worn on studded shoulder straps that crisscrossed against their armored torsos. So perfect was their discipline that not a single word passed between them. Only the sound of horses' hooves pounding into the soft turf mixing with the metallic clattering of weapons against body armor served to mark their passage.

Thankful to have left the cloying dimness of the tangled forest behind them, both horse and rider found their spirits rise at the sight of the wide vista of wild fields opening up before them. Inured to the open geography of the plains, the cavalryman had a natural distrust for woodlands and marshes, attributes that Germania possessed in abundance. In such places, the natural advantage of the horse in transport and in battle was negated. Indeed, the fear of all cavalry is to lose its ability to move and maneuver in the open. Once confined into narrow spaces, cavalry were easy prey from attack by slower moving infantry. For the Romans, it had been a bitter lesson learned at such evil fields as Carrhae and Mundus. So it was that these men, who possessed the natural apprehension of all their kind, picked their way along the barely discernable tracks that twisted and turned across the uneven floor of Thuringian forest. More than once the riders caught themselves looking furtively behind them as if sensing a malevolent presence snapping at their heels. They had all heard the stories, noised about by Druid priests in the villages and hamlets of northern Gaul and southern Germania, of the unspeakable death that awaited every Roman who was unfortunate enough to find himself lost in the shadowy realm of a Druid forest. For that reason they silently prayed as they rode, calling on the protection of the gods against any strange enchantments that might be lurking behind the fallen tree or tumbled stone. To a man they were heartily grateful when the trees abruptly ended and the welcome vista of sun-washed fields opened in front of them.

Riding farther out into the meadows, they could see on their left the wall of oak, ash and pine winding its way toward the western horizon where the late afternoon sun was already beginning to throw long shadows along their path. On their right, distant mountains tinged with hues of Tyranean purple and crowned with summits of eternal snow, peaked out above the fringe of the ubiquitous forest. Ahead of them lay the gray band of the River Rhine, the Father of Northern Rivers, the object of their journey.

With the sun on their left now sinking down into the purple folds of a line of distant hills, the troop of horsemen continued their progress due north toward the far end of the plain. There the Rhine had slashed an angular slit across fields heavy with overgrown thickets of thistle, foxglove and goldenrod. For some time they continued their pace, steady and uninterrupted, not even pausing when a pair of startled pheasants erupted from the grass in front of them. Soon the silhouette of a tall mound, like an island, appeared among the waving grasses, growing steadily in size as they drew near to it. They were not a hundred stadia from the odd hill when the lead rider held up and his hand and reigned in his mount, a signal for the escort to halt. Turning back along the waiting line of men and horses, he rode to the middle of the column where an officer sat astride a mare of mottled gray and white. Pounding a fist against his armored shoulder, the rider saluted the man and waited.

Publius Quinctilius Varus, legatus pro praetore of the newly consigned province of Germania, sniffed the humid air and sneezed.

"Wretched country!" he wheezed, pulling a silk handkerchief from his belt and blowing his nose. Varus, an officious man of fifty had until recently held the luxurious post of governor of the rich eastern province of Syria. He might be there still enjoying the sensuous pleasures of the Orient were it not for the fact that he had managed to contract a marriage to the grand niece of the great Augustus in order to further his career. His opportunity was not long in coming. When it came it did so in the unlikely form of the dour Tiberius Nero, commander of the Rhine armies and stepson of the Emperor himself. At the very moment that Varus was binding himself to the Imperial family, Tiberius was fuming in Germany from an imagined slight at the hands of his stepfather. In a fit of pique, Tiberius angrily resigned his commission and retired to sulk amidst the indolent philosophers and scholars of Rhodes, leaving the Emperor scrambling to appoint a successor. Since it was Augustus' practice to keep sensitive army commands within the jurisdiction of his own family in order to ensure loyalty to the Julian dynasty of which he was the head, he had little trouble in finding a suitable candidate. A spotless if unspectacular record in Syria kept Varus in good stead with Augustus. And once he had become a member of the family, Augustus had little qualms in naming Varus to the post. The fact that it was the Praetorians who were escorting him to the German frontier was an indication of the change in his fortunes. The Guard never strayed far from their appointed precincts in Rome and Italy unless under the pretext of accompanying the Emperor and members of his immediate family.

The man himself was typical of his class. The puffy skin surrounding pale blue eyes and the veined jowls hanging on the neck bespoke a life of privilege spent in the consuming pursuit of power and pleasure in equal portion. Thin wisps of graying hair, sporting in places the original color of youth, were repeated again in the line of the brow. The head was enclosed in a magnificent black helmet, embossed with silver tracings of laurel leaves and crowned by a glorious plumage of black ostrich feathers. The body, flabby and shapeless from years of dissolute living in Rome and the Orient, was hidden beneath the exquisite confines of his muscle cuirass. Like the helmet, it too was the color of polished ebony. Yet whereas the art applied to the helmet was restrained in its application, no such care appeared to have been taken with the accompanying cuirass. Gaudy portraits from the pantheon of Roman religion filled every space of the breastplate: Jupiter Optimus enthroned and crowned on the right breast, representing the power of the Roman state and the goddess Roma on the left, over the heart, reflecting the divine incarnation of the spirit of the City on the Tiber. But as lovely as the armorer's art had made the cuirass, Varus was never comfortable in it. It always made him sweat profusely. It had never occurred to him that the northern sun could shine with the same ferocity as that of its Syrian cousin. His misery was further compounded by the sweaty dampness of his black, knee-length tunic that clung in clammy pockets to his skin. The dark legate's cloak, pinned at the shoulders by a chain of polished gold, seemed to hold all the raging fires of Hades in its folds.

Pulling a bronze flask of water from his saddlebag, Varus tipped it back and took a deep draught. Wiping the back of his mouth with his hand, he grumbled with disgust, "Who would have imagined a German forest to be hotter than the deserts of Syria?" Removing his helmet, Varus wiped the sweat from his sodden face and neck with his handkerchief. "How much farther to Castra Vetera, tribune?" he asked the officer waiting beside him.

The tribune, a handsome, dark-eyed young Latin named Gaius Silvanius shook his head. "No more than an hour's ride, Excellency."

Varus nodded and surveyed the mound in front of them. He noticed that it was not a natural formation but a hill constructed by human hands. A stone path had been cut into the mound's sloping sides, winding its way up from the floor of the plain to the summit. The crown of the hill had been sheered away and leveled suggesting that at some time past it had been used as a fortification or signal station. But all that could be seen now was the tumbled ruin of an old stone tower.

"What is this place, tribune?" asked Varus.

"It is called Bellatorix's Tor, the tower of Bellatorix."

"Bellatorix? Who is he?"

"An ancient king of the Celtic folk who used to dwell in these lands. It is said that he was suspicious of his subjects so he ordered this hill to be raised where he built a high stone tower to watch them from his window. The story relates how one day while watching through the highest window of the tower, he spied a beautiful shepherd girl passing by the foot of his hill with her flock. Unfortunately, he forgot where he was, so intent was he to catch a glimpse of the girl that he leaned out too far and fell to his death. But the stones you see are not of the original tower but one constructed by the great Julius during his campaign against the Usipetes and the Tencteri."

Varus grunted. "An interesting story to be sure, tribune, but I am more interested in the reason for stopping here. I am eager to make camp before nightfall."

Silvanius licked his lips as if preparing himself for an unpleasant task. "Unfortunately, Excellency, we must halt here for the moment."

Varus halted the flask half way to his parched mouth. "Halt? Why?"

"We must wait for someone to arrive."

"Wait for someone to arrive? Wait for whom? Why was I not informed of this? Just who is so important that he must inconvenience the legate of the army of the Rhine?"

"His name is Segestes," explained Silvanius shielding his eyes against the lowering sun while scanning the line of the horizon. "He is a chieftain of the Cherusci."

"Just who in the infernal name of Hades are the Cherusci?"

"They are a tribe from the far side of the Rhine."

"Barbarians?" exploded Varus, nearly choking on a mouthful of water. "I demand an explanation, tribune or by the gods I will have you in chains before the hour is out!"

Since he first drew the assignment to escort the new governor-general of Germany to his command, Silvanius had dreaded this moment. In the fortnight since they had left Rome, he had played it out in his mind of how he would handle the situation when it arose. Varus was a novice when it came to the politics of the northern world; Silvanius was not. He had served in the campaigns of both Drusus and his brother Tiberius when they had originally stabilized northern Gaul by establishing the empire's boundaries on the west bank of the Rhine River. He had eaten with, marched with, talked with, and slain many of the barbarians that Augustus now intended to incorporate into the Empire. He understood their minds, their loves and hates, their passions and their desires. Indeed, he had received his promotion to the Praetorian Guard because of his exemplary service in Germany. It was no passing coincidence therefore that the Emperor chose him to escort Varus to the headquarters of the Rhine legions at Castra Vetera. By doing so, Augustus hoped Silvanius might educate and illuminate Varus' understanding of the world he was now expected to pacify. But just in case Varus proved to be a stubborn pupil, the Emperor had given Silvanius leverage to ensure the legate did as he was told.

Removing a small, metallic cylinder from beneath his cuirass, the tribune passed it to Varus. "I trust the general recognizes the Emperor's seal." The governor general stared at the raised image of a sphinx with wings spread inside a laurel halo. "What is the meaning of this?" he demanded his watery eyes narrowing with suspicion.

"Read it, sir," replied Silvanius, "And all will be made clear to you."

Angrily, Varus snatched the cylinder from Silvanius' hand, snarling, "If you wish to keep your place in my command, tribune you will learn to curb your tongue."

Varus pulled at a small exposed tab on the side of the cylinder which revealed a scroll ingeniously wound around a spindle inside the cylinder. Stretching the miniature scroll to its full length he read the following:

Gaius Julius Augustus Caesar, imperator, to Tribune Gaius Silvanius, ala commander of the IV Calvary Cohort, Praetorian Guard;

Greetings.

It is with affection for your father and grateful remembrance for your services to the Senate and People of Rome that you are remembered by us. For that reason I am convinced that I may entrust to you a duty that by its very nature must remain secret. When you receive this you will have already been assigned to escort P. Quinctilius Varus to Castra Vetera to take command of the legions in Germany. Know that word has reached us that Segestes, a noble chief of the Cherusci desires to renew his pledge of loyalty to us and offer aid in the upcoming campaign in Germany. He has knowledge important to us of the locations of certain rebellious tribes who will need to be dealt with before the frontier can be stabilized. I am told that you are acquainted with this Segestes and thus would know him by sight. He has agreed to meet you at a place called Bellatorix's Tor two days before the Kalends of August. I am also told that you know this place well and will have no trouble in finding it.

I know, tribune that I may rely on you to carry out my instructions for I perceive that the noble blood of the father runs just as truly in the son. May the gods grant you success.

Augustus Caesar, Imp.

P.S. You may find Varus a bit obstinate in accommodating you in this. You have our permission to show this order to him, should you feel it necessary to the success of your mission.

Varus' face was livid as he threw the scroll back at Silvanius. "How dare he!" he hissed, "Am I a dog of a Syrian to be treated in such a fashion?"

The tribune shrugged and replaced the cylinder back beneath his cuirass. "Caesar is the Emperor and as such may do as he wills. As for this business with Segestes, your Excellency would not have been a suitable candidate to meet with him. As Caesar has said, I know the man and I know this to be the place of which his letter speaks. But if you need further proof, turn and see for it comes now."

Varus turned in the saddle and saw to their right from the direction of the distant tree line, a trio of riders closing quickly upon them. To a man like Varus whose experience of barbarian peoples was limited to only those he saw killed during an afternoon's sport in the arena, the initial sight of these men raised a sense of curiosity and admiration. Even from their distant vantage point, Varus could discern that they were all very similar in feature and dress. Long streams of flowing hair the color of burnished brass streamed out from behind each of the men as they rode. To keep their tresses from obscuring their vision, they wore braids held in place by ties of decorative silver that hung like twisted rope down the sides of their faces and the middle of their backs. Although it was the practice of the Germanic tribesmen to wear pleated and forked beards, these men were clean shaven in the Roman fashion. They were attired in knee-length tunics of wool, so favored by the people of the northern forests, stitched in a checkerboard of blue and white and gathered at the waist with leather belts and gold buckles. Despite the heat of the day, they wore tight fitting trousers of tanned deerskin to the ankle where their feet were clad in soft calfskin shoes and full calf leggings. A heavy cloak of dyed wool pinned at the right shoulder with large broaches depicting fanciful dragons from Celtic mythology, completed their dress. Around each neck flopped heavy torques of beaten gold, handsome trophies from past battles. They approached unarmed except for the long Germanic broadsword each carried at their side, the hilt partially obscured by the folds of the cloak but kept ever ready if needed.

Time seemed to slow in its course as the waiting Romans watched the newcomers draw near. They all experienced an involuntary inward shudder at the sight of these fair-haired giants astride their sturdy Teutonic mounts. Varus particularly was drawn to the middle horseman, who it could be seen, was a head taller than his companions. Boldly they came on, so hard in fact, that for a moment, it looked as if their intent was to actually crash through the Roman column. But within a stone's throw of the Romans, the Germans pulled fiercely on the bridles of their horses, bringing them to a whinnying halt.

For a few tense moments, Roman and barbarian glared at one another in the spirit of the long enmity between the two races. Then to the surprise of all save Silvanius, the enormous German who rode in the middle said in perfect Latin, "Which of you is Tribune Silvanius?"

"I am he," responded Silvanius.

"And I am his commanding officer!" cried Varus, edging his own horse past the tribune's and placing himself between Silvanius and the barbarians. "And anything that is to be spoken between us will be through me."

The German stared at Varus with mild amusement. "I am aware of who you are, General Varus, legate of the Rhine legions and governor of the Roman province of Germania, if such a thing exists. But my instructions come directly from your Emperor and they are to treat with Tribune Silvanius directly."

The barbarian's words seemed to strike Varus like a fist. His mouth hung half open with disbelief. The barbarian seemed surprisingly well informed. Too informed for Varus' liking.

It was Silvanius who retrieved the situation. Wading into the awkward breech he asked the German, "Is it the illustrious Segestes, chief of the Cherusci, I have the honor of addressing?"

Segestes unveiled a smile of perfect white teeth, "It is indeed, good tribune. It has been many moons since last I saw your face but I have not forgotten it. Nor the pleasant times you spent amongst us when Drusus of fair memory last campaigned against the Chatti. My heart sang when word reached me that it was you I was to meet. I pray to the gods that we would have those times again."

Silvanius bowed graciously and replied, "I was not sure my lord remembered me, since many years have passed since last we parted. It pleases me that my lord's memories of those days are pleasant ones. But if my lord pleases, who are these men with you, although one I think was a young boy when last I saw him. Tell me this is not the young Arminius in your midst?"

The young man Arminius returned a slight bow from his saddle. "I am honored the tribune remembers me," he offered in flawless Latin, couched in a voice both deep and melodious. But something about his manner and the defiant angle of his body astride his horse gave Silvanius a momentary prick of concern.

"And the other with me is Siegmyrgth or as you would call him Segimerus," continued Segestes, "A man of renown amongst the tribes of the north. Both these good men have served in the auxiliaries of Rome when Tiberius was last in Germany. I can vouch for both of them. They are loyal and trustworthy and ready to die in the service of Caesar."

Silvanius nodded but his attention was still on the impassive features of Arminius who did not flinch from the Roman's challenge. Silvanius strove to recall what he knew of the young German. When he was a boy he had been sent to Rome as a hostage by the late Drusus Caesar to ensure the behavior of his father who was a leading chief of the Cherusci. While in Rome Arminius had received the formal education of all young Romans which not only included immersion in Latin and Greek literature, science and history but also an intensive training in the martial arts of war. Arminius learned not only to think like a Roman, but to fight like one as well. He proved his meddle when he was awarded the command of an auxiliary cohort of his countrymen during the campaign of Tiberius some years before and distinguished himself as a gifted commander and leader of men. Those were the days when Silvanius knew him and fought along side him on the east bank of the Rhine. After his transfer to the Praetorians, Silvanius had lost all track of the young man. Until now.

Silvanius forced himself to turn from his silent skirmish with Arminius to address Segestes again. "I could not forgive myself if I did not ask after your daughter, the fair Thusnelda. When last I saw her she was but a slip of girl with the promise of great beauty to come."

At the mention of his daughter, Segestes' face clouded over as if fallen under the shadow of a painful memory. "It does not surprise me that you should ask of her since she had a girlish love for the tribune when last you dwelt in my house. But the girl has grown into a woman and the ways of women are a mystery to me."

The tribune did not fail to observe the change that came over Arminius at the mention of Segestes' daughter. The impassivity vanished like a mist, replaced by a look that could only be described as the dreamy stare of one who is desperately in love with the unattainable. *So*, thought Silvanius to himself, *Arminius is in love with her himself. Interesting. That may be of use to us in the future.*

"It saddens me to hear you speak so," replied Silvanius. "You must tell me how this sad state of affairs came about over a tankard of your best ale."

"Tribune!"

The voice of the legate, now recovered from his initial shock, rang out across the field. "Get back to your place!"

Without a word, Silvanius submitted to the discipline of his training and wheeled his horse back into line. Varus, satisfied that the issue of command had been reestablished, now spoke directly to Segestes.

"Now I will have my say. I strongly disapprove of these arrangements made without my authorization or knowledge. I want it clearly understood that I am in command here and that I will not tolerate another incident like this one. If it were not for the fact that the Emperor himself was its architect I would, without hesitation, terminate this meeting and have you all thrown in irons as enemies of Rome."

"You cannot do that, general," interjected Segestes, "We are citizens of Rome."

"You?" spat Varus, "Citizens of Rome? I think not! You are barbarians!"

"Barbarians we may be but also Roman citizens. We have all served under the eagles of your Auxilia under the princes of the House of Caesar. Augustus himself awarded us the scrolls of citizenship with his own hand."

"As with all barbarians, you lie with the ease of your race!"

"There are many who say that Rome has lied, general, promising peace with one hand while bringing war with the other. And most of them are not citizens."

"How dare you question the policies of the Emperor and people of Rome!" demanded Varus imperiously.

"I dare anything that does not bring life but death. It is the reason why I am willing to turn my back on my own people so that in doing so, I might save them. And you. If wanting to dwell in my own lands in my own house with my own family makes me an enemy of Rome than I proudly declare my enmity."

The sensibility of Segestes' argument sobered Varus' anger. Listlessly waving a hand, he said, "Of course, Rome wants peace. We desire to live in peace with our neighbors as much as any people. It is, in truth, the gift we offer the world. But peace comes only when those who bring it are strong and our strength is carried on the javelins of the legions. By Caesar's will, I now command the legions on the Rhine and therefore I command Germany. And if I command Germany, I command you. So this is my instruction to you: you will follow my orders and my orders only. I will be the sole arbiter of the importance of any information you may bring to us and whether we will use it. When we reach Castra Vetera, you shall be under the authority of the Tribune Silvanius who will see to your immediate needs. And one thing further. I must insist you surrender your swords until I am convinced of your loyalty to Rome."

Now it was the turn of the Germans to be surprised. Instinctively, the hands of all three men went to the hilts of their weapons. If Varus had understood the Teutonic mind, he would have realized that his demand was akin to asking them to mutilate themselves. The sword of the barbarian was like a second appendage. He would sooner lose an arm or leg then be separated from the cold presence of forged steel at his side. It was his friend, his protector, his very life, dear to him as any child and cherished more than any wife. To their swords they ascribed mystical powers, believing them to actually be inhabited by all manner of spirit or demon, birthed in the dark heart of their forest home. They were as individual as any man, named with a name that reflected its very nature. Before the sons of the woodland could even walk or talk, he was taught to entrust his life to his sword.

An ominous silence descended upon the meadow, broken only by the distant buzzing of the katydid in the treetops and the snorting of the agitated horses. Arminius and Segimerus looked at one another and then to Segestes, unsure of what to do. To obey the officious legate might be prudent, given the disparity of numbers between themselves and the Romans, but it would only be done at the cost of emasculating their pride as men. To refuse would be to invite death, however glorious, for it would undoubtedly lead to an armed confrontation. They had not come to fight the Romans like this; they would leave that to their foolish brethren who believed they could actually throw off the Latin yoke with shield and axe. They had come for a different purpose.

The dangerous moment might have exploded in fury if not for the quick thinking of Silvanius. "Excellency!" he shouted from the waiting ranks of horsemen as they braced for the order to unsheathe their swords, "Do you dare ignore the will of Caesar without consequence?" Holding the cylinder with Augustus' orders high above his head, he went on, "These men have the favor of the Emperor and are under his protection. They have served as our comrade-in-arms in battles past and have lived in our camps as honored allies and friends of Rome. And for their loyalty they have been made citizens of Rome. Heed my words, Excellency! If blood is spilt here today, it will be the blood of citizens of Rome!"

Varus turned and sneered at Silvanius. "You forget yourself, tribune. What would you have me do? If they are citizens as they claim and as you say, then they will obey the authority placed over them by Caesar and deliver their swords."

"We will not surrender our swords," replied Segestes grimly. "We have brought them to add to your own and offer our services once again to the cause of Rome." Sliding his sword from its scabbard, Segestes held it at arm's length, an action that produced an immediate reaction from the Praetorians. In the blink of an eye, their own blades were out their sheaths and brought to the ready. But battle was not on Segestes' mind. Fixing his eyes to Varus', he spoke an oath. "On my honor as a citizen of Rome and friend of Caesar, I pledge my sword and those of my companions to the service of Augustus Caesar and to his noble servant, Quinctilius Varus!" In keeping with the custom of his people, Segestes spit on the flat of his blade, sealing his oath.

The ignorance of the legate involving the traditions and attitudes of those whom he was sent to govern blinded him to the gravity of Segestes' act. It served only to confuse him and push him into uncertainty. But again, it was Silvanius who retrieved the moment.

"Excellency!" he called once again. "As an officer of the Praetorian Guard, I too offer my pledge for the lives of these good men. If they should prove false in what they say or do, then my own life is forfeit."

"Very well," sighed Varus wearily, signaling for the escort to sheath their weapons. "I am satisfied. For the present. But I look to you all to hold your oaths. Now, if we have concluded our business here, you may give the order to move out."

As the column moved off in the direction of Castra Vetera, with the Germans in tow behind them, Silvanius caught a furtive glimpse of Arminius smirking behind his companions. It reminded him of nothing less than the predatory slavering of a wolf eyeing a flock of unsuspecting sheep.

Despite the heat, the thought chilled him and made him shudder.

II

"When did they arrive?"

"Last night. Just after mess."
"Who brought them in?"
"A tribune from the Praetorians. Silvanius I think his name was. But they didn't come alone. There were three barbarians with them."

"Barbarians?"

Eighteen-year-old infantryman Cornelius Strabo's eyes bulged wide with excitement. Like most Romans, his experience with the barbarian races clustered on the distant river frontiers of the Empire was restricted to the slave markets and the arena. The fact that the Emperor Augustus employed a large bodyguard of Gauls for his personal use only added to the mystique of the barbarian in the Roman psyche. As a child, Cornelius had been weaned on stories of heroic Romans of the past battling and overcoming marauding hosts of Celts and Germans bent on the destruction of their civilization. Indeed, it was for the very chance to cross swords with these fabled giants that Cornelius had enlisted with the legions.

"So what did they look like, Lucius?" he asked excitedly of his companion, an impish dark-haired Campanian from Neapolis named Lucius Bassanius. "I have heard that they are not like us at all. They say that the reason they do not wear armor in battle is because they grow scales like a lizard to protect themselves. I have even heard it said that they are not human at all but a race born from a union of Hades and a dragon of the underworld."

Bassanius looked up from the leather strap of the lorica he was repairing and grinned. He was not the usual conscript found throughout the Imperial legions. A product of the Archimedean school of Syracuse, he had been earmarked by his teachers for a career in the rarified strata of academics. But a soured relationship with a Sicilian peasant girl had caused him to enlist in the army instead. Three rigorous years under the colors had not only served to expunge the memory of his failed romance but had also dulled the keen edge of his youthful passions. Pragmatism over ideology had become his motto. And now as he looked into the eager face of his young charge, he saw a reflection of himself before the cares of a soldier's life had wrought its change. The eagerness to prove himself a man through the profession of arms was all but evident in young Cornelius. Bassanius remembered experiencing similar stirrings in his own breast before the rigors of hard campaigns in Pannonia and Germania had burned it out of him. He had earned his own mantle of manhood in the caldron of battle. The memory of the boy he had once been was now obliterated by the reality of the present man of war, a fate that would surely befall his friend Strabo before too long.

The thought produced a pang of regret in his breast for Cornelius and also, for himself. It had never occurred to him that maybe he had lost a part of himself when he willingly put off the child inside.

Perhaps, he thought, it is better not to forget entirely the excesses of youth. Perhaps one need only curb those things that dull the sharp edge of responsibility. After all, what is the harm of believing your enemy has scales? It is the kind of exaggeration that leads to unreasoning fear and fear can sometimes be a soldier's most effective protection.

Bassanius shook his head. *Lucius, you fool! Do you hear yourself, exchanging philosophy for truth? You're beginning to sound like those pompous rectors at the college. Do the boy a favor and speak plainly! Don't let him live on myths and old wives' tales told to frighten children into behaving.*

"Cornelius," he began, "You must not take to heart everything you hear, especially in the camps of the army. I would wager a hundred sesterces that the average Roman wouldn't know the difference between a German chieftain and an Arab sheik."

"Oh I would!" crowed Cornelius brightly causing Bassanius to laugh.

"Oh you would now would you? And how, by the hoary club of Hercules, would you accomplish that? Lift up the first barbarian kilt you see and check for scales?"

Cornelius tilted his head back and roared with laughter. "I might enjoy that if she happened to be a girl!"

Bassanius sought to turn the conversation from its frivolous course. "But seriously, my friend, pay heed to what I tell you. Barbarians are neither to be feared nor wondered at. They are flesh and blood men like you and I. Thrust with your sword and they will bleed and die the same as any other mortal. Surely you've seen enough of them in the arena to know that. But I have also faced them in battle and I tell you truly, I would rather put my faith in the stoutness of the Roman line then in the ferocity of the barbarian's charge. You would do well to remember that, my Cornelius, when first you hear that blood-chilling cry of imminent battle or watch them from afar as they mass their shield walls for an attack. But remember this: no army of Rome worthy of the name has ever been bested in battle by the barbarian. Never forget that."

Cornelius nodded silently, sobered by his friend's words. In reality, this was what he liked; this was what had fed his imagination as a boy growing up in the Bruttian port of Rhegium, tales of the invincibility of the legions of Rome. It was something his father would never have understood.

The elder Strabo was the harbormaster of the port city of Rhegium located on the Italian shore of the Straits of Messina. The position had become over the years, the personal fiefdom of the Strabo family. Not only was his father the current harbormaster but both his grandfather and great grandfather had held the post as well. So the elder Strabo could be forgiven for assuming that his son would naturally carry on the family tradition of directing nautical traffic and collecting the port dues for the ancient Greek colony. But he did not reckon the mettle of his strong-willed son or the possibility that he was cut from a different cloth. As he grew older, Cornelius began to disdain the fate that would ensure his imprisonment in the customs house of Rhegium. The horizon of Cornelius' world extended far beyond the suffocating provincialism of his hometown. Indeed for him a life sentence as a galley slave was more appealing than the prospect of spending the rest of his life as an insignificant Italian bureaucrat of a second-rate Latin town.

Even now, as he sat with Bassanius inside their company papilo, the long leather tent that housed eight legionaries and their gear, he recalled the stormy interview with his father when first he broached the subject of leaving. Naturally, his father, hurt by what he saw as his son's insensitive attitude, angrily refused to allow Cornelius to join the army. He loudly reminded him that he was duty-bound to fulfill his destiny as a member of the House of Strabo and become the harbormaster when his time came. Cornelius appealed to the aspiration of all parents to better the lives of their children even at the price of their traditions. The elder Strabo responded by arguing that the position of harbormaster was not only an important post to aspire to but an honorable one as well. And if Cornelius could not respect the wishes of his father and the call of filial duty than surly he should think of his poor mother. Would he allow the woman who gave him life to spend her remaining days in misery, never knowing whether her son was alive or dead upon some foreign battlefield in some God-forsaken country?

No. Cornelius certainly did not want that. So he agreed not to speak of his ambition again while his mother lived. That was in his sixteenth year. Barely a year followed before his precious mother suddenly took ill and died. With her passing, Cornelius no longer felt bound by the oath of silence to his father. The night after her funeral, while the house lay still with grief, Cornelius quietly packed a few belongings and under the cover of darkness, stole out from beneath his father's roof forever. He left neither a note nor a word of explanation to the old man (something he had since regretted) surmising that it would not be difficult for him to guess what had become of his wayward son. He wondered what would be more difficult for his father to absorb: the loss of both his wife and son or the fact that the next harbormaster of Rhegium would not be a Strabo.

Making his way northward along the paved highway of the Via Pompilia as it passed through the coastal flatlands of the Silan Plain northwest of the spine of mountains of the same name, he followed it to it's conclusion at the city of Salerum at the base of the Bay of Naples. Journeying on the old coastal road that hugged the wild and beautiful shoreline of the Bay of Naples, Cornelius passed through the famous cities of Campania until at last he came to Capua, the city of gladiators. It was while in Capua that he happened to overhear in a local tavern a piece of news that changed his life. Recruiters from Rome had recently entered the city to seek out recruits to fill a quota for three new legions that would eventually see action in the far north. Early the next day in the forum of the city, Cornelius presented himself in front of the recruiting tables erected to one side of the Temple of Castor and Pollux. With youthful elation, he affixed his name to the document of enlistment. Six months of strict training followed. Fundamentals of weapons, tactics and discipline were instilled into him by grim parade centurions until they became second nature. It succeeded in transforming the boy from Rhegium into a legionary of Rome.

Such thoughts, as they were, of a home barely remembered and a future dimly perceived were interrupted by the grumbling arrival of a third soldier into the papilo. Gaius Fibrius, a broad shouldered, bull-necked Spaniard from Saguntum, pushed his way past the two friends and flopped down onto his cot. Unlike Bassanius and Strabo who were enjoying a few hours respite from duty, Fibrius was still clad in his cuirass and helmet, having just completed a stint of picket duty outside the wooden palisade of Castra Vetera. Loosening the drawstrings under his chin, the Spaniard pulled the helmet from his head and flung it with a gesture of disgust beneath his bunk. Swinging his legs up on to the bed, Fibrius stretched himself out with a sigh and covered his eyes with a brawny forearm.

"Aren't you going to take your breastplate off, Gaius?" asked Bassanius.

"Too tired," grunted the Spaniard in reply. Bassanius and Cornelius exchanged a knowing glance between them. When men come together to share living quarters, they quickly learn the characteristics and idiosyncrasies of their companions. It is nature's way of ensuring tranquility and cooperation inside an impossible situation. Fibrius, they had quickly discovered, was a high strung and taciturn individual who, because of his size and temperament, was best left alone to sulk in his corner of the tent. More often than not, the men of this particular papilo found themselves making allowances for the brooding Spaniard whenever they could. All, that is, except Bassanius who seemed to take a perverse pleasure in making Fibrius the butt of his jokes.

Cornelius looked down at his feet to the nudging at his ankle and discovered that Fibrius' helmet had managed to roll under his own cot. Picking it up and turning it idly in his hands, he asked, "A difficult picket, Gaius?"

The Spaniard offered another low grunt. "Difficult enough," he growled, "No thanks to that bastard Fetch Another."

'Fetch Another' was the nickname of the unsavory primus pilus of the Nineteenth Legion, Sextus Pompilius. It was generally conceded by those who served under him that never in the glorious history of the Roman legions was there ever a more unworthy candidate for the office of senior centurion. A drunkard, a bully and a braggart, Pompilius was seen to possess every vice capable of attaching itself to the human race. It could be rightly said that the men under his authority would rather face the fury of a full charge of heavy Parthian cavalry without shield or pilum than suffer the injuries of Pompilius' idea of discipline. So twisted was his concept of administering the punishments associated with keeping order in the ranks that it had led to him being tagged with the name 'Fetch Another' because of his habit of beating the backs of offenders with whippet branches of willow and birch until they broke and calling out "Fetch me another!" And although Bassanius and Strabo had so far managed to avoid the displeasure of the malevolent centurion, Fibrius seemed to be centered out for special attention by Pompilius. He never seem to tire of finding fault with the big Spaniard.

"So what happened this time?" asked Bassanius.

Fibrius was suddenly up on his elbows, angry and fuming. "He assigned two hours of latrine duty after my picket because of a missing button on my cingulum. I couldn't believe it! All because of a stinking button!"

Both men nodded. Although neither voiced the thought, they agreed that Fibrius had probably gotten off lucky. There were always worst punishments to be endured at the hands of Fetch Another than cleaning out the cohort's latrine pits. Cornelius, who had a genuine sympathy for the abuse Fibrius received from Pompilius, attempted to curb the Spaniard's temper by changing the subject.

"Did you see the barbarians that came into camp last evening with the new legate, Gaius?"

"Aye, I saw them," affirmed Fibrius, lying back down on his bunk again. "So what?"

"I was wondering that if you saw them you might tell me what they were like."

Bassanius as usual, could not resist the temptation to wade in against his favorite target. "Yes, Gaius," he cooed in a voice silted with sarcasm, "Do tell us what they looked like. Our young friend here has the most curious theory that barbarians were hatched from the eggs of frogs and lizards. Did you happen to see any gills or scales upon these particular barbarians?"

Fibrius glared at the Campanian with a look of loathing. He found Bassanius' constant badgering almost as insulting as the ill treatment he suffered from Fetch Another. He was particularly offended by the latter's intellect and how he used it as a weapon to belittle those around him. Like most provincials in the army, Fibrius' education had produced only a functional literacy that served him well enough to be a soldier and little else. Until he met Bassanius, that had always been enough for him. After all, one didn't need to be familiar with the esoteric teachings of Socrates or the principles of geometry and mathematics as espoused by Aristotle and Archimedes in order to learn how to fight. One needed only a strong sword arm, a clear eye in battle and a courage refined by the discipline of the legions to be a soldier in the service of Rome.

"Why don't you tell him what they look like, Bassanius," he growled, "You've certainly seen your share."

"Alas, young Cornelius relies only on my expertise with the fairer sex. The subject of barbarians he prefers to leave to more learned men than I." At the word 'I' Bassanius motioned his head towards Fibrius provoking a snicker from Cornelius.

The Spaniard fumed as red as his tunic. "Curse the man who assigned me to the tent of a fool!" He rolled heavily over on his side to face the leather wall of the papilo, indicating their conversation was at an end.

But Bassanius was not willing to let go his prey so easily. In a mocking tone, he quoted the ancient Latin poet, Armillius:

"Make no place for evil in thy heart, gentle soul,
If I should show thee the ways of Truth,
For upon the winged feet of clouded Mercury,
Shall we ascend to the summit to the palace of immortals,
To know all there shall be to know.

"Go to hell!" swore Fibrius.

The Spaniard's response sent Bassanius and Strabo into a fresh chorus of laughter.

III

"**G**entlemen, I need answers and all you're giving me is more questions."

Governor General Varus stood at the head of a long briefing table with his hands behind his back, a large map of Germania in colored inks scribed on a roll of yellow vellum in front of him. Around the table sat the general staff of the Rhine legions, sixteen men in all. There were the three legionary commanders and one of six military tribunes assigned to command the six cohorts of each legion as their aide-de-camps, the praefectus castorum of the semi-permanent camp of Castra Vetera, a trio of praefecti fabrum or military engineers, and the prefect of the Rhine flotilla stationed at the naval base of Novaesium forty miles south of Castra Vetera. Varus had also appointed Gaius Silvanius to the post of praefectus equitum or commander of the cavalry despite their earlier unpleasantness over the Germans. Segestes too, sat in council with Varus and his commanders, boasting the long colorful wool tunic and shoulder cloak of a Cherusci chieftain. He was flanked by both Arminius and Segimerus on either side. The last man sitting before the legate was a senator, Gneaus Domitius Turtullus, recently arrived from Rome to aid Varus in his labors to construct a working framework of Roman law in the territory between the Rhine and the Elbe rivers.

Turtullus and Varus had been friends for most of their careers since meeting as young lawyers in the law courts of the Roman capitol. Like all good lawyers, both aspired to political office but it was Varus who had made the bigger splash by landing the plumb governorship of Syria and acquitting himself well by conducting the affairs of his province in an efficient if unspectacular fashion. When Augustus needed a new governor for Germany Inferior, someone who was willing to build the foundation of a stable province through the rule of Roman law and order, he only had to look as far as his own household for the inflexible legalistic mind he sought. When Varus received his commission to institute a new system of law for the German tribes based not on their own custom of tribal tradition but on the civilized precepts formed on the banks of the distant Tiber, he sought out his old friend Turtullus as a mind equal to the task. Turtullus could be trusted to act when told and react when necessary and be in lock step with Varus on every point, however trivial or insignificant.

But what had begun with such promise for the two friends was quickly turning into a morass. By nature, Varus was a man of stern and autocratic tendencies. It was a character that had served him well in the law courts but was bound to bring trouble to a responsibility that depended upon flexibility and tolerance for success. His view of the governed of the Empire was shaped by his experience with the docile provincials of the Orient. In his mind there was little difference between a northern barbarian and an eastern one. If a Syrian or Egyptian could be molded into a responsible

Roman through the introduction of Roman law, language and custom, than why not a German? Such was his thinking on the matter that he issued an edict amongst the barbarians of the Trans Rhine, that in a single stroke cancelled their own legal code while proclaiming the creation of his own tribunal before which all cases must now be tried. Thus by the stoke of his lawyer's pen, Varus had kindled the barbarians' anger by stripping them of the right to avenge themselves against injuries inflicted upon them and reserving the sole right to do so to Rome. The astonished Germans stared sullenly at the spectacle of justice now meted out by Roman lictors sent out by the overbearing Turtullus to every village and hamlet. The smallest infraction was now dealt with the endless wrangling of Roman lawyers, intent on proving points of law rather than guilt. The anger of the barbarians was kindled and fanned by the sight of husbands, brothers and fathers being dragged before a foreign bench they refused to acknowledge and scourged by the rods and axes of the lictors. Before long, the forests and hills of Germania echoed with whispers of resistance. All that was needed was a leader who could unite the tribes in their hatred of Rome. Such a leader would not be long in coming.

The council of war took place in the governor's quarters of Castra Vetera in the late spring of Varus' first year as governor of Germany Inferior. Vetera had more or less been a permanent settlement for the Romans since the first legions encamped there during the early campaigns of the stepsons of Augustus some twenty years previously. The original earthen ramparts had been enlarged and surrounded with a wooden palisade complete with four sets of gates and trellis facing the four cardinal points of the compass. High guard towers had been set into the corners of the palisaded wall as well as flanking towers for each gate and were continually manned with compliments of ten men each. The interior of the camp was sectioned into quarters by the intersection of the north/south via praetoria with the east/west via principalis. At the point of intersection, the governor's house had been raised, a two storey structure of wooden planks and beams with a large open space before it that doubled as both a forum and a parade ground. In orderly rows on both sides of the stone and curbed roadways, wooden barracks were erected to replace the dependable papilo for the common soldier. But the addition of two more legions in an area designed to comfortably house one meant that a forest of papili had grown up like a field of leather mushrooms outside the stockade of Vetera.

Inside the first floor conference room of the governor's house, Varus waited impatiently for an answer to his question. Surprisingly, it was Segestes who spoke first.

"General Varus, I warned you what would happen if you moved too quickly with this plan to install your tribunal amongst the people. If you remember, it was I who advised caution in this lest your actions provoke the tribes to disobedience. I have said before and I remind you again, you have only marched over the land, you have not conquered it. Except for the forts at Aliso and Minden, there is no Roman presence in Germany. Without your swords to back you, they will not accept your laws."

The German's words were met with murmuring around the table. Rising from his seat, Senator Turtullus puffed himself up like a toad and said, "If the barbarians will not accept the benefits of Roman law than it is high time we presented them with an object lesson and march our army right down their throats!" More murmuring this time accompanied by many nodding head's of assent.

"So you propose that we abandon our plans to pacify Germania with peaceful measures and campaign instead with the legions. Is this what I am hearing?"

A few scattered 'ayes' skittered around the table but it was clear that not all were in agreement with the assessment of the situation. Turtullus seemed to have the majority of the general staff on his side. Two of the three legionary prefects, the quartermaster general and prefect of the flotilla all concurred with the senator. Some sat in contemplative thought, unwilling to venture advice that might prove disastrous. Of this group, Silvanius was the most senior. For their part, the Germans held their silence.

"Yes I say give it to them," continued Turtullus, "The will of Caesar must be seen to be done here. Why must we hide here on the Roman bank of the Rhine hoping the barbarians will do what we want them to on their own accord when we have the means to make them do it? Your Excellency was not entrusted with three legions of Rome's best so that they could sit idle behind walls and ramparts."

Varus smiled warmly at his friend. "As usual, your counsel is sound, Senator Turtullus."

Segestes cleared his throat and said, "With all due respect to the honored senator from Rome, I suggest that it is easy for him to advocate the use of force since he will have no share in the actual fighting." The comment caused Turtullus' mouth to drop and the soldiers in the room to smirk. "But," continued Segestes, "I would advise caution. My previous words were intended only to point out a fact, not to recommend it as course of action at the present time." Beside him, Arminius clucked his tongue in undisguised disgust.

"You disagree with your chief, Arminius?" inquired Varus.

Arminius made to reply but was silenced by a withering look from Segestes. "He has nothing to say. He will do as I tell him." The face of the young German reddened, bristling at the insult. Without warning and to the mild amusement of the Romans present, he spat at the feet of Segestes and turned to the governor general. "Permission to speak, sir!" Segestes was on his feet, his hand upon the hilt of his sword.

"Segestes!" cried Varus. "Put up your weapon! I would hear what our young friend has to say."

"Regatz!" swore Segestes in the guttural tones of his native tongue. Prodding a long finger into Arminius' face, he added, "What is between us has no place here."

"I will have my say!" protested Arminius.

Varus clapped his hands sharply, cutting the argument short. "What is this all about?" he demanded. With the sullen look of chastened children, the two men glared at one another.

"It is a personal matter, general," explained Segestes through clenched teeth. "And thus should not be spoken of here. I am the chief of my people and I will see that peace is kept in my house."

"You cannot deny that she loves me!" blurted Arminius, a statement that caused Gaius Silvanius to sit up in his chair. A thought hidden somewhere in the back of his mind now came floating to remembrance. *Of course!* He thought, *Segestes' daughter Thusnelda!. Arminius is in love with her and obviously her father is not agreeable to the match! This could work greatly to our advantage.*

The tribune's thoughts were very much in keeping with the general attitude of the men under Varus' command concerning the strange relationship that had grown up between Varus and Arminius in the intervening months since the governor general had arrived in Germany. For reasons no one could quite fathom, the legate had taken a strong liking to the moody barbarian. To the consternation of his staff, Arminius began to be included in many important and sensitive gatherings that if the truth be told, should have been for Roman ears only. Eyebrows were further raised when Arminius became a permanent fixture in Varus' personal household. His ubiquitous presence by the side of the governor general had led to a rising tide of resentment against him amongst the officers and men of the army. Some spoke openly of resorting to violent means to remove the cancer in their midst while others accused Varus of 'going native' for his speech and manners began to betray the influence of things German. But it was always Silvanius who brought the mutinous talk to an end by reminding them that by uttering such things, they invited the return of the troubles and disturbances that had so recently plagued the legions of Germany and Pannonia. Ultimately, it was they who were to act as the instrument of Caesar's will and that his will was now represented in the person of his legate, Quinctilius Varus. To speak against the governor general, he argued, was to speak against the Emperor himself, a step of insubordination all were unwilling to take. The ill feeling towards Arminius, however, not only continued, but increased with every passing day. But Silvanius now believed he possessed a weapon that might pry Varus from his unhealthy obsession with Arminius.

For the moment, Varus sought to contain the situation. "Enough of this!" he barked. Pointing a finger at Segestes he signaled for him to sit. To Arminius he demanded, "Well?"

The German's face flushed as he realized his mistake. Bowing his head, he mumbled, "Forgive me, excellency. My lord Segestes spoke rightly when he said it is a private matter between us. I pray you will forget my indiscretion and continue with the business at hand."

But Varus would not be dissuaded so easily. "I would know what is so important that it threatens this conference with bloodshed." Arminius lapsed into silence.

"If I may, sir," interjected Silvanius, "I believe I can shed some light upon this affair."

Varus turned toward his master of the horse with a quizzical look. "Indeed? Very well, tribune. Since our friends are reluctant to speak for themselves you have my permission to speak for them." Arminius glared at Silvanius with a narrow-eyed wariness.

"As you may know Excellency, I became acquainted with both of these men during the time I spent amongst the tribes on the far side of the Rhine. I remember fondly the days I dwelt in the house of the noble Segestes." The mention of pleasant days of the past brought a trace of a smile to Segestes' angry countenance.

"I knew him well," continued Silvanius, "And for his part, he denied me nothing. I became an intimate of not only his people but also his family. I soon learned that the jewel of my host's life, more precious to him than gold itself, was his daughter Thusnelda. The recent loss of his own dear wife to the plague only served to increase the value of this treasure in his eyes. It would not be for all the wealth of the Empire that he would easily let her go for I perceive it to be a truth of the human heart that the father who mourns a wife cannot fail to see her reflection in the daughter she leaves behind." At this, Segestes' head sunk down upon his chest as if burdened by the weight of a memory too great to bear.

Silvanius went on. "The man Arminius I do not know for it was only the boy whom I shared an acquaintance. But even then I could see a great stirring of passion within him for the fair daughter of Segestes. When he was packed off to Rome to ensure the continuing peace of the Cherusci, I believed time and the delights of the capitol would burn it from him as it would any young man to whom civilization is foreign. But it seems that if anything, it served only to stoke hotter the fire of his passion. It is my guess that our friend Arminius has made a demand on Thunelda for his wife which her father will not honor. What we are witnessing is a bitterness born of a spurned suitor and the fear of a father who cannot bear the thought of losing his daughter."

Varus gazed down at the old chieftain, wondering how a people could submit themselves to be slaves to such ungovernable currents of emotion. A Roman would never allow the mundane matters of the heart to interfere with the more important aspects of conquering and ruling the world at large. The Greek philosophers had rendered a priceless service to Rome by imparting to them the importance of logic over emotion and the need to submerge those qualities of the human heart that caused the rot of a man's soul through useless sentimentalism. Strength of intellect and will were seen as virtues to be desired even as the domination of feeling and emotion were seen as a dangerous weakness, suitable for women and the elderly. It was little wonder that the barbarian races of the earth were subservient to the power of Rome. They possessed neither the discipline of mind nor the willingness of the soul to rein in their passions and acquire the singular balance between heart and mind essential for the building of a great nation. Slaves they were and slaves they would remain unless by chance a Germanic Spartacus should arise among them to harness the inherent power of their numbers and lead them out of their forest fastness into the very heart of the Empire. But in Varus' mind, that was unlikely as long as they behaved like children crying for a lost toy.

"Does the tribune speak the truth, Segestes?" asked the governor general. Slowly, Segestes raised his eyes to Varus and replied, "There is little point in denying it. Yes, the noble tribune speaks truly. This man has asked for my daughter in marriage but I do not see the advantage of such a match. For the good of my house and my people, I have betrothed her to another. Arminius, I fear, must look elsewhere for a wife."

"I will not!" broke in Arminius indignantly. "Thusnelda was promised to me."

Segestes shook his head sadly. "It was a promise made by her mother. It is no longer binding."

"I will bind it with this!" cried Arminius, his sword suddenly in his hand. "And seal it with your blood if need be!"

The unexpected appearance of a drawn sword provoked a predictable reaction around the table. Every officer was immediately on his feet, his own sword drawn and ready. But Varus froze the scene by shouting for order. "Away with your swords!" he cried, "This is not the practice field! Arminius, I command you to sheath your weapon and stand to." For a long moment, it appeared as if Arminius might ignore Varus' command and actually carry out his murderous intent upon Segestes. But whatever else Arminius might be, he was no fool. Twenty against one were odds best left to the fickleness of gaming boards and dice, not as surety for a fight. With deliberate slowness, he slid his blade back into its scabbard.

"My apologies to you, Excellency." he said bowing in deference to Varus. "I would not have disgraced you by spilling unworthy blood beneath your roof." Segestes bristled under the insult and half rose in his chair. A withering look from Varus sat him down again.

"Gentlemen, this is all becoming quite tiresome," commented the governor general, his arms folded across his chest. "My tax collectors are being murdered in village streets and half the province is in revolt and yet here we sit, commanders and officers of the great army of the Rhine, listening to you haggle over a woman like a pair of Arab traders. By the gods, I swear that if the illustrious Drusus Nero were standing in my place, he could have clapped you both in irons rather than tolerate such nonsense in his councils. Arminius, if you truly look to me as a friend, than heed my advice. I have no doubt that this Thusnelda is beautiful, for after all, why would you desire her if it were not so? And an alliance to the house of Segestes could only be beneficial to you if one day you hope to rule the Cherusci, but the fact of the matter is that the last word on this matter must lay with her father. While Segestes has life in his body, he is ruler of the Cherusci and the head of his household. Your wisest course is to forget the girl for now and concentrate on building your fortune in the coming campaign. I have no doubt that there will be many lovely captives who will catch your eye and make you forget the bewitchment of this woman. I insist you make your peace with Segestes and swear an oath you will not pursue this matter while you are under my command."

The change Varus' words worked upon the barbarian shocked the officers around the table. It was as if Arminius deliberately let the mask of civility slip from his face to reveal the reality of the feral being lurking beneath it. The handsome features hardened into taut blocks of colorless flesh, the eyes darkening into malignant pools of unrestrained hatred. So startling was the transformation that even Varus involuntarily stepped back from it. Through teeth clenched so tightly that it caused his jaw muscle to quiver, Arminius breathed a deadly threat.

"You are not my friend and you will live to regret your words, I promise you. I will have Thusnelda for my wife and not even Caesar or his legions will keep me from her."

Turning to Segestes, he said, "I swear by the gods of our fathers that the day is coming when I will have your head and the crown upon it!" Angrily he turned on his heel and stalked towards the door with Sergimus close behind. One of the military tribunes standing near the door attempted to bar the way but Silvanius ordered him to let the barbarians pass.

After they had gone, the room endured a deathly silence. No one either dared speak or offer an opinion on what had occurred for fear of offending the legate. As for Varus, he had been so shaken by the episode that all he could do was stare with self-recrimination down at his feet. Arminius' outburst should have led to his immediate arrest and execution according to Roman military law. But such illogical behavior from a man he had come to look upon as almost a surrogate son had taken him by complete surprise. What had he said to provoke such a change in his young friend he wondered?

After the conference he must seek Arminius out and make things right between them.

Segestes had remained strangely quiescent during the whole affair. He alone of those present appeared unfazed by either the suddenness of Arminius' turnabout or the vitriolic nature of his threat. He it was who was first to break the uncomfortable quiet around the table.

"I've warned you before, general. That man is dangerous to Rome. He burns with a fire that cannot be easily put out. If you heed my advice, you will not allow him to leave Castra Vetera."

Varus shook his head. "I have never seen him like this."

"Can you not see that you have entertained a serpent in your midst? One that is at this very moment, preparing to strike?"

"We have been through this before regarding the young man, Segestes, but I have always thought it envy on your part. I did not suspect he harbored such feelings for your daughter. If I had known, perhaps I might have chosen my words more carefully."

"Thusnelda is not the cause of his hatred," replied Segestes, "I have evidence that Arminius is one of those who is stirring the tribes against Rome. He is not unlike your own god Janus who can see in two directions at once. He has insinuated himself with you so that he might discover your plans and pass them on to those who now wait hiding beyond the Rhine frontier. Rest assured, general, they know of your every move and what you plan to do. And now you have let him go. If you were uncertain about our loyalty to the Emperor, than you should have arrested us all, myself included, so that you could sort out the truth later, after the revolt had been put down."

There was general assent around the table that Segestes had offered sound counsel. Senator Turullus spoke for all when he said, "Excellency, you know what the barbarian says is true. Give the order to have Arminius arrested." Turtullus' bigotry would not allow him to view Segestes and his companions as anything less than 'barbarians'.

The senator's observation was met with various 'ayes' and nodding heads around the table. Varus, faced with the unanimity of his general staff, reluctantly signaled to the tribune at the door to carry out the order. It wasn't long before the man returned to report that Arminius and Sergimus had vanished from Castra Vetera.

"No good will come of this," muttered Segestes glumly.

"Who now is thinking too highly of the young man?" demanded Varus. "One man cannot stand against the power of three Roman legions. I suggest we put this regrettable incident behind us and focus on the task at hand. But I want it understood that should Arminius return he is to be placed into immediate custody and brought to me. Is that clear?"

Amidst the affirmations of his fellow officers, Silvanius sat in silence trying to shut out the thought that screamed in his head:

We will all regret the hour when first we ever heard the name of Arminius.

IV

*T*he dream began with a face. A face like no other.

To say that it was strong would be to deny its delicacy. To speak of it as beautiful would ignore the inherent power of its masculinity. To describe it would not do it justice and to look into it was to gaze upon the divine. Great gentleness and calm radiated like light from behind the olive-skinned features. Eyes, luminous to the point of incandescence, enveloped all they beheld in an embrace of unearthly peace. A beatific smile stretched playfully across the full lips, framed inside the contours of a beard the color of snow. Indeed, not only was his beard white but his hair also which fell in soft curls to the tops of his shoulders. But the color was not a reflection of age for the face projected an image of youthful eternity. Suffice to say that it was a face that Cornelius could not readily recall he had ever seen but felt he would never forget.

The face now began to resolve itself into the figure of a man, clad in a tunic of such wonderful material that it shone brightly as if lit by the fires of the sun. Stretching his hand towards Cornelius, he turned a palm up and said. "Cornelius, son of Sextus, favored of God, rise and follow."

The language sounded foreign to Cornelius' ears. He was even more surprised to realize he could readily understand it. At that point in the dream he began to look around his surroundings and discovered that he was lying face down upon the muddy ground, surrounded by the bloated and broken bodies of a slaughtered army. Everywhere he looked he saw soldiers, many whom he knew, lying in various poses of death, tangled in a macabre dance of twisted limbs and shattered weapons. The man in his dream stood on the perimeter of the field opposite Cornelius against a mighty stand of

47

oak, elm and tamarack. Cornelius could dimly perceive ghostly shapes moving in the shadow of the trees behind the man, seemingly searching for something they could not find. All around him, the grim face of death and destruction pressed heavily against him. Cornelius felt a strangled cry begin to well up in his throat. The man raised his hand again.

"Cornelius son of Sextus, favored of God, rise and follow."

Cornelius had never considered himself devout when it came to religion. Like most Romans, he offered only a cursory token to the gods of his ancestors and the divine gens of the Imperial house recognizing that such practices were performed as a nod to tradition than genuine spiritual enlightenment. Yet something deep in his heart told him that this vision was more real than any temple or sacred grove he had ever entered. Whoever or whatever this strange man was, Cornelius instinctively knew that his was a heavenly presence.

Rising from the tangled wreckage around him, Cornelius reached out his hand and cried, "Lord, help me! Do not leave me to die here in this cursed place!"

The smile grew deeper and more loving, filling Cornelius' soul with a warmth he had never experienced. The dread of the scene about him began to melt away like spring ice. "Fear not," said the man of the vision, "For the hand of the Almighty shall overshadow you and protect you and deliver you from the valley of death. Rejoice for you have found favor with God and are called by His purpose. In days to come shall you become an instrument of His making to call out the faithful from amongst nations not yet born."

And although Cornelius heard the words he did not understand them.

Cornelius awoke in the darkness of the papilo, sweating and breathing heavily. Although the night was oppressively humid, he knew it was not the stifling air of the tent that bathed him in a pool of his own sweat. Nor was it the strangeness of the

dream that had awakened him but an insistent shaking of his shoulder by someone who was standing by his bunk. As his eyes grew accustomed to the dark, he recognized the toad-like features of Fortensius Machinus, optio to the senior centurion. The feeling of dread he had experienced in his dream now returned to seep back into his soul. Sitting up in his bed, he asked, "What is it, Machinus?"

Machinus, a man as corrupt as he was ugly, grinned a mouthful of crooked yellow teeth. "The Primus wants to see you on the double," he croaked jerking his thumb behind him. "Out at the latrine pits."

Despite the cloying heat of the papilo, Cornelius felt an involuntary shudder spasm through his body. "What does he want at this hour?" he whispered.

"How should I know? He just said to come and get you so you'd better get moving. The Primus doesn't like to be kept waiting."

Cornelius made to reach under his bunk for his cuirass and helmet but was stopped by Machinus. "You won't be needing those. He told me to bring you as you are. So get moving."

Quietly, Cornelius swung his legs out of his bunk and followed the retreating form of Machinus as he deftly moved between the rows of sleeping men. As they stepped from the tent, Cornelius was stunned by the sight that met his eyes. The landscape around him was bathed in the ethereal light of biggest moon he had ever seen. The lunar cast upon familiar objects around him gave the scene an otherworldly quality in which one could easily imagine seeing forest spirits peeking out from behind every tree. Cornelius stood momentarily transfixed by the awesome sight.

Machinus growled behind his ear. "Don't stand there like a nervous virgin on her wedding night. Get moving!" He grabbed Cornelius by the arm and started to pull him toward the direction of the main gate. Cornelius blinked as he tried to clear his mind of the knot of terror that had lodged there. His heart thudded dully against his chest as he wondered what awaited him when he came face to face with Fetch Another.

The main gate of Castra Vetera was set in its southern wall as the camp had originally been laid out so that its northern perimeter was protected by the river barrier of the Rhine. On this night, it was guarded by a squad of four mailed legionaries, one who stepped forward and challenged the two men as they approached.

"Password?" he challenged with hands on hips.

"Don't be an idiot, Caius, it's me you fool!" sneered Machinus. Caius cocked his head in order to get a better look from under the protruding browplate of his helmet and smiled.

"Oh, it's you, Machinus. Wondered who'd be out sneaking about the camp at this hour. Who is that with you?"

"None of your damn business!" snapped Machinus, "This is the personal business of the Primus and if you want to be on the receiving end of fifteen lashes just keep asking stupid questions."

"Alright, alright," drawled the guard signaling to his companions to open the gate. "I've got my job to do too, you know."

"Then make sure you do it and stop wasting my time." Machinus pushed Cornelius through the open gate.

Outside the wooden palisade of the camp, the road proceeded south-west for a little over a Roman mile before it began to curve back in an eastward direction toward the Imperial province of Gaul, paralleling the line of the great river as it did so. Machinus and Cornelius walked about fifty paces from the gate until they came to a well worn trail that branched off the main road to the left. Plunging off onto the trail, they followed its winding course as it cut a swath through the dense underbrush, rising steadily underfoot until it suddenly broke through into a wide square clearing. Cornelius did not need to smell the drifting stench of human feces and urine in the humid air to tell him that he had been brought to one of three latrine stations employed by the population of Castra Vetera.

As they stood in the pale light, their shadows elongated by the spectral light across a trio of rectangular pits cut into the rocky outcrop on which the station was set, a disembodied voice sounded from the far side of the clearing. "He's here?" it asked huskily with a slight trace of slurring.

"Yes, Primus," answered Machinus, "Just like you ordered."

"Did anyone see you leave?"

"Only that fool Caius at the gate. But don't worry, he won't say anything. I told him he would have to answer to you if he asked any questions."

"Excellent! You have done well, Machinus, as usual. You may retire."

"Thank you, Primus!" Machinus saluted smartly and disappeared back down the trial.

The man who emerged from the shadows was obviously drunk. He was of middle age, a half a head shorter than Cornelius but many pounds heavier. He moved into the center of the clearing with the staggering gait of the inebriated, sliding to his left a few unsteady steps before angling back right in a useless attempt to walk a straight line. Inexplicably he was dressed in the finery of a centurion's parade uniform replete with a gorgeous muscle cuirass and matching grieves worn over a wine-colored tunic bordered with gold trim. He wore no helmet so that in the pale light of the moon, his bald head and hatchet face took on the appearance of a leering vulture. A violent scar ran diagonally from the right brow, across the bridge of the flat nose to the left corner of bloodless lips, courtesy of a Pannonian broadsword. The wound had destroyed his right eye which was now only a sightless white orb perpetually staring from a folded mound of scar tissue. In his left hand he clutched a leather wineskin and in his right, the ivory and brass baton of his office. He managed to amble within a pace of Cornelius where he made a comical attempt to overawe the young man by straightening his thick body and puffing out his barrel chest.

"Do you know who I am, boy?" he demanded insolently.

The fetid reek of sour wine slammed into Cornelius' senses like a hammer. Nausea bubbled up inside him as he struggled to master the bile that threatened to crawl up his throat. Swallowing hard his reflex to vomit, he managed to reply, "Yes, sir."

"I can't hear you!" roared the man, pulling the wineskin to his mouth and tipping its contents down his throat. The wine spilled out over his chin and dripped onto the gold metal surface of his cuirass, staining it with spidery veins of ruby red. Glaring at Cornelius with his good eye, he repeated, "Tell me who I am, soldier!"

"Primus pilus Pompilius, senior centurion of the Nineteenth Legion," intoned Cornelius. The answer seemed to mollify Pompilius who nodded his bald head and pointed a thick finger in Cornelius' chest. "Don't ever forget it if you want to get ahead in this army, boy. I can be your best friend or your worst enemy. The choice is yours." Lifting the wineskin again to his mouth, he drained it by tightly twisting the skin until not a drop remained. Tossing it aside, he wiped his lips with the back of a meaty hand and began to circle around the young Strabo, surveying him with keen interest.

"You're a fine young thing, aren't you?" he cooed, lifting the hem of Cornelius' tunic with the brass end of his parade baton. "I've noticed you for quite a while now and I thought now was a good time to get to know one another, if you get my drift."

The words cut like a knife at Cornelius' wildly beating heart. He fought to control the tide of disgust rising up from the depths of his soul. Everyone knew of Pompilius' predilection for the young men under his command but it had never occurred to Cornelius that he might one day find himself the target of the primus pilus' loathsome attentions. His legs threatened to buckle under him as his muscles turned to water. Bowing his head, he wished himself anywhere but here. Pompilius forced his head back by jamming the butt end of the baton under his jaw.

"Yes I think I shall enjoy myself with you, boy," he said, caressing Cornelius' cheek with the ivory shaft of the baton. "But first, I have a little job for you to do." Walking over to the edge of the nearest latrine pit, Pompilius picked up a spade and hefting it like a weapon, tossed it to Cornelius. It fell with a thud at his feet.

"Pick it up."

Forcing his leaden muscles to obedience, Cornelius complied and stooped down to pick up the spade.

"Now, get in the pit and start digging, soldier."

The urge to flee overwhelmed Cornelius' fevered mind but fear rooted him to the ground. Pompilius was drunk, he reasoned. He was older and probably much slower than Cornelius. It would be a relatively easy matter to lose him in the dense forest around them. But if he did, what then? No one in command would side with him against the senior centurion, especially one of Pompilius' reputation. And for his part, Pompilius could concoct any nonsense he wanted and it would be believed, such was the fear that everyone held for Fetch Another. Cornelius would face the harshest punishments available for whatever imaginary indiscretion Pompilius chose to charge him with. His life, far from being filled with the glorious exploits of his boyhood dreams, would become instead an unending misery. The alternative was not much better. He could choose to become a fugitive from the legions, spending his life seeking to escape the long reach of the Roman eagle.

Running, hiding but never really finding security or peace until one day, they would catch up with him as they surely must, and consign him to either the arena or the cross. In his mind's eye he saw his disapproving father in far off Rhegium, shaking his head and scolding him, 'I told you your stubbornness and pride would bring you nothing but trouble. But you wouldn't listen to me. Now you must pay for the consequences of your poor choice.'

At that moment, a drifting bank of ragged cloud passed across the face of the moon, darkening the clearing. In the cloak of new darkness, it was now or never.

"Didn't you hear me, soldier? I said dig!" Pompilius swung his baton and caught Cornelius on the shoulder, sending sparks of pain down his right side. "Get moving or you'll get worse, I promise you." Rubbing his shoulder, Cornelius trudged to the edge of the pit. The fetid stench of human waste was overpowering. As he girded himself to step down into the rancid pool, he felt the baton flick out across his chest.

"Take the tunic off."

"No!" cried Cornelius with every fibre of his being screaming in abhorrent protest. But before he could speak further, he heard the swoosh of the baton cutting through the air. Behind his left leg he felt a terrific explosion of pain that drove him to one knee and produced a shower of stars before his eyes. From somewhere above him, the malevolent whisper of the centurion drifted down to his ears. "I said take it off, boy!" Numb from the throbbing pain in his leg, his mind deadened by the emotional maelstrom around him, Cornelius obeyed and removed his tunic. Standing naked, except for the thin covering of his linen underwear, he felt his shame complete. Even the night sky seemed to mock his pain for the moon chose that moment to free itself from the shroud of the passing cloud, shining with perverse brightness on Cornelius' disgrace.

Pompilius grinned idiotically as he eyed the young man's body in the pale light of the moon. "Yes," he slobbered to himself, "Now that's what I like. Oh, you are so beautiful, my pretty! I'll wager Ganymede himself was not half as lovely as you. I shall want you with me always, my pretty, always and forever. But first things first as they say. Dig!'" He pointed his baton to the pit.

There are hidden mechanisms of survival that are imparted into every human that manifest themselves only during times of extreme jeopardy when the very destruction of self is at stake. Cornelius now found himself in just such a situation as he began to experience the phenomenon of his spirit disengaging from the present suffering of his physical self. He found himself watching with detached fascination as his body seemed to move without conscious will into the sucking muck of the cesspool and begin to dig. Savagely he attacked his task, flinging spadefuls of filth up onto the rock lip of the pit, oblivious to the sheen of sweat on his body or the clots of feces that landed on his skin and hair. He dug as a man possessed as if seeking to destroy himself through pure physical effort. And all the while, Fetch Another watched from above, taking a perverse pleasure in watching his victim work himself to exhaustion.

He never knew how long he remained in the pit performing his useless task for Pompilius. It was five minutes if it was an hour. All he did remember was reaching a point of such despair that he knew his next shovel of dung would most likely drain his last reserve of strength. When that happened, he would sink willingly into the promise of oblivion offered by the repulsive morass sucking at his knees. Surely, he thought, such a fate was infinitely more preferable than the one Pompilius had in mind for him; even if it meant that his father would die never knowing the fate of his only son. But as to the nature of that fate, he was now about to discover.

"That's enough," ordered Pompilius, "Come up here, boy."

Dripping with sweat and stained with the offal of the pit, Cornelius climbed up onto the ground with agonizing slowness and stood panting before the centurion. A dreamy, far off look diffused Pompilius' hatchet features. He stood swaying on his feet, his one good eye staring with glassy intensity at his filthy victim. From deep in the barrel chest came an odd noise that gurgled and rumbled, rising in intensity and pitch as his face reddened under a blush of passion. Coming closer, he reached out his free hand and began to lightly stroke Cornelius' glistening forearm.

"Listen to me, my pretty," he purred, "I can do a lot for you. Make you my personal aide. Teach you the things you need to know in this man's army so that one day you can become a primus pilus like me. After the army, you can become a knight, like I will. Run for office if you like. Who knows, one day even sit in the consul's chair, if the gods will.

Anything you like or desire, I can make it happen for you. All I ask in return is that you give yourself to me, freely and willingly. Now that isn't too much to ask for, is it?"

The words barely dented Cornelius' torpid conscious. Exhaustion and shock had taken their toll. Pompilius had unwittingly shattered Cornelius' dreams for glory. And the future. His dreams of hard won victories with sword and javelin had been cruelly and mercilessly torn from him to be crushed like a child's plaything between the thick fingers of a drunken pervert. Beneath the glittering edifice of his beloved legions, Cornelius had discovered to his dismay, the body of a rotting corpse.

Pompilius now began to roughly massage Cornelius' chest, his mouth drooling in anticipation for what he had long waited for. Pushing his face to within inches of Cornelius' own, he whispered hoarsely, "What do you say, my Ganymede? Will you pleasure your Zeus in return for what I can do for you? Do you know how many young men with ambitions like yours would gladly trade places with you right now if it meant they would advance to the highest commands? You think a muckety-muck like Varus runs this army? Puh! Don't make me laugh. He's nothing but a pathetic joke just like the rest of his useless class. Everyone knows the legions are the primus pilus' to control. And I control the Nineteenth. I have the power to raise you or break you. Only a fool would deny and resist that kind of power. And you, my lovely Ganymede, do not strike me as a fool." As he finished speaking, his hand plunged down suddenly beneath the drawstring of

Cornelius' underwear, seeking to fondle the young man's manhood.

A towering wave of revulsion flooded through Cornelius, electrifying his senses and shattering the stupor of his thoughts. Before he even realized it, the spade which was still in his hand, was arcing through the air, the glint of metal tracing a deadly trajectory in the moonlight. Spurred by the force of his searing emotions, Cornelius slammed the edge of the spade into Fetch Another's unprotected temple. A look of stupefied wonder passed over Pompilius' face as a thick stream of blood oozed over and around his good eye. For a few moments, he stood tottering unsteadily on his feet. Then like the falling trunk of a great tree, Pompilius fell sideways to the ground, his skull smacking against a protruding rock with a sickening thud. He lay still on his back, his eye staring unseeing up into the night stars.

Cornelius stood above Pompilius, staring incomprehensively at the blood spattered spade in his trembling hand. He reared back and threw it into the forest beyond the pits. It clattered unseen amongst the undergrowth. Then dropping to his knees, he surrendered to a violent spasm of vomiting.

When he had sufficiently recovered his senses he staggered to his feet, his mind racing with the magnitude of what he had done. That he had just killed the senior centurion he had no doubt; the sightless eyes were proof enough. He knew only too well the irrevocable penalty for such an action, regardless of the provocation, for it meant his own life was now forfeit. Home, career, future, all vanished like a wisp of smoke before his eyes. By dying, Pompilius had ruined Cornelius' life more assuredly than if he had lived to carry out his repulsive intentions. Cornelius would forever carry the stain of murder upon his soul and the death sentence of the Roman state upon his head. There was little likelihood of escaping either.

A sudden wild thought flashed like a spark in the gloaming darkness of his mind. Perhaps he could flee to the far side of the Rhine. Take refuge with the tribes that dwelt in the rolling forests beyond the river. Blend into their society by submerging his Roman self into the flood of nameless barbarism. Life however rudely lived would be a blessing after the horror of this night.

As he stood feverishly considering his options, he was suddenly conscious of the feeling that he was not alone. Turning to look around him, he could at first see only the lifeless body of Pompilius lying where it had fallen at the moment of death. Peering into the encroaching gloom around the clearing, Cornelius was startled by the apparition of a shadowy form standing at the top of the path. He made to cry out but no sound emerged from his fear-constricted throat.

Someone had seen him! Someone had seen him kill the primus pilus!

Cornelius trembled in the humid darkness his hope for escape all but gone. A witness had seen him murder a senior officer. He was as good as dead.

The silhouette remained motionless, watching Cornelius. Suddenly, it moved into the moon-washed light of the clearing, revealing the cloaked and armored figure of the Tribune Silvanius. Without a word he went over and kneeled down beside the body of the dead centurion.

"Sextus Pompilius," he announced out loud shaking his head. Standing up again, he walked over to Cornelius and looked into his eyes. Cornelius was quick to commence his defence but all he could manage was a stuttering, "I.... I...." Tears filled his eyes and he bowed his head, his shoulders racked with sobbing.

Silvanius put his hand out and touched Cornelius' shoulder. "Easy, soldier," he said soothingly, "It's all over now. There's nothing to worry about."

"But I killed him!" sobbed Cornelius with the pathetic demeanor of a distraught child. "I killed him!"

Silvanius offered a gracious smile. "From what I saw, you had good reason. Many of us wondered when old Fetch Another's birds would come home to roost. Do you think you're the first man to want Pompilius dead?"

"But it was an accident!" whined Cornelius. "I didn't mean to do it. It's just that he was going to, I mean, he tried to, to...." The rest of sentence trailed off as the tears flooded back into his eyes.

Silvanius gripped Cornelius' arms tightly. "I want you to listen to me, soldier. I want you to forget what happened here. Do you understand? I want you to go back to your tent and forget everything you heard or saw here. Is that clear?"

"But what about the Primus? What about the body?"

"You let me worry about that. What Pompilius has done has finally had its way with him. Right now I want you to return to your papilo and get some sleep. And if anyone should ask you any questions about the senior centurion you are to say nothing. Understand? Nothing!"

Cornelius nodded and wiped his nose. "What about Fortensius Machinus?"

"What about him?"

"He knows I was here with the Primus. He brought me here on Pompilius' orders."

Silvanius' features turned grim. "Yes, well Machinus was what you might call Pompilius' chief procurement officer. I don't know which is worse, the pervert or the piece of dung who finds his victims. All I know is that the army will be well rid of both of them. Now, go. Get cleaned up and get some rest. Consider it an order."

Cornelius sniffed and wiped the trail of tears from his dirty face. Managing a salute to the tribune, he left the clearing more tired and drained then he could ever remember. Thankfully fatigue was already beginning to dull the memories of his humiliation. He hoped sleep would hasten his recovery.

When he had gone, Silvanius walked back over to the body of the primus pilus. Putting a booted foot to the side of Pompilius' ruined cuirass, he pushed the body forward until it tumbled into the nearby pit. As he stood and watched, the corpse of the dead man sank with a soft sucking noise beneath the surface of the malodorous pool. Spying the man's baton nearby on the ground, he threw it in after the body.

"Farewell, Sextus Pompilius. May Hades take your black soul and hang it over the fires of the underworld. There will be few amongst the living who will mourn your passing." And having pronounced Fetch Another's funeral oration, he left the latrine pits to find Fortensius Machinus.

V

Quinctillus Varus sat at the large oak writing table in the study of his quarters and steeled himself to compose his latest report to the Emperor. So important was the task of pacifying the province of Germany that Augustus insisted on being kept informed with monthly updates, carried to Rome through the excellent courier system of the Imperial post. Most of Varus' correspondence up to this point had been nothing more than unimportant bureaucratic tinkering or legalistic posturing concerning the Roman presence amongst the local populations. But this report would be different. It had to be. Varus had finally decided that the situation beyond the Rhine had so deteriorated that it required the armed intervention of the legions to straighten it out. To do so, however meant getting Caesar's approval. To this end, Varus now bent his energies.

Tapping the stylus against his teeth, he gathered together the strands of his thoughts and began to write.

Publius Quinctilius Varus, legate of the province of Germania to Gaius Julius Augustus Caesar, ten times consul, princeps of the Roman Senate and People, Father of his Country;

Greetings,

When Your majesty appointed me legate of Germania you also set for me the task of pacifying the territory between the Rhine and Elbe rivers in order to make it secure for Roman interests. To this end, I have endeavored to make the barbarians aware of the need to embrace the elements of civilization by issuing an edict in your name, outlawing their barbaric notions of law and order and replacing them with the more sensible Roman tribunal. The eminent Senator Gneaus Turtullus (of whom few in Rome surpass his knowledge of the intricacies of Roman law) has proven invaluable in this labor. Under his tutelage, tribunals have been set up in all tribal centers and markets, calling the barbarians to bring their cases before our judges rather than trying them in their clumsy assemblies. These assemblies were infamous for the battles and skirmishes they created than for any justice that was seen to be done. I have attempted to imprint upon the barbarian mind the need for the rule of law and how submitting to that rule will lead them to all the blessings civilization can offer. I am also pleased to report to your majesty, that for the most part, the barbarians have complied with the edict despite a few incidents that were quickly and severely dealt with. But I expected no less. These people will learn to dwell peacefully in the Empire, if not by the imposition of fair-minded and even-handed laws than by the points of our swords.

Your majesty will also be pleased to know that the taxes assessed for my province for the replenishment of the military treasury following the great revolt in Pannonia, is close to being realized. The country has been blanketed by my tax collectors who have been most efficient in procuring every last sesterce owed to the people of Rome. And although Germany is a poor land, your majesty may rest assured that I am confident that the assessment will be met. They will be made to realize that they must pay for the privilege of being protected by the legions and the laws of Rome and that that privilege does not come cheap.

But lest your majesty think by my positive words all is well in the province, I pray you will not be deceived. There are forces at work amongst the barbarians who have arrayed themselves against Rome, black-hearted scoundrels who are attempting to whip up the people to revolt. They have incited some to rise up and kill a number of lawyers and tax gatherers, loyal servants of the noble Augustus, on the fringe of their settlements, deceiving them into believing that the writ of Roman law cannot reach them so far from the camps of the legions. I intend to show them otherwise. With your majesty's permission, I propose to march with the Seventeenth, Eighteenth and Nineteenth Legions out of Castra Vetera and into the country on the east bank of the Rhine. My reason for this is twofold: first, to apprehend and punish the murderers of Roman citizens and arrest and try those rebels amongst the barbarians who have convinced their countrymen to act so rashly. Secondly, I believe that a show of force on the far side of the Rhine will be sufficient to discourage any further thoughts of rebellion and cause the general population to cower into acceptance of our authority. Once I have accomplished my objective, I will carry out your will and establish a strong defensive border of walled camps and towers on the Elbe River to link up with our fortifications on the Danube. But I can only do so if I am confident that my rear is secure and is in no danger of rising up behind me.

Varus stopped writing and leaned back in his chair. He wondered if he should inform the Emperor about the incident with Arminius but decided against it. Chances were Augustus didn't even know who Arminius was other than as a companion of Chief Segestes when they had rendezvoused with Varus and his escort that day at Bellatorix's Tor. Besides, knowing the Emperor's efficient turn of mind as well he did, Varus concluded that Augustus would probably chastise him for including such nonsense in the official dispatches. It was all so meaningless at any rate. He banished the thought of further consideration from his mind.

Turning back to his letter, he continued.

Senator Turtullus has expressed his desire to accompany the legions during the expedition into Germany and I see no reason not to allow him to do so. He shall come attended by his own staff of legal advisors for the express purpose of observing and revamping the tribunals already in place.

Chief Segestes will also accompany our forces across the Rhine to....

The sentence was interrupted by a sudden commotion in the anteroom on the other side of the double doors of the study. Muffled voices could be heard followed by the sound of scuffling. Abruptly the study doors banged open to reveal the anteroom guard struggling to keep Segestes from entering the study. Varus could see the barbarian chief was obviously agitated. His face was scarlet with rage and he looked as if he had not eaten or slept for days, unusual for a man who unlike most barbarians, took great pains to present a civilized face to the world. From what Varus could see, Segestes was unarmed.

"I must see the legate!" cried the German as he pushed back against the shaft of the guard's javelin that was pushing to keep him out.

"And I said the legate was not to be disturbed!" growled the guard redoubling his effort to move Segestes back out into the anteroom.

"What's going on here?" shouted Varus half rising from his chair. "Guard, let him pass!"

The guard reluctantly ceased his efforts to remove the intruder from the study and saluted before sullenly resuming his post outside the study doors.

Striding to the front of the desk, Segestes stood panting heavily from the effort of his struggle with the guard. He offered a cursory bow to the irate legate.

"Forgive the intrusion, general."

"By the gods, Segestes, this had better be important! You are interrupting my letter to the Emperor."

"A thousand pardons, general, but I would not have dared to bother you if it were not a matter of some urgency."

"Well? What is it?"

"She is gone!"

"Who's gone? Speak plainly, man!"

"My daughter, Thusnelda. She is gone."

"Perpol!" moaned Varus with disgust leaning forward to resume his letter. "What has your domestic problems to do with me? You are her father and must deal with her as you see fit. If she has run away than send some of your warriors to fetch her back. Now if you will excuse me, I have more important matters to attend to. Dismissed."

Segestes planted his hands on the front of the writing desk and waited for Varus to meet his gaze. "I said you are dismissed," repeated the legate.

"Arminius took her."

Varus' expression turned from annoyance to sudden interest. "What do you mean Arminius took her?"

Segestes straightened up. "Three nights ago, Arminius arrived with a company of armed men and forced their way into my house. My daughter was there alone with two of her slave women and a modest guard of trusted men. They came at night, out of the forest, and overpowered her guard, killing them all. They found Thusnelda but she was not asleep as might be assumed at such an hour. She was waiting for Arminius and his men and it is reported that she went willingly with them. They made straight away for a sacred grove nearby where Arminius had a Druid priest waiting and ready to perform the marriage troth. They are now husband and wife."

Varus leaned back in his chair and allowed an admiring smile to play across his lips.

The cheek of the man! To violate the house of his chief was one thing but to steal his daughter from right under his nose and take her for his wife was quite another. But was it truly a theft? It appears she went willingly enough. Obviously there was a conspiracy between the two to carry out the plan without her father's knowledge. It only served to prove the mettle of Arminius and that there was nothing he would not dare if the reward were great enough. Such a man would be a dangerous adversary and one that bore watching.

"Are you sure it was Arminius?" he ventured.

"There can be no doubt."

Varus nodded. "And you say the men with him were armed?"

"Yes."

"Then it would appear that Arminius has thrown in his lot with the rebels."

"I told you, general, he is their leader. It was he who incited the people of the Vasservald to rise up and kill your tax collectors. And now he has my daughter."

"Your daughter is not likely to meet the same fate as my tax collectors. I remind you that this is a matter of state and not one of blood."

Segestes was clearly exasperated by the governor general's inability to see the situation as it really was. "Are you so blind, general, that you cannot see that they are both intertwined?"

"I can see well enough to know that a friend of Caesar would not put the welfare of his own flesh before the larger interests of the Empire."

"I cannot deny that I am concerned for my daughter," replied Segestes, a look of chagrin upon his stony features, "nor can I forget that I have pledged my sword to the Roman cause. But Arminius has inflicted a grievous wound that will not heal until I have sent his shade to the underworld."

"So it is vengeance you seek."

"Yes. And more. It is already being whispered amongst the Cherusci that perhaps I have become too old or too Roman to lead them anymore. They say that if I cannot protect my own household then how can I protect theirs? They say that Arminius is the man to lead them to freedom from the tyranny of Rome. The whole country is ripe for rebellion and Arminius' knows it. If we do not act quickly and break his reputation, his auctoritas as you would call it, then you will have an entire province in flames thirsting for Roman blood."

"I intend to have three legions across the Rhine and in their midst before they realize it," boasted Varus, "That should silence any foolish talk of rebellion."

"That is not enough!" retorted Segestes, "We must slay the head of the dog not its tail. Cutting off its tail will not keep it from biting you. But lop off the head and the body must die."

"Then what is it you propose?"

Segestes leaned forward and fixed Varus with an intense stare. "Release me from service with the legions. Allow me to take a small force ahead of you into the country and search for Arminius. I am familiar with all the tracks that are in the great forest across the Rhine. I know every town and village from here to the Elbe. You do not. I would know where to look for him and once I found him, I swear to you by the gods of my fathers, I will bring him to you in chains, to parade in your triumph through the streets of Rome. I assure you, general, that if you grant this request we will both have what we want. You will have the traitor Arminius and I will have my daughter."

Pride whispered to Varus that he did not need the kind of help Segestes was proposing. It was more a father's pain, he told himself, rather than any clear-sighted stratagem on the part of his German ally that prompted him to suggest such a course. He was about to tell him so when something made him pause. Despite his skewed assessment of the situation in Germany, perhaps Segestes might still be of value to the coming campaign. A poignant question came to Varus' mind: did Segestes' desire to find his daughter really conflict with the larger scheme of Roman policy on the far bank of the Rhine? Arminius might very well be distracted from a greater purpose by having to evade his new father-in-law's frantic efforts to find him. And to that end, Segestes' proposal had definite merit.

"Very well, Segestes, I will grant your request. Take what men you think you will need for your task. Keep me informed of your movements and relay to me personally any information you think may prove useful to us. We may yet end this rebellion before it ever begins."

Segestes' bowed gratefully. "May the gods grant us both success, general."

"You may rely on your gods, whoever they may be," frowned Varus, "but I prefer to put my trust in good Roman steel. You have my leave to go."

"Thank you, general." Segestes bowed again and left the room.

Returning to his letter, Varus reread his last sentence and realized it would have to be rewritten.

VI

During the last week of August, three things occurred which broke the summer-long malaise over Castra Vetera.

Firstly, the oppressive heat and humidity covering the northern marches since the summer equinox finally lifted. The prevailing southerly winds that had been siphoning the desert-heated air of Africa up into Gaul and Germany now gave way to cool breezes off the North Sea. The men of three legions gave grateful praise to whatever gods conscience dictated for the change in the weather. Heavy spirits departed with the receding high temperatures as the simple tasks and duties of the legionaries ceased to be as odious as they had been during the weeks of unrelenting heat. Men greeted one another with restored civility, choosing to forget the quarrels and bad temper produced by the hot, humid summer. Laughter and good humor had become the order of the day.

The second and third occurrences were similar in that they both involved the emergence of seemingly unrelated rumors.

Rumor is always the unavoidable byproduct of bored and idle minds. To this end the legions were not immune. Whole armies have been launched into the jaws of destruction on the strength of a single rumor, a fact that commanders over the centuries had striven to purge, although not always with success, from their ranks. The discipline of the Roman legion for the most part provided a bulwark against the disruption of unsubstantiated rumor. Yet being a superstitious lot, the soldiers listened for it with ready ears all the same. This was especially true when troops had been forced to lay idle in one place for a particularly long time, as the army of the Rhine had been at Castra Vetera that simmering summer. The numbing sameness of duty and routine performed day after day without change made them desirous of anything that promised diversion. And so it was that the rumor of an imminent move across the Rhine into Germany spread like Greek fire amongst the rank and file of the legions. Tongues wagged loudly and men spoke hopefully of marching to glory under the eagles, to cross swords with the barbarians and bring back to hearth and home the spoils of a hard-won victory. The rumor was elevated to fact when Castra Vetera awoke one morning to the loud banging and clattering of construction. The army corps of engineers under the Prefectus fabrum Julius Memmius had set to work erecting a new wooden bridge across the swift current of the Rhine. A spirit of anticipation swept through the camps as men everywhere began polishing and repairing their weapons and armor in readiness for the order to march.

The second rumor followed on the heels of the first and had to do with the mysterious disappearance of the primus pilus of the Nineteenth Legion, Sextus Pompilius and his personal aide, Fortensius Machinus. A thorough search of the country in and around Castra Vetera had turned up no trace of the missing officers. Nor did they uncover a single clue as to what had befallen them. Desertion from the ranks in the Roman army was almost unheard of and so the possible desertion of a senior officer such as Pompilius was cause for much speculation amongst the soldiery. After a few days, the legate of the Nineteenth called off the search and ordered his clerk to strike off the names of Pompilius and Machinus from the rolls. As a consequence, all his centurions moved one place higher in rank. A man named Sergius thus became the new senior centurion of the Nineteenth to the collective relief and general approval of every member of the legion. An unforeseen consequence of the change was that it left the Nineteenth short one command centurion. To fill the vacancy it was inevitable that someone would be promoted from the ranks. The speculation of who the lucky man would be was the main topic of conversation amongst the men of the Nineteenth, at least as much as the talk of the upcoming campaign.

In one of the gigantic mess halls of Castra Vetera, Cornelius sat at one of the long tables sharing his evening meal with Bassanius, Fibrius and two others who shared their tent, Marcus Rubricus and Marcellus Bano. The conversation ranged between the two poles of interest in the camps namely the march into Germany and the disappearance of the Primus Pompilius.

"Have you seen the bridge?" asked Rubricus, a lean wiry man from the highlands of Cisalpine Gaul, "Memmius has almost finished it. I was talking to one of his men and he told me they would be done tomorrow. I'm betting we leave day after tomorrow."

"Too soon," mumbled Bano, a light haired Gaul from Arvenio, through a mouthful of vegetable stew. "We couldn't possibly leave that soon. It'll take us a week just to get ready and load up the wagons. My guess is we'll leave next week sometime."

"That would be cutting it close, Marcellus," returned Rubricus, "It's already the end of August and the campaigning season is nearly over. We'd only have a month and half, maybe two if we're lucky before the snows set in and we have to go to winter camp. That's hardly enough time to wet your sword once with barbarian blood."

"Once is all we'll need," waded in Fibrius. "You only have to kick a German's ass once for him to get the point."

"I wouldn't be so sure, Fibrius," replied Bassanius, "All of you here are novices at this game. I tell you truly that the barbarian is like a mad dog; you never know which way he will jump. One day he may flee from your boot but the next he can sneak up on you from behind to take a bite out of your ass. It will take more than one engagement to teach him who is the master of this country."

"Then when do you think we will leave, 'general'?" asked Rubricus sarcastically.

"We leave," returned Bassanius pointing his thumb in the general direction of the governor's house, "When the bigwigs say we leave." Everyone nodded.

Presently, Rubricus spoke up again and said, "Well, whenever we leave, I hope we know who the new centurion is going to be. Sergius seems like a decent sort. He's certainly a step up from old Fetch Another. But I for one would like to know exactly who is going to command our cohort."

"What do you supposed happened to the old bastard?" asked Bano rhetorically.

"Who cares?" replied Fibrius taking a healthy chunk out of his bread, "He's gone and I thank the gods for it."

"Yes I'm sure you do, Fibrius,"grinned Bassanius."Considering how much he loved you!"

The remark caused titters around the table. Fibrius reddened with anger but the effect was much greater on Cornelius. The spoon he had been holding fell from his trembling hand and clanked nosily into his bowl, splashing the contents of the untouched stew onto the table. Quickly, the laughter subsided as Bassanius stared quizzically at his friend.

"Cornelius?" he asked softly, reaching out to touch his arm. "Are you alright?"

The gesture caused Cornelius to wrap his arms tightly around his abdomen, bending forward at the waist in a continual motion like a child with a stomach ache, his mouth moving wordlessly.

"Cornelius," repeated Bassanius, "What is the matter? You have been acting strangely these past few days and this is stranger still. How has my little joke disturbed you?"

Cornelius stared miserably at his friends but said nothing. While the others gawked, Bassanius mind worked furiously to piece out the puzzle. Why would the mention of Fetch Another's attitude towards Fibrius solicit such a reaction from Cornelius unless..... unless. Realization dawned on Bassanius.

Of course! He knows what happened to Fetch Another!

"Cornelius, where is Pompilius?"

A wild look possessed the younger man's eyes. He shook his head with vehemence.

"Why ask me? I don't know anything! Nothing! Don't ask me anymore questions."

The others immediately caught the implication in Cornelius' answer. They edged their chairs into a tight circle around Cornelius as Bano took up the role of inquisitor. "Cornelius, do you know what happened to the primus?" Again the question was met with a furious refusal. "It's alright, Cornelius, you can tell us. We are all your friends here."

"I can't!" protested Cornelius, a tear sliding down his cheek. "I can't! He's gone, that's all I know. He's gone and he's not coming back." Jumping to his feet, he stumbled out of the hall.

The four companions sat staring at one another in disbelief.

"What do you make of that?" asked Rubricus.

"I would say," said Bassanius, "That our friend Cornelius has the answer to the riddle of Pompilius' disappearance."

Fibrius sucked his tongue between his teeth. "And what was that? He didn't say anything."

"On the contrary, Fibrius. Cornelius told us all we needed to know. Remember what he said? 'He's gone and he's not coming back'. That sounds very definite to me. Whatever his part in it, I would say that he knows Fetch Another is dead and most likely his toady Machinus as well."

"If he knows what happened, why doesn't he go to the legate?" asked Rubricus. "Don't you think the legate would like to know the fate of one of his senior centurions?"

Bassanius shook his head. "He can't, Marcus. You saw his reaction when I mentioned Pompilius. Cornelius knows more than just the 'what.' He knows the 'who' and quite possibly the 'why', although I dare say just about everyone in the Nineteenth would have been willing to kill that old lecher and consider it a good day's work. For all we know, he may have been personally involved. None of us needs to be reminded of the penalty for killing an officer. For the time being I suggest we keep this to ourselves, both for his benefit as well as our own. If this becomes common knowledge and reaches the ears of the legate, it will be assumed that we knew about it but chose not to say anything. We could very well receive the same punishment as the guilty. Are any of you willing to risk that?" From the looks on their faces, he could tell that they were not. "Then we are agreed. Let us keep silent on the matter for the moment and leave it to the gods to sort out. For now, we must say nothing."

VII

The day was overcast and cool, courtesy of the cold wind that had been blowing consistently for a week across the chilled waters of the North Sea. Although it was only the first week of September, the legionaries who struck down their tents and packed their kits for the march into the forest fastness of Germany, were ordered to include their heavy woolen winter cloaks and leggings. The affect of this demand succeeded only in creating widespread grumbling among the soldiers who resented the imposition of the added weight to their packs as an unnecessary hardship for a march through difficult country. They were doubly perturbed when they learned that they were being made responsible for transporting the fat senator from Rome along with his bloated retinue of lawyers and lictors and fifteen extra wagons filled with the accoutrements of the legal profession into enemy territory. What idiot, they asked themselves, would bog down the movement of troops in dangerous country by saddling them with useless civilians? What good was a bunch of fancy lawyers in a land as backward and uncivilized as Germany? Unless they could wield a sword or cast a pilum, what use were their ink pots, rods and paper if they should find themselves under attack? The whole situation reeked of overconfidence and bad planning. To the mind of every legionary, it was nothing more than the ingredients for a disaster that no amount of sacrificial offerings to the gods would prevent. And to a man, they all knew who was to blame. Varus had begun his first campaign with a monumental blunder. He had by his thoughtless actions alienated the respect of his troops.

And so it was a surly group of legionaries who gathered on the parade ground just east of Castra Vetera to hear what their commanding general had to say to them. Three legions, some eighteen thousand men in all, stood row on row in full armor facing the stand which had been erected to one side of the new wooden bridge. Before the perfect square of each legion were arrayed the legionary standard bearers, identified by the leopard skins they wore over their helmets and cuirasses. Each man who functioned in these honored positions had a specific image for which he was responsible. Three vexillarii carried upon their poles a small square banner of stitched cloth stiffened by wire sown into its edges, proclaiming the name and number of the legion they represented. Around them stood the signiferi, eighty in number to correspond with the number of centuries for each legion. The signifer carried a long pole crowned with either a spear point or an open hand with circular shields of polished silver or bronze affixed to the shaft identifying the century and the cohort to which it belonged. To the most senior and trusted of the standard bearers, the aquiliferi went the honor of carrying the splendid silver eagles that represented each legion in both body and spirit. The eagle was believed to be the incarnation of the legion itself and thus came to signify the embodiment of every member of that particular legion. Men would rather die then see their eagle fall into enemy hands, a disgrace that meant the purging of the offending legion from the Army rolls forever, a fate too hideous for any soldier to consider. To see the legions thus arrayed before their proud eagles and standards was an impressive sight that gave testimony to the power that had conquered the known world.

Presently, the wide space of the parade ground echoed with the sound of trumpets heralding the appearance on the stairs of the reviewing stand of the army high command. Led by Varus, encased in the gorgeous ebony armor of his office, the group consisted of the three legionary legates, the Tribune Silvanius as commander of the horse, Chief Engineer Memmius, Quintus Plodius, the prefect of Castra Vetera and Domitius Catullus, prefect of the Rhine fleet at Novaesium. The last to mount the platform was the obese figure of Senator Turtullus, conspicuous by the whiteness of his toga and the broad band of purple that marked his membership to the senatorial class. He wore a smirk upon his face, blissfully unaware of how he had become the target for the seething rage of the soldiery.

When the high command had taken their places on the platform, Varus stepped forward and raised his hands. "Soldiers of Rome!" he cried, his voice echoing across the wide space of the parade ground. "I greet you in the name of our beloved and esteemed Emperor Augustus Caesar!" At the mention of the name of the Emperor of Rome, eighteen thousand men drew out their swords and banged them against their concave shields in a universal act of respect and obeisance. Varus allowed the tumult to continue for a few moments before raising his hands again for order.

"You do yourselves justice by your display of affection for the Emperor. Know then that it is Augustus Caesar himself who has called you to uphold Roman honor amongst the barbarians of Germany. It is his most solemn wish that the authority of Rome should now be extended from the Rhine on which we stand to the far waters of the Elbe so that all the peoples of Germany might benefit from our enlightened government."

An anonymous voice cried out from the ranks, "Then what need have we of lawyers, general?" The question solicited a murmuring rumble of agreement from the massed legionaries.

"There can be no government or order without law," replied Varus in way of explanation. "The Germans must learn that without law there can be no peace. The lawyers are needed to teach and instruct the people in the Roman rule of law."

"Then let them carry their own gear!" shouted another voice. This time the reaction from the troops was louder and more insistent. The smirk on Turtullus' face began to fade. A realization of danger was beginning to dawn on his officious mind. Varus might agree for the need of a legal presence in Germany but the legions were of a different opinion. Turtullus wondered if he had more to fear from the soldiers in his own camp than the barbarians across the river.

Varus held his hands up a third time for silence. "Do my ears deceive me? Can these be loyal sons of Rome I am hearing today? Have the stout hearts of the men of the Tiber melted away like water? Who has stolen from you the necessity of duty and the strength of discipline? How would Gaul have ever been vanquished if the legions of the Divine Julius had refused to obey his commands?"

"Caesar never had to deal with lawyers," retorted one wag, "only senators!" It was an allusion to the fact that Julius Caesar had been assassinated in the Senate House of Rome by men of the same ilk as Turtullus. The joke sent a roaring chorus of laughter through the ranks.

Varus angrily began to pace back and forth on the platform. "Since the days of Marius, the legions have built towns and cities, theatres and aqueducts, roadways and forts. The Empire is filled with the works of your hands and yet now you cry like children because you are being asked to take a few wagons through the woods. For shame O soldiers of Rome! Where is your courage? Where are your stout hearts?"

"Where are their muscles?" came back a shouting retort. The sea of legionaries roared with laughter again and began banging their shields with their swords. Few noticed Senator Turtullus quietly leave the reviewing stand.

Varus turned and signaled the trumpeters to sound for order. When the trilling blasts had at last restored quiet across the field, the governor general stood in the middle of the platform with his fists planted on his hips scowling at the helmeted faces before him. "How dare you call yourselves Romans!" he cried. "Your fight is not with those who dwell on this side of the river. We are all citizens here. It is against those who live on the far bank who defy the authority of Caesar and the

Roman people. Yet by your behavior here today you have set yourselves up against that authority and have numbered yourselves with the barbarians!"

These last words found their mark in the wounded pride of the soldiers. A low murmur drifted between the perfect lines of fighting men, punctuated here and there with a scattered 'no' or 'never'. Sensing that he had stemmed the tide of sedition for the moment, Varus went on.

"Look!" he shouted, dramatically pointing to the forest eves on the far side of the river. "There lies your enemy! There lies the power that seeks to topple Rome! But they are cowards, hiding behind the skirts of their wives and mothers, afraid to come out and face the legions of Caesar in the open, as civilized men would do. Oh yes, the German is proud and boastful when his foe is at arm's length but let him be faced with a greater power and he comes crawling like a dog to your feet. It is well known that the harder you hit a German the more respectful he becomes and I intend to hit them hard!" Varus' bravado elicited a loud cheer from the legions followed by more shield banging.

"Caesar has commanded me to bring order out of chaos," cried Varus. Stepping to the edge of the platform he grasped the standard of Caesar's image from the nearest imaginifer. Holding it aloft for all to see, he shouted, "And it is our Emperor's will that this standard be planted upon the banks of the Elbe River for the glory of mighty Rome! Who then will follow me? Who will crush the hand that dares to raise itself against Rome? Who will do the will of his Emperor?"

Pandemonium reigned on the field as men cheered and shouted, stamping their feet and hammering on their shields. The sound swelled into a thunderous cacophony that filled the air as men strove to outdo one another in their praise of Caesar and their support for their commander. Whatever residue of resentment the soldiers harbored for the civilians in their midst, Varus' stirring harangue had succeeded in quelling it for the moment. Their minds had been turned to thoughts of glory and conquest, meat to the hungry soul of a soldier. All were eager to begin the campaign and win what they had been promised. 'To the Elbe!' became their war cry. They would have all crowded together to ford the Rhine on the new bridge, sinking it in the process, if not for discipline of their training. They remained in their ranks, banging shields and brandishing swords waiting for the order from their centurions to march. But the centurions waited upon Varus.

Even while the cheering was at its climax, Varus at the height of his own exhortation ran across the platform and down the stairs to the foot of the wooden bridge. Turning to face his troops, he raised the standard above his head and cried, "Follow me, noble Romans, and I will lead you to glory and everlasting fame! Centurions give the order to strike arms and move out! First the Seventeenth, then the Eighteenth and finally the Nineteenth! Let us go conquering to the Elbe!" Sprinting across the bridge, he reached the far side of the Rhine where he planted the standard on the muddy bank of the river and waited. Soon the head of the first column came into view over the central span of the bridge.

At its head walked the legate of the Seventeenth, leading a large mottled bay behind him. When he reached the end of the bridge, he handed the reins to Varus who swung up on the horse and unsheathed his sword. "To the Elbe for Caesar and for Rome!" he cried to the metallic gray line of legionaries who streamed down over the bridge. Swinging his sword like an axe, Varus plunged into the forest wall, followed closely by his soldiers.

Unbeknownst to Varus, however, the standard left on the bank bearing the beaten brass likeness of Augustus Caesar began to slide down the muddy bank of the river from the vibration of the columns of hobnailed feet on the planks of the bridge. Leaning precariously out over the swirling surface of the river it finally fell in with a silent plop and disappeared beneath the murky water. It would prove to be an ill omen for Rome.

VIII

The fires of the camp burned like fireflies through the angled trunks of the dark wood.

Segestes, with a band of three hundred warriors, crouched silently in the undergrowth around the encampment, watching for any sign of movement around the mud-walled huts. After days of unfruitful search, they had come upon an old swineherd tending a small group of pigs who told them of a new habitation that had recently appeared in the upper reaches of the forest. When asked if he had seen a man like Arminius in appearance around the camp, the old man replied that although he had not been to the place himself, he did remember seeing someone fitting Arminius' description during market day in his own village not three days past. Perhaps, he suggested, the man they were looking for had his dwelling place in the new settlement.

"Was there a woman with him?" asked Segestes hopefully.

"Yes," answered the swineherd, "I believe there was. She was most beautiful as I recall. She seemed very devoted to this man."

Segestes heart sank at the news. He was pleased to know his daughter was safe even though it was obvious she did not think herself in any danger. It only served to confirm the fear that had plagued him since the night of her abduction. There could be no doubt now that she had been a willing participant in the whole affair. The rebuke of his own flesh and blood served only to deepen Segestes' thirst for vengeance.

Segestes had found the encampment exactly where the old man had indicated, a half dozen circular mud huts with thatched straw roofs thrown up in the center of a clearing. In behind the clearing, providing a natural defence from attack was a wooded ridge that sloped steeply up and away from the perimeter of the huts. No wooden palisade or earthwork had been constructed for the entrance to the settlement suggesting that if Arminius was encamped here, he did not expect trouble to assail him from that quarter. Segestes had come under cover of dusk and had commanded his men to conceal themselves in the wood until they received the signal to move from him. He had sent a trusted scout forward to spy out the settlement and bring back word of possible hidden entrenchments and whether Arminius was actually present. And so he sat, watching the glowing fires through the trees while patiently waiting for the scout to return.

Presently, the man returned and gave his report. The camp was deserted. The huts were empty except for one that contained a few assorted items from which the scout had brought back an iron torque affixed with a pair of entwined serpents with ruby eyes. Segestes turned the torque in his hand and proclaimed, "It is his. He is here."

"But the place is deserted," asserted the scout, "It does not appear to have been inhabited at all."

"Then what of the fires?" asked one of the other warriors.

"They have been set to give the illusion that someone has been here. But I have searched the entire camp and found nothing. Whoever did this wanted us to believe that someone was encamped here."

"For what reason?" inquired another warrior.

"To send us a message," replied Segestes, "To taunt us by showing us that we will always be one step behind our quarry. Perhaps he hopes we will tire of the chase if we realize the futility of it. A man of Arminius' overweening pride would dare anything. Even to the point of stealing what can never belong to him." Segestes stared at the unattended campfires, nursing his thoughts while his men waited in the dark. Finally, the scout asked softly, "What are your orders, lord?"

Turning from his reverie, Segestes looked at the intent faces of his followers. "Burn it to the ground. We will send a message of our own to our adversary."

Whooping and shouting, the Cherusci warriors emerged from their hiding places and advanced on the abandoned camp. From somewhere, a torch was produced, followed by others. It was not long before the entire encampment was consumed in a conflagration of flames.

Segestes watched the bonfire with detachment. That it was a useless exercise he had little doubt. He envisioned seeing Arminius in the midst of the flames, his flesh and bones being seared away and vanquished by its fierceness. Then this merry fire would have a purpose! But for now he would have to content himself with the pleasure such thoughts of vengeance brought to his troubled spirit. One day, he was sure, the gods would bring his foe under his hand and then his thirst for vengeance would be slaked at last.

"Ho, Segestes!"

A familiar voice echoed across the hollow space of the clearing, jarring Segestes into a taut alertness. Seeking the origin of the challenge, Segestes looked up and to the right of the burning settlement to the top of the ridge where he saw a group of men with torches standing in a gap in the trees. His heart pounded in his ears as he recognized the figure standing defiantly between a pair of torchbearers.

Arminius!

"Ho, Segestes!" he called again though cupped hands. "What are you trying to do, burn down the whole forest?"

Segestes ran to the foot of the slope followed by a number of warriors, their swords drawn. "If I knew you were hiding behind a single tree, I'd burn down every forest in Germany!" threatened Segestes.

Arminius wagged his head and sucked his teeth. "Now, now, is that any way to greet your son-in-law?" The words caused Segestes to squeeze his hands into fists of impotent rage. "Where is Thusnelda? Return her to me now and I will forget the oath I swore to kill you!"

Arminius' mocking laughter boomed out across the glade. "Thusnelda is mine, now. She is my wife of her own free will."

"Liar! I don't believe you, you lying dog of a Sarmatian! Let me hear it from her own lips!"

"Alas, I could not bring my wife with me to greet you tonight. She is resting in our tent. We are expecting my son in the spring!"

Segestes doubled over onto his knees as if he had been struck in the stomach. A long strangled cry emerged from the pit of his tortured soul, wailing in the torment of a fearful dream come true. He had lost her! She now belonged to another man, body, soul and mind. And she was going to carry his child! To endure the whelp of such a man was a fate almost too hateful to bear. The thought was like a blacksmith's bellows in his mind, fanning his hatred and desire for vengeance into a white-hot ingot that threatened to sear his very being.

Rising to his feet again, Segestes looked up at Arminius, his eyes filled with hate. "By Odin's beard, I will have your head for this insult to me and mine, you son of hell. A child you may have gotten upon my daughter but I swear it will never know its father. You shall be dead upon my blade before spring. Flee to the ends of the earth, swine, even to the courts of Caesar if you dare. You will not escape me. I will have my Thusnelda back!"

Arminius gazed down at his father-in-law with a look of pity on his handsome features. "Your time is past, old man," he replied, "Our people need a new leader, one who will lead them to glory and freedom. They do not need a feeble heart to bring them under the Roman yoke. We are a free people, Segestes. But you have forgotten who you are and now you seek to blind the minds of your own people to the truth. We will not become lackeys to the Romans. We will destroy them before that happens or die in the attempt!"

"My daughter has tied herself to madman!" exclaimed Segestes. "Only a fool would deny the power of Rome. How many nations have they crushed underfoot because they refused to submit to the mistress of the world? For good or ill, the gods have given them dominion over the earth. If you stand against Rome, you stand against the gods of heaven!"

"I am standing with the gods," corrected Arminius boldly, "For say what you will, they are still only men and men make mistakes. I believe the Romans have overreached themselves. It is not the divine will that the Cherusci become a subject race to Rome. I have seen it in visions and in my dreams. Wide fields of Roman dead, broken swords and captured eagles. If the Roman comes into Germany, he will do so at his peril!"

"Fool!" cried Segestes, "Varus is already on his way with three legions! Dreams and visions cannot stand against sword and pilum!"

Arminius grinned broadly, his hands on his hips. "I am aware that Varus is coming with his legions. After all, I invited him!"

"Invited him? What do you mean you invited him?" Segestes felt a sickening pang of disquiet creep into his stomach.

"Dreams and visions, old man!" laughed Arminius, "Go and deliver this message to your master like the obedient hound you are! Tell our friend Quinctilius Varus that if he wants to find me, he must come to the Teutoberg Forest!" Suddenly, the torches around Arminius went out and the ridge was plunged into darkness.

By the time Segestes and his men and scrambled up the heavily wooded slope to the top of the ridge, Arminius and his men were gone.

IX

Cornelius lay on his bunk and stared into the darkness around him. Sleep had been an infrequent companion since the night of Pompilius' death. When it did creep into his tent, it brought with it terrifying visions and black nightmares that drove him to wakefulness again. In these nightly horrors, Fetch Another appeared as a hideous demon with fangs slick with dripping saliva and blazing lizard-like eyes. Like Prometheus of Greek myth, Cornelius discovered that he had been chained naked to a rock, shivering in fear as the demon circled about him. And in the moment when the claws reached for his exposed skin, he screamed himself awake. After that, he shunned sleep like an enemy.

He didn't know exactly when the thought to kill himself entered his consciousness but as the days passed, it grew louder and more persistent in his mind. His mood grew more morose and bleak fueled by lack of sleep and the weighty guilt he felt like chains around his soul. True to their word, his tent mates kept their oaths and avoided him when they could, making excuses when they could not. Even his good friend Bassanius, at a loss of what to do or say, made the choice to disassociate himself from Cornelius. For the first time since he joined the legions, Cornelius felt alone and alienated, no longer a functioning member of the whole but a discordant part with no purpose. In such a state of mind, the idea of suicide had little trouble in finding fertile ground.

As he lay in the darkness, fingering the sharp edge of the sword beside him, he listened intently to the sounds around him. It was the second night out of Castra Vetera and Varus had chosen to make his camp in a sheltered valley of short grasses and shrubs some forty miles northeast of the fortress walls. Outside the leather walls of the papilo, Cornelius could hear the heavy tramping of the pickets on guard duty mingling with the crackling of cooking fires, and the muffle of murmuring voices. When the wind was right, the odd snatch of the gurgling brook that ran across the floor of the valley whispered in his ear. Sometimes he fancied he could actually hear voices in the water beckoning him to come and lay down in the forgetfulness of the cool stream.

Around him, men lay asleep in their bunks, exhausted from the effort of their march through the tangled underbrush of the German countryside. The highly charged emotions of the day they embarked across the Rhine had been quickly extinguished by renewed grumbling and complaining as the legionaries struggled to drive the overloaded wagons of the civilians over the ghastly terrain. To add to their misery, rain had begun falling the previous afternoon and had transformed the soft earth into a sinking quagmire. After a day's wasting march and the intensive labors required to set up the evening's camp, it was all the men could do from falling senseless with exhaustion into their bunks. Fortunately for Cornelius, it was unlikely anyone would see him leave.

Perhaps it was the combination of the miserable conditions around him or the spreading blackness within him that convinced him it was finally time to act. Without sleep, he could not face another day's rigorous march without collapsing on the way. Should that occur, it meant an extended stay in the infirmary where they would nurse him back to health before returning him to duty. Then the cycle would begin all over again. No, if he were going to do this thing, he would do it right. He would do it quickly. He would do it as a Roman. And he would do it now.

Silently rising from his bed, he crept between the rows of cots with their compliment of sleeping soldiers, and slipped out into the night. The air was crisp and cool, befitting an early September evening. The rain that had been steady for a day and half had momentarily let up. The sky overhead was locked inside a mantle of thick cloud covering the stars and moon. Drawing his greasy sagum around him to keep out the chill of the night air as well as concealing the sword he carried, Cornelius walked with determined steps toward the main gate. Nodding to the sentries, he explained his need to relieve himself. They let him pass without comment.

Walking on in the coolness of the evening he came to the bank of the brook and stood watching the dark waters drift by his feet. The lulling sound of the water over the pebbled bed of the stream had a soothing effect on Cornelius' thoughts. In the gurgling of the water he fancied he heard the voice of the brook calling softly, "Come to me, O tormented soul. Lay down and feel my cold touch and I will make you forget." For the first time in many months, his thoughts drifted to home and his father in far off Rhegium. He wondered if he should have written the old man one last time, explaining why he had ignored his injunction to run off and join the legions. But of what use was such recriminations now? His dream had been shattered; its broken pieces would be all the evidence his father would need to confirm his judgment. The elder Strabo would have to be content with the small stipend he would receive from the government for the loss of his only son.

The squall of sad memories was abruptly dissipated by the appearance of the Man of Dreams to his mind's eye. The soft eyes were filled with an expression of compassion that seemed to look past Cornelius' outer man and into the very heart of his tortured spirit. The bearded lips smiled but spoke not a word. Yet in his mind, he heard a voice say, "Come to me, my child and I will give you rest!"

Overcome with emotion Cornelius dropped to his knees and began to weep. Crying out in the night, he said, "Lord, who are you? If you are the spirit of these waters speak to me further, I implore you! If you are one of the gods, show yourself to me. Give me a sign to show me what I must do! Give me a sign, I beg you!" He strained to listen for a reply but heard only the insistent murmuring of the running brook.

He had no idea how long he remained kneeling by the brook. No visible sign came while he waited. In the crucible of his tormented mind, Cornelius despaired of his sanity. Slowly he rose to his feet, embracing the purpose of self-destruction with a renewed fortitude that left him strangely calm. "I see the way of it now," he said to the darkness around him, "There is no hope for me except in death. The gods, if they exist, take little interest in the affairs of men. They hide themselves from the world and care not for the souls in their keeping. I curse them in their lofty places and damn them to hell even as I send my own shade to Hades." Pulling aside his cloak and tunic, he brought the point of his sword to rest over his heart. Closing his eyes and grasping the hilt of the weapon with both hands, he took a deep breath and prepared to deliver the deathblow. A familiar voice stayed his hand and caused him to turn with a start.

"I trust you are only cleaning that weapon out here, soldier."

Gaius Silvanius stood a short distance behind Cornelius, his feet apart, his arms folded across his midsection, a look of mild amusement on his angular features. Unlike their previous encounter, the tribune was not in armor but was attired only in a simple short tunic and scarlet military cloak. His head was bare, showing a manicured crown of black curls. He was armed only with a dagger that was sheathed to the thin leather belt around his waist. Cornelius stood with his mouth open too surprised to speak.

"Nice night for a walk," commented Silvanius, standing next to the young man and staring down at the water. "But I should warn you, this is dangerous country and you would do well to stay close to the camp. By the way what is your name soldier? I am afraid I didn't catch it when last we met."

"Cornelius Strabo, sir."

"Strabo." Silvanius turned the name over on his tongue. "That is Greek is it not?"

"Yes, sir."

"Where are you from?"

"Rhegium, sir."

The tribune nodded. "Been there. It is a beautiful city with a large harbor if memory serves."

"Yes, sir. My father is the harbormaster there."

Silvanius' black eyebrows shot up wrinkling the smooth brow. "Indeed? But you had no taste for that kind of work?"

"No, sir. As long as I can remember, I have always wanted to be a soldier."

"With your father's blessings to be sure."

"No, sir. I ran away from home after my mother died and joined the legions in Capua. My father never shared my enthusiasm for a military career. He wanted me to become the harbormaster after him just as he had done with his father and his father before him."

"Oh, I see, it is a hereditary position. Well then, its little wonder your father could not see eye to eye with you on your choice of professions. Still, it is not a good thing to go against a father's wishes. Here, you'd better let me have that weapon."

Cornelius stared down at the sword in his hand as if seeing it for the first time and then meekly handed it hilt first to the tribune. "As I was saying," continued Silvanius, tucking the blade in his belt, "It is not a good thing for a Roman to disobey his father's wishes. Fathers desire only the best for their sons; it is only natural after all. Would it have been such a terrible thing to become the harbormaster of

Rhegium? It certainly would have been more preferable than tramping around these infernal woods."

"I wanted to be a soldier," answered Cornelius with a tinge of petulance in his voice.

Silvanius fixed him with a steely glance and said evenly, "A soldier is not afraid of death, Cornelius Strabo. He learns very quickly that it is his boon companion, always at his shoulder, ready to extract its wage when offered. Death can be your best friend and ultimately your worst enemy. You must learn to use it to your advantage. How old are you anyway, Cornelius? Nineteen, twenty?"

"Eighteen, sir."

The tribune nodded and stooped down to pick up a pebble, which he skipped across the surface of the stream to far bank. "At the latrine pits," he asked, "Was that your first time killing a man?"

Cornelius began to tremble, his mind heaving with guilt. "I.... I...no, I, I.... I mean yes... I mean...."

"Why did you come out here tonight, Cornelius?" continued Silvanius placing a comforting hand on the younger man's shoulder. Cornelius let out a shuddering sigh and sobbed, "To kill myself. Whatever the man did to me that night changed me forever and I have hated what I have become."

"And what have you become, Cornelius?"

"A monster. A madman. A coward. I don't know."

Silvanius shook his head and smiled. "No, my young friend, you aren't any of those things. Those were the very things you destroyed when you killed that jackal Pompilius. No, the only thing you've become is a man. Death overtakes us all and in Pompilius' case it was sorely overdue. But let me ask you this: do you think you would have felt differently if Pompilius had been a barbarian?"

"Of course," retorted Cornelius, "Barbarians are enemies of Rome. They threaten to destroy everything that is beautiful, everything that is lovely, everything that is Roman. It's the reason I wanted to be a soldier in the first place; to destroy those who wanted to destroy us."

The tribune laughed and stooped to skip another stone. "Very noble. You make it sound like a spiritual quest. But has it ever occurred to you that the enemies of Rome lurk on both sides of the frontier?" Cornelius frowned, disturbed by the inference of Silvanius' question.

The tribune continued. "What I'm saying is this: that a man like Pompilius is just as much a danger to the Roman way of life as any barbarian whether you find him on the Rhine or the Euphrates or even the Tiber. Men like Pompilius eat away at the structure of empire from within just as the barbarians beat against it from without. Believe me I when I tell you I know this to be a fact. I have lived amongst the very people we now strive to subdue with our laws and our swords. In their hearts I have discovered a nobleness of spirit and a depth of courage and compassion that are lacking in Roman ones. That is why I can stand here and tell you that men like Pompilius will always deserve death no matter which master they choose to serve."

The two men fell into silence with only the sound of the brook between them. Silvanius' words had produced a marvelous affect on Cornelius. He felt the heavy darkness of the past weeks lifting off his soul, affecting a feeling of lightness of being. Pain receded like a tide and a welcome peace enveloped his heart. The crisis had passed, the night was over and Cornelius knew his life would go on, different in some ways, better in others, but it would go on. But for now he was acutely aware of how tired he was and the need to find his bunk.

As if reading his mind, Silvanius yawned and said, "It is late. Shall we go?"

"Yes, sir."

As they prepared to return to the main gate, a question caused Cornelius to stop and ask, "Sir, how did you know I would be out here by the brook?"

The gray eyes of the tribune took on a dreamy cast as if seeing something from far off. "It was strangest thing," he said half to himself, "I am not a man given to portents and signs, but I had a dream. And in the dream, a most extraordinary man appeared to me and told me to get up and go out to the stream outside the camp where I would find a young man in agony of spirit who was despairing of life. The impulse was so strong from the dream, that it literally drove me out of bed and out into the night. That was when I found you here. Strange, isn't it?"

Cornelius was thunderstruck. He had asked for a sign and a sign had been given. It was clear to him now that he owed his recovery not to so much from the arguments of the tribune but to a supernatural agency that was watching over his life. From that revelation, a single thought reverberated through his mind like a lamp in the dark:

Who is this Man of Dreams?

X

Despite Governor General Varus' seemingly rash behavior in leading his legions across the new bridge on the Rhine, he knew exactly what he wanted to do. His intention was to parallel the line of march pioneered by the Emperor's stepson Tiberius Nero to the Elbe some years before. This required him to strike out in a slightly northeasterly direction, crossing the marshy and heavily wooded countryside along the line of the Lippe River before skirting the southern headwaters of the Ems and Weser Rivers. Along with various temporary causeways and bridges fording some of the more swampy areas, Tiberius had constructed two fortresses on this line: Aliso on the Lippe River near the source of the Ems and Minden on the muddy banks of the Weser. Between these two fortified points stretched the foreboding and brooding eves of the Teutoberg Forest.

Over the intervening years, these forts had been manned with a skeleton force of auxiliary troops drafted from the surrounding population, depending upon the prevailing political climate of the time. Returning scouts reported to Varus that Aliso still possessed a small garrison of auxiliaries and that its fortifications were relatively intact. Minden, however, was a different story. It was for all intents and purposes abandoned and appeared to have been so for some time. The walls and foundations were in desperate need of repair and the front gates had been torn down and carted off, probably by the barbarians themselves.

Varus' military staff argued for restraint and suggested they make for Aliso, enlarging and strengthening the fortress by replacing its wooden walls and ramparts with stone and establishing a permanent garrison as a strategic reserve before moving on toward the Elbe. The Germans, they pointed out, were suspiciously quiet and submissive of late and that it was more than likely a ruse to draw the Romans into a false sense of security before rising suddenly to strike.

"Nonsense!" snorted Varus derisively. "The barbarians are incapable of such duplicity. If they are quiet it is because they respect the power of three Roman legions in their midst. I agree we must reinforce the garrison but I intend to leave them only a cohort. That should be sufficient. My goal is to make for Minden. Any fool can see that it is the real key to the whole province, not Aliso. It guards the approach to three rivers as well as the plain that divides the Weser from the Elbe. For that reason alone, Minden must be restored and strengthened. But my intention is to establish our winter quarters there and by doing so, move the frontier from the Rhine to the Weser."

"Excuse me, general," replied Marcus Vinicius Rufus, legate of the Eighteenth Legion and a veteran of three previous campaigns in Germany, "But if we establish our lines upon the Weser, we leave ourselves open to a hostile population behind us that could rise up in revolt the minute we shut ourselves inside Minden."

"And besides, general," broke in Caecilius Mentor, legate of the Seventeenth, "We can't possibly make the Weser before the first snow falls with the amount of wagons and baggage we're carrying. The men are tired and grumbling as it is with the effort required to move the trains through this cursed country. Won't you consider the alternative of heading for Aliso instead?"

Varus allowed his irritability to show. "Do my ears deceive me? Can these possibly be Romans saying such things that only women would say? What has made you so faint of heart? The Germans know they are beaten and will not assail us. When they see the eagles standing on the battlements of a new fortress on the Weser they will realize their resistance is futile and they will have no choice but to submit to the authority of Rome and the Emperor. The will of Caesar will be carried out and we will plant our standards on the Elbe before midsummer."

It was at that inopportune moment that a message arrived for Varus from Segestes. Taking a cursory glance at the note, he ordered it read aloud to his staff.

To Quinctilius Varus from Segestes, chief of the Cherusci.

Be warned Excellency, that I now have proof that Arminius is leading and inciting the people to revolt against you. The chiefs of the Chatti, Marsi and Brueteri have joined arms with those of the Chersusci who follow him and have gathered to prepare themselves for war. Although I have managed to burn his encampment at Volgisces I was unable to apprehend him or those who were with him. I did, however, speak with him and your Excellency should know that he told me if you wished to find him you must come to the Teutoberg Forest.

Do not go there, your Excellency! It is a wild and dangerous place filled with ghosts and evil spirits. Few of my people dare to venture in its wood and even then only when necessary. It is my opinion that Arminius is setting a trap for you as it is a place ideal for a hidden assault. The wooded hills will conceal the enemy from your sight before it is too late and the marshy valleys make it unsuitable for maneuver by the legions. Those who do not die by the dagger in the dark will perish at the hands of the malevolent beings in the forest. Pay heed to my warning! Do not approach the Teutoberg Wood under any circumstance! If you must pass that way, my advice is to make for Aliso as quickly as possible and fortify it for the winter. Arminius will not be able to hold his forces together long nor will he dare attack you behind stockade, moat and ramparts. The winter will weaken him while you gather your strength so that come the spring, you will be able to march unopposed to the Elbe.

I pray you will hearken to my warning and remember me as a true friend of Rome.

SEGESTES

"It seems, gentlemen," commented Varus, "That our friend Segestes shares your opinion. I, on the other hand, do not. Nor is there anything in this note that would dissuade me from abandoning a march to Minden."

Gaius Silvanius spoke up and said, "Sir, if I may venture my own opinion. I have been in the

Teutoberg Forest and the noble Segestes is right when he calls it a dangerous place. There are few places in the world that have filled me with an inexplicable feeling of unease and terror than those dark woods. Even the dullest German knows enough to steer clear of it for it has an evil reputation. It would be most imprudent as well as foolhardy, to attempt a march through it, especially if Arminius is planning an ambush there."

Varus glared at his cavalry commander with knitted brow. "Your sympathies for the barbarians are well known, tribune. But I think I understand their minds better than you. The German is incapable of orchestrating and implementing the kind of attack Segestes suggests. He is by nature a coward and although he might conceal himself behind a tree, it is not for the purpose of an ambush but to hide from being beaten by a Roman stick. If by your argument I understand you to say that the barbarian has the capacity for the kind of organization required to engage in an ambush of three Roman legions, would it not follow that perhaps he also possesses the attribute of subterfuge? Are you willing to entertain the possibility that this threat of ambush is only a ruse forcing us to go around this forest and thereby to a place more suitable for Arminius' purposes? I for one do not believe it."

"I am willing to entertain any possibility, sir," replied Silvanius, "Arminius is a lot smarter than you are giving him credit for."

"I am well aware of Arminius' capabilities, tribune."

"Are you, sir? Arminius is the most dangerous of barbarians: one trained and fashioned by Rome herself. He knows well the Roman ways. He has served and commanded in the auxiliary and wears a gold ring of citizenship on his finger. He is more like us than you imagine."

"Once a barbarian always a barbarian," retorted the governor general.

"Just as once a fool, always a fool, Excellency."

"What does that mean, tribune?"

"Just this. That Arminius fooled you once. Do not allow him to do so a second time. For if you do, it could very well mean the death of us all."

"Not while there is life in my body."

"Then stay away from the Teutoberg Forest," said Silvanius grimly. "And don't go to Minden."

With equal grimness Varus ended the discussion. "I will reach Minden any way I must and I will not allow tales of a haunted forest spread by a renegade soldier turn me from my purpose! You are all dismissed!"

XI

The fortress of Aliso was constructed on the crown of a bald hill overlooking an ancient Celtic pathway that ran from the Rhine to the Weser. It was built ostensibly to provide a fortified point for any future Roman offensive into the upper reaches on the river Elbe. Whenever the legions chose a site for permanent occupation, it was always with an eye to the merchants and colonists that would inevitably follow on the heels of the army. It was they who transformed such outposts into the Roman municipia, with its forums, basilicas, marketplaces. Some were even fortunate enough to boast the luxuries of a theatre or arena. After the departure of the legions, these municipia became effective instruments of Romanization through daily interaction with the surrounding natives. The indigenous populations quickly learned that in order to obtain the material advantages offered by Rome they would have to adopt the language and practices of the Roman way of life. In this way, not only was a common Latin framework established to foster a grassroots unity and loyalty to the Empire, but goods from all over the Mediterranean world found their way into the strangest places. Thus could Syrian copper pots and bolts of royal Tyrhennean cloth turn up in villas and marketplaces all over Gaul and Spain just as easily as amphorae of Gallic wine appear in the great Agora of Athens or the

111

exotic bazaars of Alexandria and Damascus. It will be understood then, that this was what Tiberius had envisioned for Aliso when he laid out its fortifications. It must also be noted that he was not unmindful of the need to have a military presence beneath the looming shadow of the Teutoberg Forest.

Five days following Cornelius' brush with the miraculous at the nameless brook of the second night's camp, the Army of the Rhine straggled wearily through Aliso's gates. It had rained three out of the five days making their progress frustratingly slow. Precious time was lost to the remaining campaign season because the legionaries were constantly struggling to free the commissariat wagons from the grip of muddy tracks and marshy ground. Their already smoldering resentment and anger against the civilians was fanned further by the infuriating behavior of the lawyers and their lictors who insisted on standing to one side while the soldiers strained to free their carts. Around the evening camp fires, the air was filled with more threats against Turtullus and his rasping crew of magistrates then against the barbarians themselves. In one unfortunate incident, the bank on which a group of lawyers were perched as they watched the soldiery work on righting their tipped cart, gave way from the rain. They tumbled beneath the heavy wagon just as the men were pushing it back in place. Seven magistrates were caught in the muddy soup beneath the wagon. By the time the troopers had succeeded in freeing the cart, two had drowned and the rest were badly injured with a variety of broken bones and cuts. Turtullus vented his rage on

Varus, irrationally blaming the soldiers for what had happened. Varus cut him short and told him for the sake of their long friendship, they had best forget the whole incident. And although the episode had somewhat cheered the flagging spirits of the legionaries, it had forever put a shadow on the relationship between the two men.

Sensing that he was overtaxing the endurance of his troops and exasperating their evil temper, Varus agreed to modify his plans slightly and gave the order for the legions to stand down and rest for three days. However grateful they were for the three days of rest, every man knew that it would not be sufficient to quell either the pain of their tired bodies or the feelings of resentfulness in their breasts. The prevailing talk around the camp fires betrayed their impatience with the men who were leading them into what they clearly saw was a hopeless morass. And that danger came on them full force by an incident that occurred on the night of their second day at Aliso.

The night in question was cloudless and clear, the sky brilliant with the hazy illumination of the Milky Way. A pair of soldiers, seeking to break the boredom of the mind-numbing routine of camp life, decided to explore the mysterious forest that hung like a dark curtain just east of the fortress. Carefully evading the perimeter sentries, no one saw the men slip into the shadow of the Teutoberg Wood except an old large horned owl perched upon an overhanging branch. With the morning, their disappearance was discovered at roll call and a number of search parties were organized to reconnoiter the countryside around Aliso. It was only by chance that one of the parties spied a blood-spattered rock near the entrance to the forest. Upon entering the wood they discovered the grisly remains of the men. They had been subjected to hideous torture that left them without eyes, ears or tongues. Their broken bodies had been nailed to the trunks of two massive oak trees, their skin tattooed by unknown symbols of red ochre that suggested they were victims of some Druid religious rite.

News of the mutilations spread like wildfire through the camp. The affect on the soldiers chilled their martial ardor, already eroded by the wet weather and their ongoing feud with the civilians accompanying them. Men spoke openly of defying any further order to move east and argued for turning back to the west bank of the Rhine.

But Varus would have none of it. He railed against his staff who argued with renewed fervor for a return to Castra Vetera or at the very least, fortifying their present position at Aliso until the subsequent spring. Varus in turn accused them of cowardice and possessing the faltering hearts of women. "Need I remind you of why we are here?" he wheedled them at a noonday conference in his tent. "It is to bring law and civilization to a land that has none. What happened to these unfortunate men serves only to confirm the need for the rule of law here. I for one will not allow my imagination to get the better of my good sense. There are no ghosts or evil spirits lurking in the Saltus Teutobergensis, only criminals who have committed a horrendous act of murder. I will not permit an attack on Roman citizens to go unpunished and unanswered in my jurisdiction. As governor of Germany, it is my responsibility to see that these murderers are brought to justice. I promise you, I will level the whole forest if I have to in order to see that justice is done."

In the end, the legates and officers of the army reluctantly acknowledged that a man as stubborn as Varus could not be prevailed upon to change his mind. His character was such that he would sanction the destruction of half his legions just to prove his point. And once a mind as intransigent as his was made up there was little anyone could say or do to move it from its course. As they filed from the meeting in an air of gloomy resignation, there was one who was determined to head off disaster if he could. Gaius Silvanius promised himself that when the opportunity presented itself, he would remove the governor general by whatever steps necessary before he got them all killed.

XII

Arminius was a happy man.

He was sprawled upon a pile of thick wolf pelts in the sleeping chamber of his hut, drinking in the warm silence around him. He listened to the soft even breathing of his beautiful wife Thusnelda as she slept beside him. Their lovemaking had, as usual, left their fiery passions and straining bodies temporarily spent and satiated. Intoxicated with the wine of his life's great love, Arminius usually had no trouble falling into a heavy sleep of contentment. But for a reason he could not fathom, he now lay awake, his thoughts alert to the rhythm of the night. Perhaps, he thought, it was the anticipation of the coming battle with the Romans that electrified his senses. He believed whole heartedly that victory was not only possible, but inevitable. There was not a shred of doubt in his mind that he had been chosen by the gods to enact divine punishment upon the overweening pride of Rome. He could not remember a time when he was not aware of his destiny, even during those years when he had served in the Roman auxiliary and had been granted the coveted citizenship, not easily obtained by those born outside the Roman pale. Yet he had nourished and harbored a hatred of Rome in his heart that burned ever fiercer with each passing year of service under the eagles. He longed for the day when he would lead his people out of their forest homes to inflict a defeat on Roman arms that would forever be remembered in the annals of war. And now that day was about to dawn into reality.

"Hermann?"

The soft whisper of his German name broke the reverie of his thoughts.

"What is it, my love? I thought you asleep."

"I was. But I had a dream."

Turning to face her, Arminius laid his head in his hand and with his other hand, began to stroke her arm. "Tell me about this dream that keeps you from your rest."

Even in the darkness of the room, Arminius persuaded himself that he could actually feel her loveliness radiating out toward him. He smiled when he thought how the blush of motherhood made his wife's beauty more tangible. He pictured the heart-shaped face, framed in flowing tresses of gold, turned up toward his own, her sapphire eyes gazing wistfully over the classical lines of nose and cheek, the fullness of her lips parted slightly to reveal perfect teeth. Beside such a face, Helen of Troy would not have caused a single ship to sail to her rescue.

Thusnelda rolled upon her back and stared up at the darkened ceiling above their bed. "Before I tell you my dream," she said, "You must tell me something."

Arminius arched his brows. "And what would that be, my dearest love?"

"What is going to happen?"

"What do you mean?"

"With the Romans."

Arminius smiled indulgently at his wife although she could not see it. "These are things you need not concern yourself with, my dear. They are the affairs of men and only the gods may know their outcome."

"I am a daughter of a chief of the Cherusci," she retorted proudly, "You need not lecture me on the affairs of men as you call it, my husband. I am not so naïve as to believe that in the coming days, there will be no killing."

"There will be killing but it will be Romans who will die."

"How can you be so sure?"

"Because I know Quinctilius Varus. He will not be able to resist the challenge I have offered him."

"You mean those poor men whom the Druids butchered?"

"Yes. The Romans believe in the sanctity and the justice of their law. They will allow an entire population to be massacred before they let one criminal escape the retribution of murder! Varus may dress himself up in the costume of a general, but underneath beats the heart of a true lawyer. He would rather die than see his precious law compromised. That is why he will come. He must, he cannot help himself. He will come into the Teutoberg Forest and there he shall meet his doom."

Thusnelda lay in the dark and thought about what she had heard. Her reply was so long in coming in fact that Arminius surmised she had fallen back asleep. Testing his assumption he leaned in toward her ear and whispered, "What are you thinking?"

He was surprised when she replied, "I was thinking about the tribune."

A pang of jealousy shot through Arminius' soul like a javelin thrust. "You love him still?"

Thusnelda's sweet voice chimed out in laughter. "Your jealousy is most becoming," she jested, adding, "It was a girl's fantasy that once loved the tribune of Rome. But it is a woman's heart that loves you. Whose child sleeps even now in my womb? Rest your fears on that score, my dearest Hermann, for that was not why I was thinking of the tribune."

"Then why do you?"

Thusnelda sighed. "Because I have fond memories of him when I was young and the days he dwelt with us in the house of my father. He was so unlike anyone I had ever met! He was kind, considerate, thoughtful, and wise enough not to betray the confidence of his host by indulging the childish attentions of his daughter. I remember thinking that all Romans must be like him which was why my father adored them so and aspired to be like them. It wasn't until he took me to Rome, long after the tribune had left us that I realized how foolish my assumption had been. After that, I could never understand why he wanted to become a Roman. Still, the tribune was different. He loved our people and understood us as no other Roman could."

"Then why is he in arms against us?"

"Because he is a soldier, just as you are, my love. You, more than anyone else, should understand the duty of soldier."

Arminius snorted his disdain. "He should have stayed in Rome. So what is it you require of me?"

119

She turned again on her side and held out her hand to his. "I would not see him die. Promise me that if he comes under your hand, you will spare his life. For my sake. Send him back to his people."

Arminius mulled over his wife's request with mixed feelings. If he should grant Thusnelda's wish and save Tribune Silvanius, than what would be the result, he wondered. Gratitude from the heart he loved above all others? Or a possible future rival should the war go badly against him. He loved Thusnelda with all of his being but a part of him could not help but question whether she returned that love in equal measure. Why else would she care about this Roman? Was there still a residue of girlish love for this man somewhere behind the impenetrable curtain of her woman's heart? How could he ever be sure? And was he willing to live in the shadow of the tribune's memory if he should die by his hand? For one of the few times in his life, Arminius was unsure of how to answer.

"Hermann?" She touched his shoulder lightly sending a quiver of excitement through his muscular body. "What say you? I have asked for nothing since I became your wife but I ask this of you now."

"I think you care too much for this man," he pouted.

"But I love you, with all my heart. This you must believe."

"I do."

"Then will you not grant me this one favor?"

"It is much more than that, Thusnelda," he explained. "You ask me to spare the life of an enemy that would, if given the chance, burn every village in Germany and butcher our people giving it no more thought than an afternoon's sport in the arena. If Silvanius survives and I send him back to Italy as you desire, rest assured, he will be back and this time with more than just three legions."

Thusnelda remained firm. "I do not ask this lightly, my lord. I know full well the possible consequences to such an act of mercy."

"And still you ask."

"Yes."

Arminius sighed. Outside, a light rain began to fall, tapping against the thatched roof of their hut in a syncopated patter. "I have never seen so much rain at harvest time," he mused, halfheartedly attempting to steer their conversation away from its present impasse.

But Thusnelda was adamant. "I await your answer, my lord." Arminius could not help but notice the sudden formality in her speech. Puffing his cheeks, he blew out a long breath.

"Very well, wife," he said, "I will grant your request and spare the life of your precious tribune, if it is in my power to do so. But I warn you. The fortunes of war are fickle and do not always cooperate with the wishes of men. Or women for that matter. The winds of conflict blow where they will and take whoever stands in their way."

Thusnelda placed her hands upon her husband's shoulders and kissed him softly, "In that case, I shall rely on the mercy and generosity of my lord and husband."

Without knowing exactly why, Arminius suddenly felt quite guilty.

XIII

The third day dawned over Aliso dull and gray with the threat of rain in every angry cloud. The soldiers awoke to the blaring trumpets of muster, calling them to assemble at the foot of the hill fortress in preparation to resume their eastward march to Minden. Striking down their leather papili and packing their kits with everything they would need for the journey, the legionaries trudged to the appointed staging area, a flat, semi-circular meadow bordered by the old pathway to the north and the brooding eves of the Teutoberg Wood on the east and south. By nine o'clock in the morning, the entire area was a mass of seething activity. Men scrambled to find their appointed places in the ranks in front of their company standards. Slaves and legionaries together strained and pushed the massive commissariat carts of Senator Turtullus' lawyers into their assignations between the assembled cohorts. Everywhere centurions could be heard bellowing out orders, attempting to bring order out of the chaos, one century at a time. Elsewhere, cavalrymen saddled up their mounts and rode up and down the iron-clad columns as if on maneuver, assisting where they could in forming up the ranks. Close by the dense wall of gnarled timber and tangled undergrowth where the pathway intersected with the forest, the Roman high command stood waiting upon their commander.

Varus however, seemed more concerned with the proceedings at a portable altar then in the grand commotion of a legionary army on the move.

To quiet the fears of the men and show to all the superiority of the gods of Rome over their barbarian counterparts, Varus had arranged for a public sacrifice by members of the Augustan priesthood. He himself had very little use for the trappings of religion, considering it the personal business of the individual. But he knew that soldiers were a superstitious lot, prone to listen and take to heart anything remotely connected with the supernatural. Should the auspices prove favorable it would auger well for the success of the campaign. The men would enter into the conflict with a renewed confidence and a belief that they carried the invincibility of Roman arms upon their shoulders. Success, as Varus well knew, was dependant upon keeping the spirits and expectations of his men at a fever pitch.

The priests, members of the pontificate college in Arausio, were a comic pair. The senior of the two was a tall, gaunt man who possessed a large hooked nose, thin lips and underdeveloped chin that gave him a severe overbite which lent a noticeable lisp to his speech. He carried with him an air of severe austerity, presiding over the auspices with a disapproving gaze from his fish-like eyes. The other man could not have been more different. He was at least twenty years younger, a head shorter and great deal more plump. He wore a perpetual smile on his face that produced prominent dimples on either side of his cherubic mouth. Where the first priest walked with a solemnity born of his grave nature, the second hopped and jumped along like a magpie, chatting and talking to himself in short bursts of incomprehensible banter. Together they stood on a small hillock overlooking the approach to the forest. In front of them were the tools of their trade: a copper brazier spouting a fire of blue flame in its pan, a folding table on which the implements of sacrifice and divination were laid and a wooden cage holding a pair of sacred chickens and mourning doves.

The tall priest was lifting his hands to the gray sky while reciting a litany in Latin dedicated to the war god Mars Ultor and Fortuna, the goddess of fate, seeking a sign of divine favor for the coming enterprise. Occasionally, the fat little priest would move over in front of the brazier and throw a handful of glittering dust onto the fire causing it to burst into sudden flame. At various points in the ritual, the elder priest would stop, open his eyes, and study the sky overhead, looking for any celestial observance his prayers might have managed to evoke. After satisfying himself that none was forthcoming, he would raise his hands once more, close his eyes and continue with the liturgy. All the while Varus stood off to one side watching the proceedings with growing impatience.

When finally the prayers were concluded, the tall priest moved to the table and scanned its contents until he found what he was looking for, a sacrificial knife made of iron with a carved wood handle. Nodding to his aide, the fat little man went to the wooden cage and opened the door. Reaching a pudgy arm into the cage, he pulled out one of the chickens. It squawked loudly in his grasp as if already suspecting its fate. Bringing it to the table, the rotund priest handed the sacred chicken to the elder priest who made a cursory inspection for any imperfections or abnormalities. When he was satisfied that there were none, he gave it back to the younger priest who deftly wrung its neck with practiced hands. Once accomplished, he laid its body on a piece of midnight black silk cloth. The tall priest raised the blade to eye level invoking a quick entreaty for good omens and then plunged the knife into the bird's breast. Using a series of intricate strokes to create cuts and patterns designed to have symbolic meaning, he swiftly removed the heart, lungs, stomach and kidneys of the bird, reading each bloody organ in turn. He spent the most time over the kidneys, examining everything from their color, weight and shape to even the array of veins embedded in its flesh. Once his divination was complete, he nodded again to the younger priest who gathered up the entrails and the carcass of the chicken and threw them into the consuming fire of the brazier. In this way, the priests emptied the cage of its sacrificial contents.

For a long time after the slaughter of the last bird, the priests stood beside the table conferring with one another in low tones. When he could stand it no longer, Varus' impatience broke and angrily he stalked over to the hillock.

"Well?" he demanded with hands on hips. "What do the gods say?"

The priests looked at one another, their expressions betraying their reticence. The fat little priest began to busy himself with cleaning up the blood-stained surface of the divination table while the elder priest wiped his bloody hands with a towel.

"The art of divination is sometimes not an exact science, Excellency," he explained evasively.

"Save your lame excuses for someone who believes in your mumbo jumbo. Tell me what you saw."

The priest shrugged his shoulders. "As you wish. The auspices are not good, Excellency. The favor and protection of the Lord Mars which has long rested upon Roman arms has been withdrawn from your army."

"Why?"

"I know not, Excellency. The gods are easily offended and not always easily placated."

"It is worth your life to find out, priest. I need a favorable omen."

"The favor of the gods is not a thing you can call to your will, Excellency. The gods are capricious creatures who do not give their love willingly."

Varus snorted. "I do not desire their love. I desire only a token of their good will to show to the army that the gods of Rome march with them."

"But they do not. They side with your enemies. My counsel to you is to return to Castra Vetera and wait until the auspices are clearer and more in your favor."

"Damn you, priest!" swore Varus, "I will not turn three entire legions around and run back to the Rhine just because one of your damned chickens disagreed with something it ate!"

It was now the priest's turn to become angry. "I warn you, Excellency, you risk the displeasure of heaven by your blasphemy. You called me here to read the signs and I have done so. I believe I have interpreted them correctly and I believe that if you persist on your present course, you will die and Rome will suffer a disaster greater than ever she has known. Believe it, Excellency, for I have seen it. If you refuse to listen, you will earn the doom that sits even now upon you and your army!"

Varus was nearly apoplectic with rage. "How dare you!" he sputtered sharply, "How dare you come here with your ridiculous toys and stupid birds and curse my legions! No intelligent man worth his salt would give credence to such nonsense. Let me show you what I think of your foolish portents, priest!" Before the fat little priest could stop him, Varus stepped forward and pushed over the brazier with a booted foot. It fell heavily to the ground, its flammable contents spilling out igniting the tufted grass underfoot. It was only by the frantic efforts of the rotund priest and a trio of military tribunes that the fire was quenched and kept from spreading down the little hillock and onto the field of men below.

Varus' demonstration, however, did not seem to make an impression on the tall priest. Staring intently at the governor general, he pointed a long, bony finger and said, "You have sealed your fate this day, Publius Quinctilius Varus! The gods will not forgive this sacrilege to their altar. By your actions the lives of you and your men are now forfeit and have been given over into the hands of your enemies!"

"Enough of your pronouncements!" shrieked Varus, "If you are not gone from my camp within the hour it is your life that will be forfeit. Now get out!" At that moment, a crack of thunder sounded overhead and rolled across the billowing sky. The priest looked up and felt the first droplets of rain splash onto his upturned face. Turning to Varus a last time, he said, "Thus speaks the will of the gods. Your blood will not be on my hands. If you step into the forest beyond, you shall not return." And with that he was gone, trailed by the fat little priest and their attendant slaves who carried away the brazier and table.

Varus silently watched them as they skirted the edge of the marshalling field and headed westward along the ancient footpath towards the province of Gaul. They were almost out of sight, before the Legate of the Eighteenth Legion stepped forward and asked, "What are your orders, general?"

Varus turned and glared at his commanders. "My orders are what they have always been. Once the army is ready to resume the march, we will strike out for Minden. Through the forest. We have murderers to apprehend."

XIV

Bassanius was the first to notice the movement out of the corner of his eye.

It was the second day's march inside the huge forest. The long armored columns of three legions had only managed to snake their way seven miles along a barely recognized woodland track. The rain that threatened on the day they left Aliso unleashed itself on the army almost from the minute they entered the dark wood. Word had spread quickly through the ranks of Varus' run in with the priests of Mars and how the omens produced were of an evil rarely seen since the days of civil unrest under the Divine Julius. To their minds, the rain was a confirmation of their worst fears that the favor of the gods had been shut up against them.

For his part, Varus was neither unduly concerned nor even mindful of the danger around them. From the very outset, he treated the march as if it were being conducted within ten miles of the Capitol itself. So oblivious was he to the precariousness of the situation that he refused to employ skirmishers and flank guards to protect the head and sides of his column. Much of the time was spent clearing a path wide enough to admit the mass of men and material through the dense woods. This required a massive effort in felling endless trees and using the trunks and branches to construct bridges across the marshy streams that ran everywhere along the forest floor. The presence of the commissariat wagons in their train succeeded in slacking the pace of the march to a snail's pace. One cart had already been abandoned on the first day when an axle snapped on a broken tree trunk. When a military tribune happened upon the scene of the damaged vehicle and saw the men standing around unsure of what to do, he ordered them to leave it where it lay.

"But you can't do that!" protested a pernicious clerk rushing up to the retreating officer. "We have valuable papers on that wagon!"

The tribune looked contemptuously back at the clerk and replied, "I can and will. But if you are that concerned about your precious papers, ask one of the soldiers for a sword and you can stay here and guard it."

The drenching rains added to the whole army's misery. The leather shields of the legionaries became so sodden they doubled their weight, making them heavy as lead. With their suppleness gone, they became useless for combat. The company of four hundred auxiliary archers who were attached to the army from service in the East, labored in vain to keep their bowstrings dry. Underfoot, the clay track which they were following became slick and slippery, making walking difficult and causing muddy pools to form in which the carts became stuck. With every passing hour, the space between the individual legionary formations became dangerously extended so that by the afternoon of the second day, the distance between the head of the column and its tail had grown to over a mile and half. By not insisting on keeping his forces concentrated, Varus had left himself open to a classic hit and run assault along any point of his straggling columns.

The men of the Nineteenth were the last of the three legions to enter the forbidding maw of the Teutoberg Forest, their position dictated by Varus' unimaginative placing of the legions in numerical order. Their task was to protect the rear of the Roman line of march, the most vulnerable and dangerous point of the entire train because of the ease by which an enemy could attack. The rearguard had to be able to look ahead and behind simultaneously to see not only where it was going but to watch for an enemy that might be following. Knowing the difficulty of his assignment, the legionary legate, Marcus Didianus Florus, decided to divide his legion in a such a way that the four forward cohorts would lead the other six in the same manner as a the sighted lead the blind. The trailing six cohorts would have to literally walk backwards, keeping their eyes on the forest as it closed in behind them. And as with the other two legions, their task was made infinitely more difficult by the added responsibility of moving five of the commissariat carts along with them. But they did have an advantage over their comrades in that the way had already been cleared of trees and underbrush and the streams forded by hastily erected trestles courtesy of Memmius' crack team of engineers. Still, the passage proved to be just as dark and ponderous for the Nineteenth as it had been for the other two.

The century to which Cornelius and his companions had been attached was the primus pilus of the Nineteenth's last cohort. The flexibility of the Roman legion was in its divergent parts and how those parts could operate singularly or together, breaking off to form smaller units before coming back together into their original components. The smallest unit of the legion was the century, a group of eighty men commanded by a centurion. Six centuries were grouped together to form the larger cohort formation and ten cohorts constituted a full legion to which was usually added an ala or cavalry wing of 120 horsemen and a scattering of weapons specialists such as slingers or archers. All together, a legion comprised five thousand, five hundred men under the command of the legatus legionis, the legionary commander. Serving as his personal staff were the military tribunes, ten in number, to correspond with the number of cohorts. To each of them belonged authority over six centuries. In this way did the Roman genius for war find it's most perfect and irresistible expression, providing the means whereby the seven-hilled city on the Tiber had made herself mistress of the known world.

But the closeness of the damp, pressing wood of the Teutoberg Wald negated much of the legions' inherent tactical advantage. For the most part, the legionaries were used to marching ten abreast across good Roman roads or wide open fields, making a massed square invulnerable to attack. The narrow forest track and the tall trees meant that the centuries could only squeeze through the corridor hacked out by the engineers three to four at a time. The effect of the difficult geography on the Roman forces was not unlike pouring a large quantity of water through the narrow neck of a jar. Thinned out and stretched into web-like strands, the cohorts and centuries surrendered the strength of their formations to the miserable conditions of the surrounding terrain.

And so it was that the men of the primus pilus of the Tenth Cohort of the Nineteenth Legion, of whom Cornelius and his companions were members, found themselves skidding along the slippery clay pathway and muddy earth, churned up in the wake of the army' passage. They walked along side the last of the heavy transports, keeping an eye upon possible ruts in the way ahead as well as signs in the woods of a pursuing enemy. Bassanius was so engaged when he thought he saw something moving in the stand of tall pine off to his left.

At first he thought it a bird taking flight through the trees, no doubt startled by the movement of so many men and creaking wagons past its nest. It was an explanation he would have been satisfied with except that the initial motion was soon followed by a glint of metal. Remembering the plume of smoke they had seen a few hours earlier and took for a distant village, Bassanius nudged Cornelius beside him. "Did you see that?"

"See what?" replied Cornelius, stopping to wipe a glob of mud from his sandal on a broken branch.

"Just there, to the left. I saw something moving in the trees. I thought it was only a bird or an animal in the brush, but I saw a flash of something bright afterward."

Cornelius started to walk again. "Maybe it was someone from the cohort relieving himself in the bushes."

Bassanius shook his head. "I don't think so, Cornelius. If it were, don't you think he would make damn sure we knew he was one of us? No, I've been thinking about that smoke we saw a little while ago."

"What about it?"

"I'm beginning to think it wasn't a village."

"Then what was it?"

"I think it was…" Bassanius' explanation was interrupted by a loud thwack over their heads. Looking up they saw an arrow embedded in the elevated canvas side of the wagon, its head ignited in flame by a ball of tallow and tar. If it had not been for the fact the canvas had been soaked by the constant rain, the transport would have been engulfed in a number of seconds.

"A signal!"

Bassanius reached up and tore the arrow from the transport's side. As he did so, the air was rent with a piercing, blood-chilling shriek. Suddenly from both sides of the wood, a wave of barbarians descended upon the cart and its attendant guard under the cover of a murderous volley of assegais and darts. Cornelius barely got his heavy shield up in front of his face to deflect a dart meant for his eyes. Everywhere around them, men who were not so quick to protect themselves fell writhing and screaming to the ground with various wounds inflicted by the hail of murderous weapons. One of the first to fall under the initial assault was their centurion, Gessius Appula. Confusion reigned in the Roman columns as the soldiers milled about the now stationary commissariat wagon, attempting to ward off the second volley while trying to attend to the wounded. The barbarian infantry closed in. They crashed heavily into the Roman lines, thrusting their swords up underneath the raised shields of the legionaries to find vulnerable throats and faces. Cornelius felt his heat pumping wildly as he managed to catch a glimpse of the face of an onrushing German, his features contorted by battle rage, coming at him with broadsword drawn. Without thinking, Cornelius' body reacted on pure instinct. Bringing his shield down to meet the point of the thrusting blade of the barbarian, he simultaneously shifted his weight upon his heels and stepped aside. The momentum of the attacker, already committed to the assault, carried him past the young Roman and into the side of the wagon head first. The blow snapped his neck with an audible crack that turned Cornelius' stomach.

Beside him, Bassanius was entangled with a tall barbarian whose braided hair flowed out from beneath his iron helmet to half way down his back. The barbarian was swinging a great battle axe with both hands, driving Bassanius back against the side of the cart. The axe blows had succeeded in splitting Bassanius' leather shield and the Roman was doing all he could to ward off the relentless strokes with his short gladius. With one particular nasty swing, the longhaired German succeeded in pinning Bassanius up against the wagon and roaring with laughter, raised the axe high above his head to administer the death blow. But he hadn't reckoned on Cornelius, who having dispatched his own man, came at the barbarian from the blind side. With a quick thrust, his sword entered cleanly between the top two ribs directly into the heart. The big man stiffened and groaned. A trickle of blood seeped over his bottom lip as the axe fell from his grasp and he toppled over onto the wet ground.

"My thanks!" gasped Bassanius fighting to catch his breath. Cornelius nodded and looked about them. A battle was raging on all sides of the transport. Everywhere men were locked in combat, the Germans moving in on the hard pressed legionaries who seemed to be disorganized and unsure of what to do. Casting about for the presence of an officer, Cornelius quickly realized there were none about except for poor Appula who still lay motionless in the wet grass where he fell. Over the din of battle, Cornelius was shocked to hear his own voice shouting out a command he had heard parade centurions use during basic training.

"Legionaries! Form four squares! On the double!"

Immediately, the spell of indecisiveness seemed to lift from the soldiers as the voice of authority recalled them to their discipline. Within moments, groups of four men arranged in perfect squares, their backs to each other, their weapons forward, materialized all over the field. Now it was the turn of the barbarians to momentarily blunt their attack with indecision, unsure of how to react to this new development. Sensing the advantage, Cornelius cried out,

"Four squares counter attack! On them now!"

In almost perfect unison, the squares pushed out from the transport and slammed into the waiting Germans. Every square broke through the line of tribesmen, cutting through them as easily as if they were made of paper. Once behind the barbarian line of battle, they wheeled around and launched their counter attack upon their rear. Many of the Germans were cut down where they stood, unable to turn in time to meet the attacking Romans. Some seeing the fight lost for the moment, retreated back into the dimness of the surrounding forest.

When the last German disappeared from view, the legionaries raised their arms in a shout of triumph. Just then, a military tribune rode in on the scene, reigning in his horse in front of the wagon. "What happened here?" he demanded of celebrating soldiers.

The nearest legionary sheathed his sword and said, "We were attacked by barbarians out of the woods. They came out of nowhere and surprised us. We couldn't get on top of them at first until our centurion gave the order to form up squares and counter attack. We bloodied their nose after that, I'll tell you! The bastards ran like scared rabbits back into their holes in the woods."

"Where is your centurion?"

"He's over here!" called another soldier standing over the still form of Gessius Appula. The tribune dismounted and walked over to the small knot that was now gathering around the fallen centurion. Kneeling down, the tribune saw the glazed, staring expression of death on Appula's ashen face. The cause of death was obvious. The wooden shaft of a broken dart protruded eight inches from a ghastly wound in the side of the neck.

"This man couldn't possibly have given that order," exclaimed the tribune.

"He didn't!"

Everyone in the group around the dead centurion turned to face Bassanius who had wandered up from his side of the transport. "Appula was killed in the attack."

"Then who gave the order, soldier? You?" demanded the tribune.

"No sir," replied Bassanius, "My friend did." He pointed his finger toward a figure standing rather forlornly by the corner of the wagon. The tribune motioned for him to approach.

"Your friend here says you gave the order to form squares," declared the tribune of a rueful Cornelius. "Is this true?"

"Yes, sir."

"Who told you to do that?"

"No one, sir."

"Then why did you?"

"We were about to be overwhelmed by the enemy," explained Cornelius, "And I knew that Centurion Appula had been badly wounded. If someone did not take control of the situation, we would have been in serious trouble."

"Indeed. And just where did you learn the command to form up squares?"

"From watching the parade centurions in basic training, sir."

"What is your name, soldier?"

"Cornelius Strabo, sir."

The tribune nodded, impressed by the young man's confidence and coolness under fire. Bending down, he removed the distinctive centurion's helmet from Appula's head and tossed it to Cornelius.

"Well, Cornelius Strabo your century obviously needs a new centurion. Looks like you're him. We will need more men like you if we are ever going to get out of this alive. Now, gather your men together, centurion, and move them out. I will inform the legate of what has happened here. We'll have to prepare ourselves for more attacks."

The tribune saluted the new centurion who returned it smartly. Mounting his horse again, he rode off to find the legate. For a few awkward moments, the men of the century stood gaping at Cornelius as if they couldn't quite believe what had just transpired. Cornelius sensing their mood, decided that if he was now a centurion, he'd better start acting like one. Pulling his own helmet off his head, he cast it aside and put the centurion's helmet back on in its place. To his surprise, it was almost a perfect fit. Tying the drawstrings under his chin, he looked around at the ring of expectant faces about him and shouted, "Alright! You heard the tribune! Get back to your places and let's move out! On the double!"

To a man, the company scrambled to obey the order.

XV

In the wake of the attack on Cornelius' century, it seemed as if the army was at first being victimized by a few bands of barbarians who were shadowing their march through the forest at a discreet distance. The attacks were for the most part, beaten off with ease as the barbarian pattern of volley, assault and retreat was repeated along various points of the armored columns. But on the third day, it was obvious the enemy was growing in size and in boldness. It was also obvious that there had been a change in the barbarian strategy.

Through most of the day, the Germans stepped up their attacks and sorties against the extended armored columns. Their new strategy seemed to be designed to separate the legions from one another in order to reduce them piecemeal. To this end, they set about erecting barricades in the way of the advancing legionaries by breaking the wheels of some of the captured carts and laying the wreckage, along with large tree trunks, across their path. Each time the columns stopped to remove the barriers, they were assailed by tribesmen hiding in the surrounding thickets. In this way, a wedge was opened and widened between the legions, especially between the leading Seventeenth Legion and the other two. The men of the Eighteenth and Nineteenth Legions became so alarmed at falling behind and losing touch with the vanguard, that they soon abandoned all their wagons and transports and hurried to catch up, hoping the Germans would forget their pursuit and busy themselves with plundering the carts.

But the barbarians proved themselves equal to the famous discipline of their adversaries. They left only a few of their fellows to strip the valuables from the transports while the bulk of their forces followed closely on the heels of the retreating Romans. In the gloom of the forest produced by the incessant rain and dense vegetation, the famous legionary discipline began to quickly unravel. Men became separated from their centuries and cohorts, making them easy targets for the waiting tribesmen. New units of anywhere from fifty to two hundred men had to be hastily organized. Cornelius' command, being one of the last in the entire Roman array, had suffered horribly since the first attack, losing over three quarters of its compliment, including his friends Rubricus and Bano. He had led his men forward under some fierce fighting to join the hastatus posterior of the Sixth Cohort who had lost only five men. For his part, Cornelius was more than willing to lay down his new authority to the Sixth's more experienced centurion.

Meanwhile, the Seventeenth under Varus' personal command, had managed to gain a hilltop which had been cleared of most of its vegetation by a recent forest fire. They had seen very little action up to that point and were still in possession of all of their transports and supply wagons. Varus, however, was not ignorant of what was transpiring behind him. All through the day, dispatches and reports had come up to him from the rear informing him of the growing disaster that was engulfing his army. He had been searching for a suitable spot to place his camp so he could provide a safe haven for the trailing legions when they finally reached him. To him, the hilltop was ideal. Yet by the time he gave the orders to construct the earthworks and ramparts of their camp, the woods around them were literally teeming with Germans. Sentries and patrols had to be mounted around the perimeter of the hilltop even while the construction of the fortifications was going on in order to fend off the relentless barbarian attacks and to admit the weary survivors from the other legions as they appeared. When finally they were able to settle in behind their stockade and earthen ramparts to light their cooking fires for the evening meal, they looked out and saw the forest about them filled with the mirror image of other fires as countless as the stars. The barbarians had all but effectively surrounded the Army of the Rhine.

Too late did Varus realize his peril. It was a grim and haggard looking group of faces that attended the governor general in his tent for the evening staff meeting. Varus tried in vain to put on a brave face but the gravity of their situation was apparent to all. The meeting began on a dismal note when the quarter-master of the army reported that nearly a third of the army had failed to answer the nightly roll call.

"That is equal to an entire legion!" commented the quarter-master as he finished giving his report "At this rate the army will be decimated in two days."

"Thank you, Titus," replied Varus smoothly, "But I do not intend to see my army 'decimated', as you put it. There may be thousands of them in the woods as we speak, but they are still barbarians and no match for a Roman legion."

Gaius Silvanius clucked his tongue in disgust and spoke for all present. "After all that has happened, how can you still hold such contempt for an enemy that has us at their mercy? Face the facts, general. If it had not been for your foolish pride and your reckless insistence on pursuing a course you knew was wrong from the beginning, we would not have found ourselves in this predicament. And now you expect the men to salvage your reputation by hard fighting in impossible circumstances. If it were in my power to do so, I would have you arrested for incompetence and sent to trial in Rome."

"That's enough!" commanded Varus evenly. "I understand we're all tired and on edge, tribune, but I believe it is clouding your judgement. I will forget your words just now since we must all rely on one another if we are to survive. Now, what are our options, gentlemen?"

"We have none," shot back Legate Florus of the Nineteenth Legion bitterly. Since his was the last legion, it had predictably suffered the most damage, boasting only a thousand men from its original compliment of five thousand.

"There are always options, Legate Florus," replied Varus.

Caecillius Mentor, legate of the Seventeenth Legion spoke up. "You have left us with little to offer, general. One legion gone. Another badly crippled. The third left to tend with the wounded of the other two. The woods around us literally alive with an enemy thirsting for Roman blood. In such circumstances, what would you have us do?"

Varus frowned at the legate's grim assessment. "I would have you act as Roman officers. The picture is not as dark as you paint it."

"No, it is darker," said Silvanius. "And made more so by a foolish old man. Will you not admit you have been played for an ass, general? Arminius was never a friend of Rome. He used those men as bait, hoping to draw us into the forest and into his trap. And you have obliged him. You've damned us all. You backed the wrong horse by putting your trust in Arminius when it was Segestes who has proven to be the true friend of Rome."

Varus' eyebrows shot up at the mention of the Cherusci chieftain. "It may interest you to know, tribune, that I sent this so called 'true friend of Rome' out ahead of us to track Arminius' whereabouts and lead us to him. I have not received a single word from him since we left Aliso. It would not surprise me to learn that he too has gone over to the enemy."

"You have no proof of his disloyalty," maintained Silvanius.

"Of the father, no. But the son is another matter."

"What do you mean?"

"A prisoner who was taken today turned out to be an ex-auxiliary who had served with Arminius under Tiberius. He could speak Latin and so he was questioned about the movements of the barbarians and their intentions on the morrow. During the interrogation it was revealed that Segestes' son, the one who was made a priest of Augustus among the

Ubii last year in reward for his service to the State, was seen in the inner councils of the German high command, beside Arminius himself."

"That's a lie!"

"Is it? Think, tribune! Arminius is now the man's brother-in-law. That binds him to Arminius through ties of kinship as well as race. And if that reasoning is not enough, consider that the story was confirmed by other prisoners as well. It would seem tribune, that none of us have friends left on this side of the Rhine."

Silvanius lapsed into a brooding silence, reeling from the revelation of the governor general. Was it true? he wondered. Was Segestes a traitor as well? No! It was impossible. He knew the man too well. The picture didn't fit with what he knew of Segestes. But could the son possibly be false? Silvanius dredged his memories and recalled a scrawny, pimply-faced boy who constantly sought acceptance and affirmation from his father. When he didn't receive it, Arminius had been only too glad to take on the role of surrogate father. Arminius indulged the lad when he should not have, creating more of a syncopate than a friend in the son of Segestes. Silvanius chided himself for not seeing the connection earlier. It all made perfect sense.

"And now," continued Varus, "I ask again. What are our options?"

"It is my opinion that we must return to Aliso," offered Mentor of the Seventeenth. "It would be folly to continue on to Minden, especially if we do not know what awaits us there."

Varus stared down at the scroll unrolled in front of him. On it was displayed a map of the lands between the Rhine and Weser Rivers. Staring at the square representing Minden, he let his gaze wander back west across the empty space marked Saltus Teutobergensis to a similar symbol that represented the fortress of Aliso. Stabbing his finger on the point, he said, "I must agree with you, Legate Mentor. Wisdom would dictate that the most prudent course of action would be to return to Aliso and wait for reinforcements."

"We will have to breakout of the vice we're in to do that," complained Legate Florus. "And that will require speed, surprise and mobility. We will have to shed whatever baggage and wagons we have left."

"I agree."

"You can't leave the remaining wagons filled with important legal documents to the mercy of savages!" cried Senator Turtullus peevishly.

"Don't sorry, Senator," retorted Florus. "We won't leave them. We'll burn them."

Turtullus burst into an apoplectic rage. "Do you hear what they are saying?" he demanded of Varus. The governor general smiled. "I do indeed, my friend, and once more, I concur with the legate's judgement. We will have to burn the wagons if we want to increase our chances of escape. The burning of the remaining vehicles should provide a diversion long enough for us to break through the barbarian lines."

"Publius, I have already lost enough on this journey. I will not allow you to burn what is left of a lifetime's work for the sake of a piece of military posturing!"

"Posturing!" fumed Varus, "Do you value a pile of useless scraps of paper over your own life? Will you die in the wilderness for the defense of a single pot of ink? You must learn to think like a soldier, Senator. Cut your losses while you can. The battle may be lost today, but the war can be renewed tomorrow."

"I won't allow it!"

"How will you stop it, Gneaus?"

"I will strap myself to the wagons if I have to."

Varus looked at his friend sadly and replied, "In that case, I will order the wagons burned with you on them." Turtullus was aghast at the threat. He could see in the governor general's eyes that Varus meant every word of it.

XVI

The cohort to which Cornelius and his men had attached themselves was one of the last to reach the hilltop.

Halting at the foot of the mound after a day of hard marching punctuated by constant skirmishing against attacks from the surrounding woods, they were dismayed at what awaited them. Above them they could see the comforting lights of the camp beckoning them with the promise of safety. They could even hear the voices of soldiers shouting encouragement to them from the breast works. But to reach the summit, they realized they would have to run up the steep wooded slopes between a gauntlet of frenzied tribesmen, braving a hail of deadly arrows and darts. The centurion of the cohort raised his sword above his head and called to his troops, "C'mon lads! We've come this far! We're almost there! Don't let these bastards keep you from ever seeing your wives and children again! To the top with you now! For the Emperor and the Fatherland!"

Immediately, the centurion began to charge up the hill, followed by a knot of stout hearted men of like mind. He had not gone more than ten paces when an arrow sang out of the gloaming and caught him square in the throat. Other arrows and darts made short work of the rest of the group. The remainder of the cohort huddled pathetically together at the foot of the hilltop, seemingly incapacitated by the fate of their centurion. Again it was Cornelius who stepped into the breach.

Looking at the men about him he counted quickly that half the cohort still had their shields.

"Cohort attention!" he cried. To his relief he saw that discipline had not yet slipped from the exhausted legionaries. "Those of you without shields, form a line in front of me. Those of you who still have shields, form a tortoise on the double quick!" The men sensed immediately what Cornelius had in mind and moved swiftly to execute the command. The testudo or tortoise was a formation usually employed during sieges, so called because it took on the appearance of a tortoise's shell when used. It was composed of three lines of legionaries. The two outside lines presented their shields to the sides, front and rear, locked together so that except for their feet, the entire torso of the soldiers inside was protected. The middle line raised their shields above their heads, also locked together and joined with the others to form a moving, metallic box that could go anywhere beneath the besieged walls all the while protecting the besiegers from aerial assaults from above. Even so, it was quite unusual to witness the tortoise being employed anywhere but a siege. Given their current circumstances however, Cornelius' was convinced it was there only hope.

As the tortoise formed up, Cornelius could see it would not be a perfect fit. There was still plenty of spaces between the shields, especially on top, to permit penetration from the barbarian volleys. But, he reasoned, with luck and the advantage of surprise (he couldn't be sure, but he didn't think it possible any of the tribesmen had ever seen anything like the testudo) they might make the top with minimal losses.

"Noto! Animus attentus!" he bawled, "Those of you without shields are responsible for picking up any shield that goes down and taking their place on the line. If you are hit and wounded, I can't promise anyone will stop to give you aid. Once the tortoise starts, it won't stop until we reach the top. Does everyone understand?" The men nodded and grunted their assent.

"Alright, then. On my command, the tortoise will head straight for those lights just there!" he said, pointing to a pair of bright lantern points on the camp walls. "Tortoise, at the ready! Move now!" Ducking inside the front line of shields, Cornelius joined the rush up the hill.

Cornelius' assumption was correct insofar as many of the Germans did stand momentarily amazed at the sight of the moving shield wall as it scampered up the slope. Ten paces. Fifteen. Twenty. And still there was no reaction from the enemy. Hope of reaching the top unscathed temporarily quieted Cornelius' misgivings as the tortoise moved briskly up the hill. At twenty-five paces, the shield to Cornelius' right rang loudly as if it were a bell. Soon all around them, the sound of steel-tipped weapons echoed noisily inside the cramped confines of the testudo. Near the rear of the shield wall, a Roman voice cried out in agony and the tortoise gave a lurch. One of the shield men had been hit and had fallen away from the tortoise, causing those behind him to stumble over his fallen form. Hands reached down and picked up the downed shield, replacing it in the breached line of the tortoise before the barbarians could exploit their success. Three more times, the same pattern repeated itself with the same result. As the panting and exhausted cohort came within bowshot of the camp gates, they could hear a mighty cheer go up from the large throng assembled on the ramparts. Word had spread throughout the camp about the astonishing drama that was unfolding at the foot of the hilltop and many had come out to the walls to watch and cheer on their comrades, including many of the officers.

The frustration of the tribesmen was evident by the fierceness of their attack as the tortoise neared the gates. Two more Romans fell and were just as quickly replaced. Cornelius himself felt an iron-headed dart glance off the top of his helmet after it found an open seam in the shield wall above him. Peering through the small opening in the forward shields, he saw the front gates swinging open to receive them. Only a short distance and they would be safe! He felt the tortoise rushing on around him, eager to make the gate as quickly as possible.

Then with heart-sickening abruptness the ground fell away from Cornelius as he felt his right leg buckle under a stabbing wave of pain. Tumbling to the ground, he rolled twice and lay faced down on the wet turf of the hillside. Around him the tortoise seemed to lose its momentum and stutter to a halt. Above him he heard the familiar voice of Bassanius say, "Don't worry, centurion, we have you."

Well meaning hands pulled him to his knees, but he screamed at the agony in his leg. Looking down he saw the broken shaft of an arrow protruding from the top of his calf, just below the knee. Gritting his teeth, he shouted, "Leave me, you fools! I said don't stop for anything! Go to the gates! Hurry before it's too late!"

The testudo pitched slowly forward again under a renewed hail of barbarian artillery, leaving Cornelius dangerously exposed. "We'll be back to get you!" cried Bassanius near tears, a vow neither one believed he could keep. Oblivious to the thumping of weapons dropping around him, Cornelius watched with satisfaction as the tortoise gained the gates under the thunderous ovation of the soldiery on the walls. He wasn't going to make it but thanks to him, the men under his command would. He could die content with the knowledge that he had discharged his short-lived duty as a Roman officer with efficiency and success. Despite his earlier misgivings, it comforted him to think that his father would be proud of his wayward son.

Raising himself up on his sword hilt, Cornelius looked up to the gates that were so close yet so unreachable and waited for death. Unbelievably, none of the javelins, arrows or darts cast his way found their mark. It was as if some invisible hand was directing them away or causing them to fall harmlessly short around him. Suddenly, a mounted figure bolted out of the open gates of the camp and galloped towards him. As he drew near, Cornelius was surprised to see the intent face of Gaius Silvanius bearing down upon him. In one swift movement, Silvanius brought his horse around the stricken centurion, swinging it back toward the gates while reaching his hand down to Cornelius.

"Quickly, man, get up here!" Agonizing pain shuddered through Cornelius' body as he stood up and swung his injured leg up over the back of the horse. Once safely in behind Silvanius, the tribune whistled and the horse raced back toward the gate. Everywhere around them, the weapons of the enemy thumped into the wet turf or whizzed by their ears like angry bees. It seemed impossible that the riders would not be brought down before they made the gate by the deadly hail directed at them from all sides. Closing his eyes and steeling himself against the inevitable blow he knew must come, Cornelius was astonished when, upon opening them again, he saw the line of the stockade sweeping past as the doors swung shut behind them. As Silvanius reared his mount to a stop, the air was filled with the sound of raucous cheering and the banging of many swords against a multitude of shields. Helping hands reached up and gingerly lowered Cornelius from the back of the tribune's horse and onto a waiting gurney, ready to transport him to the surgeon's tent. Around him, many smiling and laughing faces were offering their congratulations and admiration for the author of the extraordinary scene they had just witnessed. In the midst of the celebration, the ring of well wishers abruptly moved back to admit the stocky figure of the Legate Florus who knelt down and pumped Cornelius' hand vigorously.

"Young man that was the greatest bit of soldiering I've seen in a long time. What is your name?"

"Cornelius Strabo, sir," he replied, wincing from the pain in his leg.

"Well, Cornelius Strabo, I am personally going to see that you receive the gold crown for what you just did out there. Well done! Who would have thought to use a tortoise like that? It was absolutely brilliant! And you lost but five men. We've had cohorts lose three quarters of their compliment coming up that hill and yet you managed to do it with the loss of only five. But I must tell you, I don't seem to remember a Cornelius Strabo as one of my centurions."

Cornelius offered a wan smile, the wound beginning to throb with every pounding heartbeat.

"I am not one of your centurions, sir," he grimaced, "That is until yesterday when our own centurion was killed during a barbarian attack. It was only after we had beaten them off that one of your tribunes rode up and made me the acting centurion."

Florus clapped his hands together. "Of course! I might have known! You're the young man Flavius told me about! My boy, we are in desperate need of men of your kind in this army. When we return to civilization, I am going to see that you be admitted into the college of tribunes for training as an officer. The commandant, Caius Ligurius is a personal friend of mine. Such initiative is wasted in the rank and file. But in the mean time, I am confirming your appointment as centurion and will see to it personally that your command is restored from the stragglers in camp. The gods know the Germans have created enough of them!"

"Thank you, sir," said Cornelius weakly, "But I fear if I do not get this leg seen to shortly I may lose it."

"Yes, yes, of course. My apologies. Orderly! See to this man and hurry. Get him to the surgeon's tent as soon as you can. We need him on his feet as soon as possible." Patting Cornelius on the shoulder he added, "We will talk later, Centurion Strabo, when you are up and around." With that the legate hurried off. As the attendants lifted the litter to take Cornelius to the waiting surgeons, he caught sight of the Tribune Silvanius leading his mount back to its stable. He motioned for the tribune to come over to the gurney. Silvanius turned his head toward the salutation and waved. Turning his horse around, he came to the edge of the stretcher where Cornelius grasped his hand tightly.

"I want to thank you, tribune," Cornelius said fervently, "Twice now you have saved my life."

"I rather think it is the good fortune of the gods that has spared you, centurion. Not I," laughed Silvanius. "Perhaps that same good fortune will yet deliver us from this catastrophe!"

Cornelius pursed his lips and tried to rub away the throbbing in his leg. Growing serious, he replied, "You speak more truly than you know, tribune. I for one believe there is One who has helped me. I do not know his name or why I have his favor. What I do know is that I have seen him in a dream and he has given me a warning."

"A warning? What kind of warning?"

"In the dream I saw an army, a Roman army, broken and destroyed on a field soaked with blood surrounded by the hedge of a great forest."

"Look around you, centurion. The dream has become reality."

"But there was more."

"I suspected as much. Say on."

"There was a man," continued Cornelius, "or at least what appeared to be a man, standing on the edge of the field calling for me to follow him."

"Why do you say he 'appeared to be a man'?"

"Have you ever seen a man glow, tribune?"

"Glow?"

"Yes. And the most peculiar thing about it was that the light seemed to be shining out of him and through his clothes."

"Interesting," commented Silvanius who was beginning to wonder if Cornelius had received more than just a leg wound. "And you say he wanted you to follow him?"

"Yes. But where, I could not say."

"Was that all he said to you?"

"No. There was one other thing. He said I was favored of God."

"Which god?"

"He did not say. But I suppose he meant the God, the One the Greeks speak of as being the Creator and Sustainer of the universe."

A flash of irritation passed across the tribune's tanned face. "You don't actually believe such nonsense, do you, centurion? We are fighting men, you and I. We have no time for idle speculation or empty philosophy. The only truth a soldier can rely on is a sharp sword and a strong shield."

Cornelius ignored Silvanius' reaction. "I had no belief in the gods or religion, considering such things to be useful only for the weak and foolish. Now I am not so sure."

Silvanius' brow ruffled thoughtfully. "So why are you telling me this?"

"Because I believe you have seen him yourself. The night you found me by the stream what was it you said? A man appeared to you in a dream and told you to come out and find me. And you did."

Silvanius bit his lip. "The stuff of dreams, centurion. Your wound is affecting your senses more than you realize. If you wish, we can discuss it later but right now we have to get you to the surgeons. Orderlies! Get this man to the infirmary on the double!"

In a sudden motion that caught Silvanius by surprise, Cornelius grabbed the tribune's arm and pulled him down to within inches of his face. In a fierce whisper he said, "Tribune, heed this warning! The army is doomed. Nothing can save it. Don't ask me how I know this but I am convinced of it! But you can save yourself. Leave this place tonight and save what little is left to save!"

Silvanius was aghast. "Centurion, you forget yourself. Are you suggesting I desert my command?"

"I am suggesting you save yourself, tribune."

"I will not abandon my duty because of a dream."

"Then you will die!"

"Better to die with honor than live a life of shame," retorted the tribune. "I suggest you look to yourself, centurion and do not worry about me. If the Fates cut the thread of my life tomorrow than let it be so. I will die like a Roman with a sword in my hand, stained red with the blood of Rome's enemies."

"You cannot change what will be, tribune."

"Perhaps not. But I also cannot change what I am."

"Then it is my earnest hope that the One who has sheltered me go with you tomorrow into battle," replied Cornelius with a depth of compassion that Silvanius found strangely compelling.

"And may you continue to enjoy his favor," rejoined Silvanius, "But please, no more talk of dreams and warnings for the present. You must get to the surgeon's tent without further delay. Orderlies!"

This time, Cornelius did not protest but allowed himself to be carried to the infirmary. He could not help wondering if he would ever see Silvanius again.

XVII

"**I** say we attack tonight and make an end to them once and for all!"

In the center of a clearing a short distance from the foot of the hilltop that held the Roman encampment, seventeen chiefs and captains sat in a council of war around a roaring bonfire. The ring of men had gathered at the summons of Arminius, their war chief, representing a cross section of the four tribes now engaged in the life and death struggle with the hated Romans. The principal leaders of the Catti, Cherusci, Marsi and Bructeri clans had agreed to temporarily put aside their ancient feuds with one another for the common cause of ejecting the Italian invaders from their woodland homes. And to that purpose, they had placed their trust, albeit with some apprehension and suspicion, into Arminius' capable hands. It was only through his boundless energy and forceful personality that the confederacy was gathered and forged into a powerful weapon. They had reluctantly agreed to his strategy and then watched disbelieving as the Romans marched blithely into the Teutoberg Forest just as Arminius said they would. They adopted his tactics and were shocked at the ease in which they had bloodied and decimated the peerless ranks of the legions, just as he argued they could be. Yet despite their success, there were those around the fire who, even now, continued to doubt his ability to lead them to victory. And those dissenting opinions had found their voice in a bellicose Bructerian chieftain named Banto.

Banto had been the first to stand up before the chiefs and demand they attack the Roman camp immediately. "Let's go up there and pull the rats out of their holes!" he bellowed soliciting a strident response from his supporters. "Why are we wasting our time sitting around a fire down here when we can set the whole mountain on fire with the Romans in the middle of it!" More hooting and clapping followed from a small group of six chiefs who were obviously his allies. Arminius sat silently in a carved chair and listened, marking in his mind the faces of those who were setting themselves against him. Looking around the circle, he could see others watching and listening with interest to Banto's blustering harangue. If he continued to allow the fool's tongue to wag, there was a real danger his work would be undone and the Romans would escape his trap.

"Why?" demanded Banto, pointing an accusing finger at Arminius, "Are you keeping us here? We have all seen how the Romans have been delivered into our power. Why then are we just sitting here? Let me tell you why! Because Arminius' ambition is the only thing that is greater than his pride! It is well known that he has served in the legions himself and holds their citizenship. No doubt he has many friends on top of that hill he cannot bear to harm. Why else would he hold us back from destroying them where they sit? The answer is obvious. He intends to use his Roman friends against the tribes in order to make the Cherusci lords over us all. He intends to make himself a king!"

A sullen murmur traveled around the campfire as the chiefs put their heads together to debate the validity of Banto's charge. Segimerus, Arminius' trusted lieutenant and confidant, leapt to his feet from his place beside Arminius and cried, "Noble chiefs how can you doubt your own eyes? Did not the Lord Arminius promise to deliver the Romans into your hands if you would follow his counsel? He has done all he has promised and more! The enemy is at our mercy! Will you now let him go because you give ear to a fool's nonsense?"

Banto's piggish features flushed with anger at Segimerus' insult. He took a few menacing steps toward him. "Who are you calling a fool, Segimerus? We all know what you are, you miserable cur! You are nothing more than a lapdog for your master Arminius, coming when you are called and barking when you are told."

Segimerus slid his sword from its sheath and brandished it in the firelight. "You shall find this dog has more bite than bark, you son of a Bructerian sow!"

"Enough!" Arminius was on his feet. "Put your sword away, Segimerus. Save your fighting for the Romans. This is an open council. Banto is free to give his opinion." Segimerus reluctantly sheathed his weapon and returned to stand beside Arminius. Banto stood with his legs belligerently apart and his arms akimbo, grinning like an idiot. He was disappointed it had not come down to a fight. Killing Segimerus in front of all the chiefs would have damaged Arminius' position, perhaps fatally.

But Arminius had deftly assessed the situation and its possible repercussions. He had moved quickly to contain it. He was not about to give his adversary the upper hand so easily.

Seating himself again, Arminius offered an open palm to the big chieftain as an invitation for Banto to continue.

"As I have said," growled Banto testily, "I know a lover of Romans when I see one."

"It is true," answered Arminius above the murmuring that followed Banto's statement, "I do have friends in Rome. Powerful friends. Both at court and in the army. Indeed, I will even go so far as to count the commander of the legions who opposes us as a friend, as well as some of his officers with whom I have served. Since when is it a crime to possess acquaintances who happen to be Romans?"

"They are our enemies!"

"True. But not all Romans are our enemies just as not all Germans are our friends."

The chiefs nodded sagely at Arminius' clever turn of a phrase. A wolfish grin spread over Banto's face. In the red shadows of the firelight, it gave his flat features a demonic cast. "Remember what you have said, Arminius. It may turn out to be more true than you know." Signaling to one of his warriors, they suddenly pushed a fettered man into the midst of the council of war. He was dressed in a torn toga adorned with a broad purple stripe down the right side. The white material was stained with dirt and blood, presumably from an ugly gash on the man's temple above the left eye. The vacuous look of the hunted transformed the eyes into empty windows staring but seeing nothing.

Banto grabbed him roughly by the shoulder and held up before the council. "Behold, my lords, a nobleman of Rome!" The chiefs jeered and laughed as Banto took the man and threw him at Arminius' feet. "A friend of yours, Arminius?" he asked sarcastically.

Arminius sat rock still, glaring at Banto. "A friend, no." he replied quietly, "But I know who he is."

"I thought you might," retorted the Bructerian. "Suppose you tell this illustrious council who this man is?"

"His name is Turtullus. He is a lawyer and senator of Rome."

At the sound of his spoken name, Turtullus seemed to break out of his semi-comatose state. Regaining his focus, he stared harshly into Arminius' face. "Arminius!" he cried in an accusatory tone. "You traitor! So the stories are true! You are leading the rebellion!"

"It seems he does know you, Arminius!" roared Banto, coaxing a bantering snicker from the chiefs.

"How did you come by this man?" inquired Arminius.

"Oh didn't I tell you?" laughed Banto, "We caught him outside the camp relieving himself. He was carrying an armful of scrolls at the time. I guess he was planning to wipe his ass with them." The crude joke sent the council into peals of raucous laughter.

"They were my life's work!" cried the miserable Turtullus. "I was trying to save them."

"Save them from what, senator?" asked Arminius.

"From Varus."

"Varus?"

"Yes. Tomorrow he plans to set fire to the rest of the transports and go back to Aliso. All my papers, everything I have accomplished in my life, are in those wagons. He threatened to commit them to the flames as if they were mere straw! A lifetime's work reduced to cinders! I had to salvage what I could."

Arminius stared uncomprehending at the Roman. "You would risk your life for a collection of scrolls? Are you mad?"

Turtullus raised himself up to his full height and stuck out his chin defiantly. "You would not dare lay hands on a senator of Rome. My person is inviolate. I demand you release me and grant me safe passage back to Roman territory. I have no quarrel with you."

From behind, Banto grabbed his arm and twisted it up between his shoulder blades causing the senator to yelp in pain. "Not until you have answered a few questions, my lord," he rumbled menacingly.

"Banto, let him go!" ordered Arminius. The Bructerian chieftain looked up at Arminius, his eyes filled with hate.

"So, he is a friend of yours." Tightening his grip on Turtullus' arm, he told him, "Tell them what you told me, dog!"

Turtullus' face blushed crimson under the barbarian's painful grip. Through clenched teeth, he managed to utter, "At Castra Vetera... I saw Governor General Varus meet secretly with

Arminius.... on numerous occasions. Just before Arminius left the camp.... I heard him whisper, ow, the pain! I... I heard him whisper... to Varus that all was in ready....aaah! You are going to break my arm....ow! He...he told Varus that they would be waiting at....at the agreed place." Banto pushed Turtullus to the ground where he lay, panting and moaning. Boring his piggish eyes into Arminius' own, he said to the gathered chiefs, "You have heard it for yourselves, my lords. Arminius is a traitor. By his own admission, he has told us that Varus is a personal friend. And now we know he has made some sort of a bargain with the Roman to deliver us into his hands. Can there be any doubt now as to why he will not advance against them? He has betrayed us to the Roman yoke in exchange for a tin crown!"

The damaging testimony of Turtullus followed by Banto's accusation succeeded in provoking an ugly mood in the council. All eyes now turned to Arminius, as voices were raised in anger and disgust. The leader who had brought them to the verge of a glorious victory with his quicksilver mind and strong sword arm had suddenly been found to possess feet of clay.

In the center of the rising storm, Arminius sat coolly detached. He recognized the folly of his attempts to undermine Varus' position through ties of a close personal relationship. He had seen and was aware of the Roman disapproval of his friendship with the commander of the Rhine army but it had never occurred to him that it might also have a negative impression amongst his own countrymen. But there was little he could do about that now. What was left was to show the council that Turtullus was lying. He had never said any such thing to Varus but at that point, with the possible exception of Banto, he was the only one who knew it.

"I would like to ask the senator some questions," he announced to his circle of accusers.

"We have heard all we need to hear from him," snorted Banto, kicking the prostrate Turtullus in the ribs.

"I would like to question him without your threats, Banto. Stand back and let him up." Reluctantly, Banto stepped back a few steps and waited, keeping a close watch on his prey as a cat might with a wounded bird. To Segimerus, Arminius instructed, "Help Senator Turtullus to his feet and unbind him." Segimerus moved quickly with another warrior loyal to Arminius and pulled Turtullus up from the ground. The warrior cut the senator's bonds with his long-bladed dagger. Rubbing his wrists, Turtullus glared sullenly at his benefactor.

"Senator Turtullus," began Arminius.

"I don't have to answer your questions, barbarian!" sneered Turtullus.

"If you want to live, you will do just that, senator," replied Arminius evenly. "Now, I would like to know exactly what Varus' intentions are."

"You should know considering how much time you spent with him, traitor." The response elicited a satisfying smile from Banto.

"I remind you again, senator. Your only hope of survival rests with me. Banto and his friends will not allow you to leave our camp alive."

"And you will?" asked Turtullus sarcastically. "Do you expect me to believe there is honor in the heart of a barbarian? You have already proven your worth, Arminius. There is nothing you can say that will persuade me to believe you."

Arminius clasped his hands behind his back and began to pace back and forth in front of the Roman, his brow furrowed in thought. Clearly he would have to try another tact if he was going to get what he wanted from Turtullus. Presently, a new avenue of inquiry entered his mind and he readily seized upon it. Turning to the senator he asked, "The scrolls you were carrying when we found you. You say you were trying to keep them from being destroyed by Varus, is that correct?"

Turtullus taciturn expression confirmed Arminius' answer. "And that the Romans plan on setting fire to the rest of their transports and making a dash for Aliso?" Again no response.

"So as I see it, his plan is to create a diversion to enable him to take us by surprise when he comes charging down that hill tomorrow. Not very imaginative I'm afraid. Even for Varus. But I had anticipated he might try something like this. So you have your answer, Banto, as to why I would not attack their camp tonight. It seems that the fox is going to come out of his burrow and run right into the teeth of the hounds. Unless, of course, you think the honorable senator is lying about the transports."

The big Bructerian wiped a meaty hand across his lips. How had Arminius done it? He had taken the only true part of the idiot Roman's story and put doubt in the minds of the chiefs of its validity. And if he could make them disbelieve the truth with the force of a simple question, how much more difficult would it be to uncover the lie? The council would be left to question whether any of what he had forced out of the senator had been true. He was beginning to feel his advantage crumble beneath his feet. He knew he must do something quickly or see his challenge wither away.

"A senator of Rome does not lie!" exclaimed Turtullus indignantly. "What I have said is the truth. As a lawyer, I have dedicated my life to the pursuit of truth. That is why I could not bear to see my scrolls burned!"

"What have you done with the senator's scrolls, Banto?" demanded Arminius.

"I have them."

Turtullus whirled around with a look of rapturous relief.

"Where are the- ugh!" The question died in Turtullus' throat. Banto's sword had thrust him clear through the abdomen, the point erupting from the folds of the toga, dripping bright red with blood. Turtullus' face became a pale contortion at the moment of death as he slid awkwardly from the deadly blade to fall in a crumpled heap to the ground. Almost at that exact moment, a dagger whistled through the firelight and caught Banto in the throat. The force of the blow caused the big tribesman to stagger backwards a couple of paces before crashing onto his back where he lay thrashing in his death throes. Moments later he was still, a trickle of blood oozing from the corner of his open mouth, the eyes staring unseeing into the night sky.

The council watched impassively as Segimerus walked calmly over to Banto's dead body and removed his knife, wiping the bloody blade on the dead man's wool tunic. Stepping over the corpse, he leant down and stared down at the still form of Turtullus, placing his fingers on the neck to check for a pulse. Looking up at Arminius, he shook his head.

Three young Bructerain warriors with swords drawn, elbowed their way past the silent chiefs and stood next to their fallen leader, pushing Segimerus away from the bodies. "I demand satisfaction," cried one of them to Arminius, "Your man has killed my father without cause. It is my right to exact vengeance and cancel the blood guilt."

One of the older chiefs, a well-respected Chatti leader named Ariovistus, held up his hand. "Dagomar!" he said, addressing the young son of Banto. "There has been enough blood shed this night. There is no bloodguilt here. We all knew that one day Banto's stubborn ways would be his undoing. Your father was in the wrong. He had obviously stuffed the Roman's mouth with lies to turn this council against Arminius. Both have paid with their lives. We are satisfied that Arminius has not played us false. We are content to pledge our lives to him against our enemies. So I say to you: bury your dead and return to us as brothers so we might destroy the Roman invaders together."

Dagomar listened in seething silence, his eyes blazing with rage. "The Bructeri have but one enemy now," he gritted through clenched teeth, "The man who killed my father. We will bury our dead but we will not return. Arminius! Know that

169

from this day forward, I vow before this august council that I will not rest until you and Segimerus have paid for your crime!" Turning on his heel, he stalked off into the darkness, followed by the other two warriors who bore Banto's corpse between them.

Ariovistus turned to Arminius and said, "The Bructeri are a small tribe. Their loss will not be significant."

"I wonder," mused Arminius quietly, "Gentlemen, I suggest we call an end to this council. It has been a long night and tomorrow promises to be even longer. We know now the Romans plan to fire their camp and attempt a breakthrough in the confusion. So be it. Let them burn every wagon and cart in their possession. They shall still find us waiting for them in the forest." One by one, the chieftains offered their salutations and drifted back to their own lodgings until only Arminius and Segimerus were left by the dying fire. Walking over to the dead body of Turtullus, Arminius squatted down on his haunches and observed the bloodless face. For a long time, he sat squatting, picking up a stick and drawing idly in the dirt beside the body. Finally he said, "Segimerus?"

Segimerus came and stood next to his chief. "Yes, lord?"

"How many men did the Bructeri come with?"

"About six centuries."

Arminius nodded. "Ariovistus was right. They are a small company. But they are now a very dangerous company. Killing Banto was a reckless thing to do, Segimerus. You could have ruined everything."

"Perhaps," replied Segimerus, "but I only did what I knew you wanted."

Arminius nodded again and tossed away his stick. "Yes, you are right. However, there is now something else I need you to do."

"Name it, lord."

"Do you know where the Bructeri are encamped?" Segimerus nodded.

"Very well. Gather a thousand men quietly within the next hour and go there with all speed. Ensure that not a single Bructerian survives the night."

"What of Dagomar?"

"You may kill him if you wish."

Segimerus bowed and turned to commence his work but was momentarily stayed by his master's hand.

"And Segimerus," said Arminius, looking down at the rumpled folds of the blood stained toga, "See to it that Senator Turtullus receives a proper Roman burial."

XVIII

Cornelius' leg wound was not as grievous as he had first feared. The surgeons managed to extract the arrowhead with little difficulty and after bandaging the area with clean, white strips of cloth, gave him a draught of laudanum to act as a sedative. Before long, the exhaustion and fatigue which had been temporarily checked by the rush of his narrow escape came full upon him and combined with the calming effects of the laudanum to envelop him in a deep sleep. While he slept the dream returned.

The scene was the same.

The terrible battlefield piled high with armored corpses. The grass wet with blood. The strangling forest, omnipresent and menacing. Shadows drifting through the trees. The sky above burning with ethereal fire. And standing serenely to one side of it all, the Man of Dreams. But this time, Cornelius was not in the midst of the carnage on the field but standing beside the Man of Dreams, surveying the scene with a strange sense of detachment.

"What does it mean, Lord?" he heard himself ask the Man of Dreams.

The wonderful smile played gracefully across the divine visage. "Behold the judgement of my Father!" he exclaimed.

"Our army is to be destroyed?" asked Cornelius disbelieving, his heart chilled by a sudden fear for his own mortality.

"These are things that must be," replied the Man of Dreams. "For in ages long past were these things ordained by my Father in heaven. But fear not, Cornelius son of Sextus. The favor of the Lord is upon you. You shall not share in this judgement."

"Who are you, Lord?" asked Cornelius in a querulous voice.

The Man of Dreams gazed across the field to an unseen horizon. *"I am the Alpha and the Omega. The Beginning and the End. I am the One Who Was, the One Who Is and the One Who Is To Come."*

"What does that mean, Lord?"

The Man of Dreams turned smiling to Cornelius. *"All things will be revealed in their time. Have faith that God will deliver you from the spreading shadow of evil and keep you for the day of His purpose. Rise and follow, Cornelius son of Sextus, for the time of His purpose has come!"*

Cornelius awoke to the sound of muffled voices at the far end of the medics' tent. He could not quite make out what they were saying but he recognized one of the voices as that of the doctor who removed the arrow from his leg along with his assistant. The half-light inside the tent told him it was no more than a half hour before dawn.

As he listened to the drowsing tone of the voices, he absently reached down to the fresh dressing on his wound and began to massage it, expecting pain. He was startled to discover there was none. Rubbing it a little harder, he could not coax even a dull ache from it. Sitting up in the cot, he felt refreshed and strangely renewed in spirit. Swinging his legs over the edge of the bed, he put his feet on the floor and gingerly put a little weight upon the damaged leg. It supported him easily with no pain. Standing up, he pressed the full weight of his body on both legs and walked around in small circles, testing their strength. He could scarcely believe it! His leg felt perfectly normal as if it had never been injured at all! Why, there wasn't even a tell tale stain of blood on the bandage to indicate where the wound had been!

When the doctor saw his patient walking toward him on two apparently good legs, his mouth dropped open in disbelief. "Centurion what are you doing out of bed?"

"Doctor," exclaimed Cornelius somewhat hesitantly, "I can't explain how but I think I've been healed."

"What? Impossible! You shouldn't have been able to walk on that leg for at least a week. Let me see. Calistus, fetch some light."

The doctor's assistant ran out of the tent and returned with a lit oil lamp which he held above Cornelius' leg while the surgeon unwrapped the dressing. When the last strip fell away, the flickering light of the lamp revealed what they all knew to be impossible. Where the wound should have been there was now only a perfect patch of new pink skin.

The doctor stood back and stared doubtfully at Cornelius. "How is this possible? In twenty years of medicine I have never seen anything like this! I have had patients heal more quickly than they had a right to but nothing like this! Tell me, centurion! Tell me how this happened!"

Cornelius wondered whether he should tell the doctor the truth. What would he think when he learned that his patient had been healed by a dream? For Cornelius knew without a shadow of doubt, that the Man of Dreams had somehow been responsible for his miraculous healing. Likely, the doctor would think him mad. No matter. The reality of the healing was proof enough.

Cornelius decided it would be better not to become entangled in any kind of supernatural explanation. How would he explain it in any case? So he merely shrugged his shoulders and wanly replied, "I don't know. I'm only a soldier. You're the doctor. I was hoping you would be able to tell me how this happened." Outside, the trumpet call for assembly sounded.

"Excuse me, doctor," apologized Cornelius. "But duty calls. I have to get back to my unit."

"I want to see you when we return to Aliso!" shouted the doctor at Cornelius as he ducked out of the tent. "I intend to get to the bottom of this one way or another!"

The camp was already a buzz of activity when Cornelius emerged from the surgeons' tent and stood looking around him. Dawn had just lit the eastern horizon, reveling the welcome sight of a patch of pale sky, growing and brightening in the wake of the retreat of the heavy storm clouds of the past week. The day promised to be sunny if on the cool side, the first real break the haggard Romans had had since entering the Teutoberg three days before. All around him, men scrambled to strike down their tents and find their places in the many new units that had been formed out of the shattered remnants of the Eighteenth and Nineteenth Legions. Cornelius wondered where his own century was or whether the Legate Florus had had time to organize the new command he had promised. The answer was not long in coming. A mounted tribune came suddenly into view and headed straight for the surgeon's tent, rearing his mount to a stop in front of Cornelius.

"Woe, there centurion! I am surprised to find you out of bed." To Cornelius' delight, it was Gaius Silvanius.

"Did the sawbones give you permission to stand out here? Do you want to lose your other leg?" he joked, a wry smile on his face.

"Hail to you, tribune," answered Cornelius good naturedly. "You will find I have two good legs this morning."

Silvanius looked down at Cornelius' legs and then back over his shoulder at the medics' tent. "That sawbones is a better doctor than I ever gave him credit for."

"Don't change your opinion because of me, tribune. The doctor had nothing to do with my recovery."

"Indeed? Well, I'm sure you have an interesting explanation for it. But it will have to wait for the moment. For now, I thank the gods for your swift restoration. The Legate Florus sent me to get you, to see if you were well enough to take up your new command. I can see that you are. If you will follow me, I will take you there now."

Dismounting from his horse, the two men began to walk toward the opposite end of the encampment. For awhile they walked in silence, oblivious to the bustle of activity around them. Cornelius broke the mood by asking, "Have you thought about what I said to you yesterday?"

"About your warning you mean? I have spent most of the night seeing to our dispositions. I haven't had time to even think about relieving myself let alone trying to interpret your dreams!"

"I must tell you. I had another dream last night."

Silvanius sighed but said nothing.

Cornelius continued. "The Man of Dreams came to me again. He showed me the army is doomed."

"Speak no more about this to me, centurion," replied Silvanius testily. "Your words verge on treason. As Roman officers, we are expected to do our duty to the utmost of our abilities. But I see defeat is already in your mind. Take my advice, centurion. If you are smart, you will forget all this nonsense about dreams and unknown gods. Rely on the power around you. Look to the pride of the legions! Look to Caesar as your god and protector! Not some ghost conjured from the stuff of your dreams!"

Cornelius felt a mixture of gloom and frustration prick his heart. He liked the tribune very much, a man to whom he owed much. It saddened him to see how willingly Silvanius insisted on riding to his doom.

Sighing, Cornelius said, "Tribune, my debt to you is more than I can pay. I wish I could impart to you why I believe that these dreams are from God."

"God? Which god? The Empire is filled with gods from the west to the east. The barbarians worship as many gods as there are trees in the forest. Of which god do you speak?"

"His name is unknown to me but I know now this Man of Dreams must be God. How else do you explain his appearance to you the night you found me by the brook? Look at my leg! You saw the wound there yesterday. There is no trace of it this morning. How do you explain it?

"I don't. I'm a soldier not a doctor. Nor do I care to offer an explanation."

"What must it take to convince you that what I'm saying is true?"

"Convince me of exactly what, centurion? That an omnipotent being, if He exists at all, intends to destroy an entire Roman army in the middle of the Teutoberg Forest. Is that what you want me to believe?"

"If we are to die it is not by God's hand but by our own."

"By 'our own', I take you to mean Varus. He has already lost one legion. Perhaps today he will make it two. I'm sorry but I don't blame the gods for bad generalship."

"You prove my point. It is men who are weak and apt to fail. For that reason alone we should consider putting our trust in a higher authority."

"I'm beginning to see more of Socrates in you than Alexander, centurion. But I agree with you when you say we must place our confidence in something greater than ourselves. I believe I did so when I took my oath to serve the Emperor. The same oath you took I might add. A soldier needs no higher authority than that."

Cornelius decided there was little profit in continuing the discussion. Stories of mysterious figures prophesying doom in dreams while producing miraculous healings in the dreamer were hardly the kind of thing needed in their present situation. Silvanius' concern was the same as that shared with every other man who had survived the ordeal of the past two days. To survive what must surely come with the next dawn and somehow reach the safety of the far Rhine. He would not allow himself to think beyond the boundary of his own fears.

Cornelius cast a glance up at the returning wall of gray–black cloud overhead and sighed. "Looks like more rain," he commented glumly.

"Yes," agreed Silvanius. "As if we haven't had enough all ready. It will only make our breakout that much harder to accomplish."

Cornelius nodded. "I am not afraid to die. Not now."

"I'm pleased to hear you say it, centurion. You will fight better against it if you're not afraid of it."

"There is however something else I fear."

"And what is that?"

"I am afraid for you, tribune."

"For me?"

"Yes."

"Why?"

"I have tried to tell you…"

"Your dream you mean."

"Yes. I am afraid you will not survive the destruction of our army."

"Centurion, we have been over this…"

Silvanius was surprised when Cornelius suddenly reached out and grabbed his forearm in a vice-like grip. Dropping his voice to a fierce whisper, Cornelius said, "How can I make you understand, tribune? I have seen it! It will happen! Nothing will stop it now. Just promise me this: that when battle comes, seek me out. Allow me the privilege of adding my sword to yours. Let me be your shield and your eyes. If we must die then let us die together! Tell me I have your word on it, tribune. Promise me!"

Silvanius was taken aback at the change of Cornelius' demeanor. His eyes had the same strange illumination to them that he had once witnessed in Athens when he had accidentally come upon a group of crazed devotees of Bacchus whose drunken ritual had gotten out of hand and had spilled out of the doors of their temple and into the street. It was frightening to see how their fanaticism had gripped them with a religious ferocity that had completely submerged their personalities. He was witnessing the same phenomenon in the young centurion.

He tried to remove Cornelius' hand but could not. It felt like stone upon his skin.

"Centurion, you forget yourself."

Cornelius continued to stare wide-eyed into Silvanius' face. "Promise me!" he hissed again.

"If it is the only way I can get you to release me than yes. I promise I will seek you out when the time comes. Is my word enough for you or must we draw blood in a formal contract?"

Immediately Silvanius felt the grip on his arm relax. The fierceness drained away from Cornelius' features. The eerie light faded from the blue eyes.

"I'm sorry, tribune," he mumbled, passing a hand over his eyes. "I don't know what came over me just now. It was suddenly very important that I know you would be near in the battle. I don't know why."

Silvanius looked at Cornelius with a mixture of compassion and pity. It was obvious that the strain of these past few days had proven too much for the young man. He was at the breaking point. Silvanius had seen the phenomenon often enough in the past not to recognize the danger signs now. Its manifestations were as varied as the individuals who succumbed to them. Yet there was little doubt in the tribune's mind that Cornelius was not in his right mind. And if there was one place in the white hot heat of conflict Silvanius would not put himself, it was beside a madman, promise or not.

Putting his hand on Cornelius' shoulder, he gently guided the centurion toward the center of camp. "Enough talk for now, centurion. The general is waiting for us." Neither man spoke as they made their way toward Varus' command tent.

XIX

The spirals of blue-black smoke from the evening cooking fires curled lazily in the late afternoon sky towards the surrounding treetops. A small cluster of mud-baked huts, arranged haphazardly around an open space dominated by a crudely carved totem of Germanic deities identified the place as the hidden settlement of Arminius. Apart from a few older warriors armed with long spears and leather shields cracked with age, the population of the encampment was primarily women, children and slaves. The remoteness of the area had suited Arminius' purposes admirably. It was a place he had sought to shelter his pregnant wife and his extended family and retainers from his many enemies; enemies who would think nothing of using the most precious thing in his life against him if they could. Despite his confidence in the plans laid for the ultimate destruction of the invading legions, he still harbored a fear of reprisal should the unthinkable happen and his quarry escape. But it was in his most private moments that he dared admit for whom these elaborate precautions had really been prepared. His father-in-law had never given up the search for his daughter. Nor had his desire for revenge weakened in the pursuit.

The center hut of the settlement, distinctive because it was slightly larger than the rest, served as the personal quarters of the Lady Thusnelda. She was busy kneading a lump of hard bread dough for the evening meal, lost in thought as she bent the dough in her hands. Although her husband had ensured she had slaves about her to attend to the drudgery of daily tasks such as cooking, mending and sewing, she usually preferred to do them herself . She found that keeping busy even with such mundane endeavors as making bread, helped to keep the constant worry she felt in these past few days at bay. Even as a young girl she found comfort in the simplicity of such work. Now as a married woman, she discovered the dividends of that earlier apprentiship had served her well. It allowed her to bear the long, lonely hours alone and keep her mind from engaging in any soul-weary speculation on the fate or whereabouts of her new husband. As much as she loved Arminius, it was a love that had not prepared her for the role as wife of a high chief. The time they should have been spending enjoying and exploring the joys of marriage were now spent in increasing isolation and separation. Very quickly she had learned that hers was a secondary role to the ultimate purpose to which her husband believed himself to be been called; namely, the leader who would unite the disparate tribes and interests in Germany in forging a power unknown to the northern world. Fortunately for Thusnelda, she had been blessed with a mild and understanding temperament that allowed her to carry the burden of an absent husband with dignity and good humor. The 'cause' was not a threat to her as much as it was an inconvenience. It was but for a season, she told herself, and like all men of war, he would return again when the clouds of war had lifted. Her fervent prayer was that Arminius would one day come home for good. Together they would watch the child now growing in her womb hopefully live his life in a world far removed from the storms and troubles of their present circumstances.

Kneading the bread dough with strong hands on the flat of a stone slab, she sang softly to herself a lullaby her father had sung to her when she was just a little girl.

> *And now the labors day is done,*
> *In forest, hill and field.*
> *I walk home in the setting sun,*
> *With sword and helm and shield.*
> *And as I lay my head upon,*
> *My pallet I will dream,*
> *Of glories that are left to win,*
> *On forest, hill and field.*

She smiled at the pleasant memories the song evoked in her memory about her father. As a child, he was her hero, a shining standard by which she measured all other men. In her girlish dreams she found all lacking save two. The former was her husband Arminius, as strong and vital then as he was now. The latter, a handsome young tribune from Rome with a shock of curly dark hair, beautiful eyes and a full, sensuous mouth by the name of Silvanius. He had been both a friend and confidant of her father's and had spent nearly two years as his guest, becoming in the end a trusted friend of her entire family. To the Roman she had first given her love, albeit secretly in the refuge of her dreams. She was sure neither he nor her father ever suspected the depth of her feelings. How could they? She had never given them cause to think otherwise. Nevertheless, for the sake of that long ago impossible love she had taken a chance with her husband. By pleading for Silvanius' life, she had aroused Arminius' suspicions and jealousy. Although he had granted her request in the end, it was her earnest hope that she had not driven an immovable wedge between them. She had meant what she said when she told Arminius that the love she had for Silvanius was only a girl's fantasy. Thusnelda had freely given her woman's heart to Arminius without reservations. However, try as she might, she could not deny that somewhere in that woman's heart there still glowed faint embers for the Roman tribune. It was the reason she despaired of his life when she learned of Arminius' plans for the Roman army. And should Arminius keep his promise to spare Silvanius' life, she knew she could never prevail upon his good nature again. She understood only too well the magnitude of her request. It could not be easy for a man like Arminius to spare his rival especially when it concerned the torn affections of his own wife.

A shadow passed over her as she worked. She heard the rustling of the heavy curtain that served as the door to the hut. She looked up to see Thrond, captain of her guard, standing in the doorway.

"Excuse me, my lady," he apologized, bowing at the waist.

"What is it, Thrond?" she asked, wiping flour from her cheek with the back of her wrist.

"We have a visitor."

"A visitor?" She frowned. "My husband assured me we were quite safe here, that no one would find us."

Thrond, once a warrior of renown on both sides of the Great River, but was now only an aged shade of his former self, grinned showing a row of worn teeth through his gray beard. "And so it is, my lady. Our visitor is an old man begging bread."

"Oh," replied Thusnelda hollowly. Returning to her task, she added without looking up, "See to it he receives supper and lodging for the night."

"Excuse me, my lady, but he wishes to speak to you."

"To me?" Thusnelda's heart began to beat harder in her ears. Could this possibly be a messenger from Arminius with news? She sat silently and pondered the possibility.

"My lady?"

Thusnelda broke from her reverie. "Yes, of course. Send him in, Thrond. If you believe it to be safe, of course."

Bowing again, Thrond replied, "I do, my lady. I will bring him to you now." Thrond went back out through the curtains whose rustling barely ceased before they parted again to admit the stranger.

The man was indeed old, as Thrond had said. He was dressed in a black, travel-stained robe that covered his bent form. He features were hidden inside the deep folds of a large hood. Only the fall of a white beard on his chest gave any indication as to his age. He was bent at the waist, supporting himself on a knobby, wooden staff.

For a few moments, he regarded Thusnelda in the dim firelight of the hut. Thusnelda felt uncomfortable under the old man's scrutiny. For her part, she felt a tug at her memory as if pricked by a vague sense of familiarity with the old beggar. She moved to break the awkwardness of the moment by speaking first.

"Good sir, you are welcome. I am told you wish to speak to me?"

The old man wavered for a second, seemed to make to reply before he straightened up, and threw back his cowl, revealing a crown of golden hair. Pulling the false beard from his face, he flung it to one side of the room while throwing off the black robe. Beneath it, he wore a leather Roman cuirass and a short Roman sword.

"Thusnelda!" he breathed.

"Father!" She stood petrified with shock, unsure whether to embrace him or scream for Thrond.

"Father," she repeated still stupefied, "What are you doing here?"

Segestes set his face into a grim mask. "I came to take what was taken from me. I have come to take you home, daughter."

"No!" she answered in a horrified whisper. "I can't go with you, father. My place is here, with my husband."

"He is not your husband!" cried Segestes angrily. "He is nothing but a thief and a liar. He took you from my house by force without my blessing. Your marriage is nothing but a sham and a lie!"

"I love him, father."

Segestes spat in disgust. Pointing his finger at Thusnelda to emphasize his point, he said, "You are the daughter of the high chief of the Cherusci. It is not for you to choose the way of love. That is for commoners and slaves. As my daughter, I would have chosen a husband for you when the time came."

"Who, father?" she laughed, bitter tears welling in the corners of her large, blue eyes. "Who? Some ancient chief who would most likely have died from exertion on our wedding night? Or perhaps your choice is the brutish son of some ambitious leader you wish to neutralize. Or was your plan to pack me away and use me as a pawn against your enemies until I was too old to be of use to anyone? I am sorry father, but I wanted more. Much more!"

Segestes rubbed his chin ruefully. "By the gods of my fathers, you would have made a fine high chief's wife, girl!"

"I am a chief's wife," she corrected him, "And I will bear his son."

At that, Segestes grew grim again. She was so much like her mother! When her mind was set like standing stone, as it was now, he could deny her nothing.

Sighing heavily, he said, "I see your mother in you, Thusnelda. Is it any wonder I loved her so? The heart was taken from me when she died. But knowing I still had you gave me comfort. When I looked at you, I saw the perfect reflection of my Cara staring back. When I looked at you, it was as if I had never lost her. But when he came and took you from me it was as if she had died all over again. It was more than I could bear. My only desire was for revenge. To kill the man who taken the very heart out of me! But I see now how foolish it was to think that way. Yes, Thusnelda, you are right. You are a chief's wife."

Thusnelda's face brightened with hope. "Does that mean you will make peace with Hermann, father and confirm him as your heir? As high chief of the Cherusci?"

Segestes shook his head. "No, child. That is impossible now. Arminius has made too many enemies in his overweening pride and ambition. Do you think I am the only one he has offended? Men like Arminius gather enemies as easily as fruit in the autumn harvest. He will never be able to command the loyalty he needs to exercise the authority of the high chief. And you my precious one, will never know peace."

"But father, has he not already proven his worth by gathering the tribes against the Romans? Who else could have done such a thing! Would the tribes have willingly joined Arminius if he did not already possess the mantle of authority?"

"You speak foolishness, girl," retorted Segestes sarcastically. "They fear him more than the Romans."

"Not so, father. They follow him because they know he is the only one who can break the Roman yoke from their necks. And once the Romans are gone it will be too late for you to stop him. Victory will serve as Arminius' anointing, with or without your blessing. After that, the tribes will follow him anywhere."

Segestes shook his head sadly. "You know my view on the matter, daughter. I have always said the Romans are not our enemies. Whatever success Arminius might claim today will be answered by ten

Roman legions tomorrow. Our future lies in cooperation with Rome not waging useless war against her. We can learn so much from the Romans, things we need to know if we are to survive and grow as a nation."

Thusnelda pinched her delicate features into a frown that did nothing to belie her natural beauty. "Your way would make us all Romans, father. Arminius' way would make us free. Which would you rather be?"

"I would rather be alive and a friend of Rome than lie dead in a lonely grave as her foe. Arminius' way will bring only death and destruction to our people. Let me tell you something, Thusnelda. If I have learned anything from being high chief, it is this: that a leader must act like a father wanting only what is best for his children. I am afraid it is a lesson that overweening men like Arminius can never learn."

"Better death as a free man than life as a slave."

Segestes smiled indulgently at his daughter. Secretly, he was stung to the heart by realization of the true breadth of the gulf between them. The Thusnelda he had nurtured and loved was gone, never to return. She had become the wife of a man whose values and beliefs were alien and repugnant to him. A ruthless man who would heedlessly destroy everything that Segestes had labored to build. She had indeed become a chief's wife. The thought filled him with a pang of regret so sharp; it threatened to move him to tears.

"Your husband has taught you well, my daughter," he offered finally. "I came to find you and to take you as you were taken from me. I see now that that is impossible. So be it. I leave you to the life, to the husband and to the fate, you have chosen. May the gods grant you a long and prosperous life, Thusnelda, with many children and grandchildren to comfort you in your old age. As for me, I say only this to you. From this day forward, you will see my face no more. After today, I have no daughter."

The declaration was like a slap to the face of Thusnelda. She unconsciously recoiled at the words overwhelmed by the finality of their meaning. Reaching out with doughy hands she caught her father's cloak as he turned to go.

"Father, please," she pleaded tearfully, "Do not leave me like this. Try to understand. I love you just as I love Arminius. What will become of my children if you go?" Segestes remained unmoved. He started to duck under the doorway when she tugged more urgently upon his cloak causing him to pause one last time to look down at her. Sniffing back her tears, she said, "A word before we part."

"We have had enough words between us already," rumbled Segestes gravely. "What more is there left to say?"

"If this is to be the way of it between us, grant me these last words since we are never to see one another again."

"Very well. Speak on."

Thusnelda let go of Segestes cloak and bit her bottom lip. Hesitantly she asked, "Have you any news of my husband? Is he well? I pray you do not spare me if the news is bad."

Segestes held the beautiful, teary eyes of his precious daughter to his own. In a tone stripped of all trace of emotion, he replied, "If you want to find your husband, look for him in the Teutoberg Wood."

XX

Varus could not remember feeling so tired or more discouraged in his life.

Sitting at his field desk in the dark of his papilo, his eyes moved automatically to the ceiling at the familiar drumming of rain on the canvas. The respite of two rainless days was at an end. Tomorrow, he would have to fight the last leg of the trail back to Aliso in what promised to be a deluge. If the task of contending with the hidden hordes of barbarians in the forest were not enough, now they would have to contend with the elements as well. Fortune, it seemed, had turned her back on him after all. Perhaps it was divine retribution for his ill-considered desecration of the altar of Mars. Who was he to think he could fight the gods themselves? The Greeks had a perfect word for it: hubris, the act of overweening human pride against the stated will of heaven. On the face of it, Varus could not disassociate himself from his own guilt in the matter. He wondered if it were not too late to assuage the divine rage by repenting of his foolhardiness. Instantly, the thought jarred against the pragmatic leaning of his mind. He was not the kind of man to give in to irrational flights of religious fancy. For him the gods of Rome had no more power over his life than the cold marble from which their images were carved. He had always believed that the demands of religious convention had spread more misery and ignorance in the world than any lawyer ever could.

Varus sat back and closed his tired eyes. One legion gone! Another practically decimated! How had it gone so badly? And so quickly! We must get back to Aliso or all will be lost!

He wanted very much to sleep but his mind would not allow him to put his head to the pillow. The events of the day played themselves endlessly through his consciousness, taunting his confidence and challenging his judgment. The stubborn bedrock of his will began to crack under the direness of their current circumstances, leaving him wondering if anything could be done to alter their inevitable conclusion.

In the hour after dawn that morning as they prepared to fire their transports and launch their assault against the barbarian lines, Gaius Silvanius had come to Varus with a young centurion in tow, desiring a word.

"It is my opinion, Excellency," began the tribune, "That we do not set fire to the wagons."

"Why not?" asked Varus perturbed that Silvanius chose now to question the previous night's decision.

"Burning the transports will provide only a short diversion. When the Germans discover there is nothing of value for them in the ashes they will be howling on our heels in no time. If, however, we leave them intact, the Germans will be too busy plundering their contents to follow us. We will gain the time we need to break their lines and make straight for Aliso without further hindrance."

Varus rubbed his chin in thought. As much as he hated to admit it, Silvanius was by far the best staff officer he had. He found his recommendations sound and his insight clear despite his affection for the barbarians, which Varus considered a dangerous weakness. However, what he was now proposing did make a great deal of sense.

"Very well, tribune. Give the order not to burn the transports. But fire the gates and walls when the last cohort has left. That will keep the barbarians even busier fighting a fire while attempting to retrieve their booty. See to it, tribune."

Silvanius saluted smartly. "Yes, sir."

"And who is this?" asked Varus eying Cornelius sharply.

"This is the man I told you about, sir. Centurion Cornelius Strabo, late of the Nineteenth."

"Oh, yes. The young man who used a tortoise to get his men into camp yesterday. Well done, centurion. We will need more of that kind of soldiering if we hope to get back to Aliso. I was told you were injured. You look fine to me."

"Yes, sir," replied Cornelius. "I'm fully recovered and ready for duty."

"Good. That's what I like to hear. I have need of competent officers at the moment to lead some of the temporary centuries we've managed to pull together from remnants of the Eighteenth and Nineteenth. Do you have a preference of where you wish to serve?"

Silvanius interrupted before Cornelius could answer. "Pardon me, Excellency but may I suggest we assign the centurion to command the men we leave behind to fire the gates? The officer we chose must be resourceful as well as be able to think quickly on his feet. Centurion Strabo has more than adequately demonstrated he possesses both qualities in full measure."

Cornelius stared back at Silvanius with open-mouthed astonishment. Varus nodded stiffly. "Yes, I suppose you're right, tribune. The centurion here would be our best bet at the gates. Very well. Carry on, gentlemen. See to your dispositions and report back to me within the hour."

Varus strode off to another corner of the camp leaving the two men alone in front of the command tent.

"Why did you do that?" demanded Cornelius.

"Do what?"

"Tell the general I would command at the gate. I told you I wanted to stay with you. What's so important about the gate that I have to be assigned there instead?"

A mischievous grin spread across the tribune's handsome face. "You heard the general After we've all left camp, you're going to set fire to the gates."

"I'm going to what?"

"Set fire to the gates."

"Why would I do that?"

"To create a diversion, of course. To buy us the time we need to put distance between us and the barbarians."

"So not only will I have to escape the howling enemy outside the gates but now I have to escape a raging fire inside as well. How do you propose I work such a miracle?"

Silvanius' grin deepened. "Oh I'm sure you'll figure something out. After all, that's the reason I recommended you for the job in the first place! And if you can't work a miracle, centurion I have no doubt your God can!"

At the appointed hour, the trumpets sounded for the advance. The wood gates swung open and the armored mass of the Seventeenth Legion trotted double time down the hill. Surprisingly, there was little reaction from the trees, aside from the odd dart or javelin, as the formation made the foot of the hill in good order, plunging noisily into the forest proper. A second, smaller formation constructed from the survivors of the ill-fated Eighteenth and Nineteenth Legions, followed the route blazed by the Seventeenth. This time, the response from the surrounding wood was more intense. A shower of weaponry filled the air, finding a number of unfortunate Roman targets. Here and there, legionaries fell wounded from the jogging mass of men, raising helpless cries and hands for aid to their retreating comrades. Unfortunately, for the wounded, their orders were explicit and every man knew it. Do not stop for any reason. Advance until the order to halt is given. Not once did the famous Roman discipline waver from the hailstorm directed against them from the screen of encircling trees.

At the gates, Cornelius watched and waited with a small knot of soldiers given to him for his task. Each man had been issued a crude torch and a small pot of flammable pitch. When the second ad hoc legion had reached the halfway point on the hill, Cornelius gave the order to light the torches. Quickly the legionaries dunked the rolled cloth at the end of their torches into the pots before thrusting them into the flames of a prepared campfire burning just inside the palisade wall. With torches blazing, the soldiers went to work. The wooden walls and ramparts had been stuffed with a portion of the cavalry's remaining stocks of hay as well as a flammable concoction of tallow and tar. Within minutes, the walls were transformed into a raging wall of flame. Prior to igniting the blaze, Cornelius had ordered the pins removed from the iron hinges of the gates. Now as the blaze grew in intensity, he instructed his men to push over the gates. They fell heavily to the ground, stamping out a section of the flame wall, which had the effect of creating an opening for their escape. Quickly, his men ran across the makeshift bridge and down the hill. Cornelius and Bassanius were the last to leave the fiercely burning hilltop. Everywhere flames were beginning to shoot up through the downed gates, making it difficult for the pair to find places to plant their feet as they ran for their lives. Fire began to lick the edges of the gates, creating a low wall of flame that the two men had to hurdle before hitting the soft turf in stride, heading down the hillside at a dead run. As Cornelius neared the bottom, his heart thudding in his chest, rivulets of sweat running down from under his helmet and cheek pieces, he glanced back toward the top of the hill. Many of the Germans were attempting to beat down the fires while others were desperately laboring to pull the wagons and carts clear of the conflagration.

For the rest of the morning, it appeared that Silvanius' stratagem had proved successful. Until the first watch of the afternoon, the Romans marched relatively unhindered from flanking enemy fire from the woods. As the sun rose higher in the clouded sky, it warmed the backs of the sodden troops and raised their spirits. For them, the chances of reaching Aliso's safety seemed infinitely better than twenty-four hours previously.

The optimism of the morning, however, was soon shattered by the events of the afternoon. For most of the day's march, they had made their way steadily up the wooded heights that formed the spine of the Teutoberg Forest, formed between the headwaters of the Ems and Lippe rivers. Just past noon, they appeared to reach its summit for the ground now began to slope down ahead of them into a low tableland of sucking marshes and trickling creeks, passable only through a series of winding, twisting pathways. As they trudged down the opposing slopes, they were suddenly cognizant of shadows mirroring their movement on either side. The realization for the Romans was a sober one. For all their efforts at subterfuge on the hilltop camp, it had bought them only a half-day's grace.

Almost from the moment the first legionaries placed their hobnailed sandals on the spongy turf of the marshland, the Germans renewed their assault. It wasn't long before the Romans realized that these attacks were different in nature than that of the previous day's, more coordinated and much more disciplined. They originated primarily from the Roman left flank, coming in short, sporadic bursts like hammer blows along the entire legionary line of march. When the initial reports of the new attacks reached the ears of Varus and his staff, they recognized that the barbarians were attempting to force the Romans to their right, more than likely toward a prepared point of ambush. Varus immediately gave orders for the columns to remain firm and not give ground behind them. Scouts had reported a wide, raised clearing four hours march ahead of them and it was here that Varus resolved to make his camp. Reaching the open ground would enable him to utilize the striking power of his troops, which had hitherto been denied him in the cloying confines of the hilly, wooded terrain of the Teutoberg. To reach their objective, however would entail a hard fight. Toward that end, the grim legionaries of the Army of the Rhine steeled themselves for another bloody afternoon.

And so the exhausting cycle of marching, attacking, retreating and regrouping repeated itself as the sun drifted toward the western horizon. The Germans launched their assaults with a surprising boldness and unexpected purpose, trying to turn the Roman left with an almost fanatical intensity. In turn, the Romans stiffened their resistance, refusing to give a single inch of solid ground to the enemy. Unfortunately, the conditions of the fight were not in their favor. They were restricted in their movements, unable to launch effective counter attacks or even bury the growing number of dead that littered their line of march. The barbarian attacks on the other hand, were short and brutal, inflicting the maximum damage without committing to a full-scale engagement they knew they could not win. As the long hours dragged on toward evening, the pathways became choked with more Roman corpses than barbarian ones.

Near the end of the second watch of the afternoon, the lead cohort finally broke through the last stand of pine and spruce and stumbled out into a wide-open space of short, coarse grass. Quickly, their centurions moved them up the rolling incline of the open ground forming them up into a tight defensive square where they awaited the arrival of the rest of the army. Slowly, more centuries and cohorts, each smaller in number than when the day began, joined them in the clearing. In the next hour, the remnants of the mauled Seventeenth stood exhausted but defiant in the waving field of grass. Orders soon went out from Varus to begin construction of another camp.

When the perimeter of the new camp had been cleared away, it was obvious that it would be only half the size of the previous night's site. When the roll call was finally taken prior to the meager evening meal, barely a third of the original compliment that had marched so boldly across the Rhine scarcely a week before was left to answer it. In the space of two dreadful days, Quinctilius Varus had managed to lose two full legions in the Teutoberg Forest.

Varus closed his tired eyes and listened to the mournful pounding of the hateful rain against the thin leather walls of the papilo. The tent's single oil lamp had gone out some time ago but he had neither the energy nor the inclination to light it again. His fingers groped forward in the darkness and found the sharp edge of the officer's dagger he had put in front of him on the desktop. He rubbed the keenness of its edge with the pad of his index finger and contemplated the clean cut it would make when it broke the skin. For the past hour, Varus had been debating on whether to use it on himself or not. Death was eminently more preferable to the shame that would be his, indeed that was already his, should he lead the rest of his depleted forces into further disaster. Toward that end he had even begun composing a short farewell message to his army, appointing Silvanius to succeed him in command. Varus was convinced that the tribune was the only man left capable of extracting them from their present dilemma. The gods knew Varus was not.

The drumming rain began to lessen as Varus stood up to stretch the stiffness from his aching muscles. As he did so, a sudden thought took hold of him giving him a mercurial thrill of hope. Quickly re-lighting the lamp, he returned to his field desk and scratched a few hasty lines on a scrap of papyrus. Calling for his orderly, he gave the man the papyrus and whispered some terse instructions. The orderly looked at his general as if he had taken leave of his senses. Varus sternly ordered the man to carry out the orders. The orderly saluted and reluctantly went out into the rain.

Varus sat back down at the desk and prepared to wait for a reply. *All is not yet lost, he thought. Providing Arminius is willing to listen to reason. Who knows? I may yet save my honor! And my army!*

XXI

The dense vault of the forest roof provided a natural cover from the incessant beating of the night rain. In a sheltered grove a little more than one hundred and fifty paces inside the eaves of the forest wall, a Roman officer waited against the massive trunk of an ancient oak. He was bundled in a heavy, red military cloak against the rain and the coolness of the late hour, his head protected by an ornate iron helmet. Although the clearing was dry and protected from the chill of the night wind, the officer shivered as he waited, pulling his cloak tighter against him for warmth. The sound of a broken twig in the darkness off to his left caused him to pause and look up expectantly. Presently, the grove was illuminated by sputtering torch light as two men entered the clearing from the opposite side. Both were attired in tunics, breeches and cloaks of heavy German wool. Each was armed with a long broadsword.

Seeing the newcomers were armed and suspecting treachery, the officer reached for the hilt of his own short sword sheathed at his side. One of the men, the one who had led the other bearing the torch into the grove, put his hand up signifying their peaceful intent.

"Peace, my lord," he offered, spreading his hands to show the Roman they had no other weapons than the swords at their sides. "This is not a trap."

The Roman relaxed his grip. "I expected you to come alone."

The first man shrugged. "I didn't think you would mind seeing Segimerus again."

Quinctilius Varus nodded and looked past the first speaker. "Hail to you Segimerus. I rejoice to see your face again. I only wish the circumstances were different."

Segimerus, holding the flickering torch, smiled and gave a cursory bow. "I too, general," he replied laconically. Varus was unsure for which part of his salutation Segimerus' response was meant.

"I trust the general is well?" interjected Arminius, taking little trouble to disguise the sarcasm in his voice.

Varus chose to ignore the jibe. "Well enough, my friend. I am pleased you received my summons."

"Summons?" echoed Arminius disdainfully. "You are hardly in a position to summon anyone, general. By now you must surely realize that it is I who wield the power in Germany not you."

Varus glared at Arminius through narrowed eyes. "Until now, I had not believed it possible for you to be a traitor. How distressing to discover otherwise."

Arminius pushed back his head and roared with laughter. "Traitor? My dear general, I am more of a patriot than you realize."

"You are a worthless barbarian who is a liar and an oath breaker. You attack the hand that fed and nourished you and made you what you are today. If it were not for Rome you would still be wallowing in the mud like the rest of your cursed race, killing one another over women and cattle!"

A red sternness clouded Arminius' features. Standing with legs apart and his fists planted to his muscular thighs he replied, "Such words are cheap, general, coming from a man whose very name is a stench in the nostrils of free men everywhere. But you are not wrong when you say I am indebted to Rome. Indeed I am. It was Rome who instructed me in the arts of war; how to seek out the weakness of an enemy and use it to one's advantage to utterly crush him."

"Rome is not your enemy, Arminius," argued Varus. "We have come to bring peace and progress to the tribes."

"With three whole legions?" demanded Arminius. "Who brings peace at the point of a sword?"

"Rome has pacified the earth with such as these, bringing peace to all who acknowledge the authority of the Roman people. But I don't need to tell you this, Arminius. You yourself have spent time with the Eagles. You know of what I speak."

"I have served you Romans for one reason and one reason only. To gain the knowledge I needed to throw off your yoke. If you need further proof, look at the state of your mighty army, general. I would say I have learned my lessons rather well, wouldn't you?"

"What do you want, Arminius?"

The German leader took a few steps toward Varus and stopped. "What I want, general," he said in a voice hard as flint, "Is what all people everywhere want. To be left alone. To be able to live our lives in peace, to raise our children without fear they will be taken from us and sold in your slave markets or slain before our very eyes if we resist. To grow old by our fires and hearths and tell stories to our grandchildren on long winter nights. We want nothing from you or your Caesar except the freedom to think and live for ourselves. Is that so very hard for you to understand?"

"You cannot have freedom without peace and it is the gift of peace that Rome offers the world. We have found that when peace comes, freedom invariably follows."

"Save the rhetoric for fools like your friend the fat senator from Rome."

"Senator Turtullus? What do you know of him?"

"He's dead," sneered Arminius, his features leering in the flickering torch light. "And tomorrow you shall share his fate."

The steely tone of the barbarian's threat caused Varus' stomach to tighten to stone. Whatever ephemeral hope he had placed on this face-to-face meeting with Arminius had now dissipated like smoke. It was obvious Arminius could not be made to return to his former allegiance. He sought only to destroy the remnant of Varus' army now cowering at his mercy behind the feeble shelter of their tiny encampment.

"I can see I am wasting my time here," said Varus pulling his cloak close to his body to ward off the night chill. "It is obvious your mind is set on this thing. So be it. I will of course fight you with everything I have left to me."

"One legion at best, general."

"It is enough."

"You will never reach Aliso."

Varus stared stonily at the German. "What makes you think I am going to Aliso?"

Arminius frowned. "Don't insult me, general. Where else can you go? Even a child can see that in your present predicament Aliso is the only place that makes sense."

"And if I am planning to march to Aliso will you allow us safe passage?"

"No."

"Not even for the sake of our friendship?"

"Not even for that."

"Do you hate us that much, my friend? Even one who has loved you as a father?"

"Yes."

"Why?"

"Because by destroying you, I destroy the myth of Rome's invincibility. When the world sees it, it will rejoice. Those whom you have enslaved will realize that it is possible to throw off the yokes of their slavery. Your deaths will be the sacrifice on an altar of freedom, which will bring down your precious Empire. Everywhere, men will crawl out from under the darkness of your rule into a new dawn of freedom where all men will be free to choose their own destinies and live in peace. A world without Rome! And I will be the instrument that accomplishes it!"

"You're mad! Such a thing can never be."

"We shall see."

"I will reach Aliso ahead of you."

"And I say you will not."

"As you have said, 'we shall see'. Since we have nothing further to say to one another I shall take my leave. Let the Fates bring what they may in the morning, Arminius. By this time tomorrow evening, I will either be safely in Aliso or dead in the trying."

"We shall see," replied Arminius grimly.

XXII

With no transports to burn as a diversion and little cavalry left to offer flanking protection, the Romans had no other choice but to fight their way out of their encampment. The rain, which had begun during the night, intensified toward dawn until it became an unrelenting downpour. It did not appear to hamper the Germans in the least while further eroding the already miserable morale of the legionaries. Indeed, if anything, the rain seemed only to pique the boldness of the barbarians and whet their appetite for blood.

The hours of darkness had allowed Arminius to move a number of warriors out of the woods and into positions around the enfeebled Roman fortifications. When day at last broke in the east, dreary and cheerless, the Romans were surprised to find their way barred by more tribesmen than they had ever seen. Looking out across the field he must cross in order to pick up the forest track toward Aliso, Varus felt his heart sink. Arminius had been true to his word. He had little intention of allowing even a single Roman soldier to reach the haven of the fortress, a mere seven hours march away. Varus would now have to be just as true to his own declaration. Glumly, he gave the order for the trumpets to blow assembly and marshal his remaining troops.

When satisfied that all was in readiness, Varus called Tribune Silvanius to his side.

"How many horse are left to us, tribune?" he shouted through the loud drumming of the cold rain.

"Thirty-six, Excellency," shouted back Silvanius.

Varus stated up into the rolling sheets of rain as they cascaded down out of a sky the color of cut slate. Thirty-six out of an original compliment of three hundred and sixty! Nine in every ten gone! Horse and rider! What a waste!

"It will have to do, I suppose," he mumbled half to himself. "Very well. I need you to cut a hole through those lines out there so I have clear path to the forest. Make it large enough for all the legions to pass. "

Silvanius shook his head in disbelief. Legions? We've barely enough men left to fill three urban cohorts! The gods preserve us!

"Is there a problem, tribune?"

"Ah, no sir."

"Well, get on with it. I want to be in Aliso by nightfall."

The tribune shivered and saluted. "Yes, sir. I will do my best under the circumstances."

Varus, who appeared to be slipping into a catatonic state, gazed vacantly up into the rain, oblivious to the sting of the drops on his face. "Yes, I am sure you will," he commented indifferently as Silvanius rode off to gather his remaining cavalry. It was becoming obvious to Silvanius that Varus was quickly losing his grip on reality.

Silvanius formed up his men in the shape of an arrowhead with himself at its point. If they could keep the formation, he reasoned, then there was a good chance he could actually open the breech in the enemy's lines they needed to begin sending the men through. If they could not and their tiny force was scattered and overwhelmed piecemeal, than Varus would be left to his own devices. Should that happen, Silvanius thought grimly, he would be far from caring. He would be dead.

In order to keep the Germans off balance while maximizing the slight advantage they still had in surprise, Silvanius ordered his trumpeters to stow their gear in their saddlebags. He did not want to alert the enemy to their intensions before he was ready to move. The rough-hewn gates of thin tree branches were to be opened only at his signal. Turning in his saddle, he gave the command to his ragtag company to unsheathe their swords. Feeling the moment ripe for action, he signaled to the soldiers at the gates to get them open as quickly as possible.

"Romans forward!" he cried, brandishing his sword high above his crested helmet. "In the name of Caesar Augustus and the majesty of the People and Senate of Rome, let us avenge our dead and cover ourselves with glory!" With one voice, the thirty-six cavalrymen shouted their acclamation and followed their commander out through the open gates and into the fray.

Silvanius was gratified to discover his stratagem had succeeded beyond what he had dared hoped. The dimness of the day caused by the gray shade of ceaseless rain concealed the truth of the puniness of the attacking force from the tribesmen. To the Germans, it seemed as if they were suddenly facing a thousand charging horsemen. Panic struck their lines like surf breaking upon the shore. The Roman attack carried everything before it as the startled barbarians scrambled to get out of the way, running heedlessly for cover in the nearby woods.

Inside the camp, the legates Blassius and Florus watched, barely believing their good fortune. Together they ran to where Varus sat motionless on his horse.

"Excellency!" cried Blassius excitedly. "Silvanius has done it! The way is clear! Now is the time to give the order to move!" Varus looked down, his dripping face twisted into a quizzical blankness. "What? Oh, yes, yes, of course. You have my permission to move out, legate."

Trumpets blared and centurions barked hoarse orders over their companies. The last, pathetic remnant of the mighty Army of the Rhine lurched and trotted forward into the rain-soaked fields. Without realizing it, Varus edged his mount into the human flow and found himself in the middle of the troops commanded by Centurion Strabo. Reaching the forest wall without incident, the Roman columns plunged once again into the damp, airless recesses of the Teutoberg Wald, seeking out the pathway that led to safety. Despite the rain, whose effect was somewhat lessened by the tangled canopy overhead, the Roman scouts managed to pick up the trail within minutes of entering the forest. Before long, the Romans were making their way along the slippery confines of the path, heading in a southwesterly direction through soggy ground that sloped down in front of them. Now and then, a solitary axe or javelin came flying at them from out of the surrounding wood but these were easily deflected or fell harmlessly short of their intended targets. Nevertheless, it assured the fleeing Romans that the Germans were still close on their heels.

As they proceeded on a stiff pace through the forest, Cornelius stole an occasional glance at the mounted figure in their midst. General Varus appeared to be in another world, content to be pulled along by the momentum of the trotting soldiers around him. Piqued by a morbid curiosity about the man who had led them into disaster; Cornelius edged his way beside Varus' horse and peered into the pale face inside the beautiful, black helmet. Immediately he was struck by how the strain of command had aged Varus. His skin had taken on a sallow tinge giving him the appearance of a man much older than his fifty years. The eyes were faded and glassy, framed inside the swollen and wrinkled folds of lids and skin. The nose, once straight and full befitting his aristocratic heritage, was now pinched and thin upon the nasal bone. His mouth was an attenuated slit of bloodless tissue. Stringy and knotted muscle and skin hung from his neck like the gizzard of a turkey.

Placing his hand lightly upon Varus' leg, Cornelius asked, "Does the general wish to rest?"

Varus appeared to rouse himself from his reverie. "Rest? No, I will rest when we reach Aliso." Returning to the refuge of his darkened mind, he continued to stare blankly ahead of him, saying nothing.

Before long, the forest about the exhausted Romans began to thin out. The massive columns of oak, pine and spruce soon gave way to shorter and less dense stands of tamarack, elm and birch. As they walked, they felt the ground give way under their feet to an increasingly steep descent. All the while, the track kept veering to their left where the forest appeared to grow denser. Whenever a soldier attempted to get off the path to enter the woods on the right, a barrage of spears and arrows either drove him back to the struggling columns or killed him where he stood. At the bottom of the descent, the track opened into a wide space of open marsh grass and shrubbery ringed by a living wall of standing oak. The Roman columns poured into this vast clearing like water from a narrow spout. Cold, wet and tired, the legionaries stood shivering at the mouth of the marshy fens, their hearts failing at the sight that greeted them. For there standing shoulder to shoulder and shield to shield was the largest horde of barbarians any of them had ever seen.

XXIII

For Cornelius, the shock of the scene on the fens threatened to overwhelm his reeling senses. He knew this place! He had seen it many times before. For here, laid out before him with sickening familiarity was the very field on which he had seen the destruction of the army played out in his dreams.

There was little time to recover from the blow of the revelation for suddenly behind the Roman rear there emerged a piercing war cry. Looking back, they could see the forest behind filling with baying tribesmen, running forward from their hiding places in the underbrush to push the Romans into the maw of the waiting horde. Arminius had planned his ambush well. There was no escape for his quarry either in front or behind. He had sprung his trap so effectively, that the Romans could do nothing but stand incomprehensively to meet their fate. They were pinned between the jaws of a giant vice that once closed, would seal the doom of the Army of the Rhine forever.

As the rear cohorts turned to face the threat from the woods and the front ones made ready for the inevitable attack from their quarter, the battle witnessed another unforeseen twist. The blaring note of a trumpet echoed across the edge of the plain, temporarily distracting the attacking Germans in the woods behind. With stunning suddenness,

Silvanius' cavalry exploded from the cover of a row of low spreading tamarack trees and drove into the exposed flanks of the barbarian line already engaged with the Roman rear, effectively splitting it in two. Wheeling to his left, Silvanius led his men back up into the woods, scattering the attacking tribesmen into the surrounding trees. The suddenly active Romans quickly cut down those unfortunates who found themselves cut off between the woods and the bulk of the Roman army. As Silvanius reappeared on the field, he was met with cheers from the cohorts. His daring charge had effectively lifted their flagging spirits and depleted energies. Riding up along the columns, he found Varus waiting, the reins of his horse held by Cornelius.

"Excellency," he called standing in his saddle. "We must get back under cover in the woods while the way is open! It will not be long before the enemy regroups and tries again. And when they do it will be with twice the numbers! Hurry, now before door is closed to us!"

The acrid clash of battle seemed to jar Varus from his dream state. The fogginess of his vision cleared and the focus of his purpose returned. Craning his neck to see the place the tribune indicated as the way out, he nodded and cried, "Cohorts about face! Run on the double time! Hurry now! Run!"

Varus' last word was lost in the thunderous clamor of metal on metal at the front of the Roman columns. Arminius, who had taken a position in the middle of the barbarian array on the plain, had not remained idle during Silvanius' unexpected counter stroke. Sensing he was losing the rear arm of his pincer, the arm that should have funneled the Romans ahead into the maw of the assembled forces on the open fens, Arminius ordered the main body of his army forward to engage the enemy before they could take advantage of the narrow window of escape. The noise of sword and axe against shield and helmet created a deafening cacophony that drowned out Varus' shrieking command to retreat. The distraction proved fatal. At that moment Silvanius' fears were realized when the barbarians returned in force to assail the Roman rear thereby effectively cutting off their escape route and sealing them inside a hedge of steel. There was now little left for the desperate Romans to do but fight on to the last man.

As the ebb and flow of battle began to assert itself on the marshy field, Cornelius fixed himself with a steely determination to defend his commanding officer. Arranging the few men left under his command in a defensive square around Varus and the aquifilers of the Seventeenth and Eighteenth Legions who had planted their standards and regimental eagles in the wet ground around him, Cornelius prepared for the worse. It was not that he was afraid to die. He felt as if had been walking in its shadow since the night of his perilous encounter with the predatory Pompilius. The thought of his own death neither frightened him nor gave him pause to reflect on how it might come about. At the moment he was more concerned with the fate of Tribune Silvanius than with his own. He glanced around the milling masses of men for any sign of the tribune but there was none. Silently, he whispered a prayer to the God-with-no-name for the life of the man who had twice saved Cornelius' own in the few short weeks they had known each other. The prayer had barely begun when a brawny arm clutching a barbarian sword reached out between a pair of grappling soldiers in front of him and cleaved a corner from his rectangular shield. The force of the blow nearly wrenched his arm out of its socket.

Stepping forward into the raging struggle before him, Cornelius began to swing his sword into the crowd of braying tribesmen, jostling against one another to strike the first blow against the hated Romans. Chopping his sword backward, he felt the blade bite into flesh and bone, causing a yelp of pain from an enemy he could not see. Swinging the weapon back across his body, he saw the neat, red line of a throat wound open across one man's neck while the blade lodged itself in between another's unprotected ribs. For the next fifteen minutes, the deadly cadence of swinging, chopping, stabbing and slicing raged along the swaying line of battle. Cornelius' forearms, thighs and calves were soon covered with a criss-cross welling of bright blood courtesy of sword cuts and spear thrusts that his battered shield had failed to deflect. As the minutes of intense fighting wore on, the continual motion of his sword caused his arm to ache and the muscles to become like lead. It would not be long, he knew, before he would be unable to lift his weapon at all. His reserve of strength would fail him long before they succeeded in repulsing the inexhaustible hordes that pressed in against them from all sides. For every German who fell bleeding to the earth, two more appeared to take his place. For every legionary who succumbed in battle, none was left to fill the gap.

As the Roman columns began to shrink under the pressure of the German assault, the once great Army of the Rhine entered into its death throes. The exhausted legionaries were pushed back onto each other as the Roman line became constricted and twisted, threatening to break apart at a number of points into smaller, less viable formations. Cornelius could see the men of his own command falling all around him as he was gradually forced back toward the place where Varus waited with the legionary eagles. Sweating heavily from the exertion of combat, his throat parched and his eyes blinded by stinging rivers of sweat and rainwater, Cornelius longed to rest. At the limit of his physical and emotional endurance, only the primal instinct for survival kept him from collapsing. The blur of moving shapes at the periphery of his vision caused him to swing his sword in a wild blind thrust to his right. He felt the blade bite into flesh and bone. A surprised tribesman stopped struggling with a desperate legionary and put his hand below his armpit. When he pulled it back, the hand was drenched in blood. Before he could cover the wound again, another sword thrust into his belly. The soldier with whom the barbarian had been fighting had taken advantage of the distraction and finished off his man. The tribesman made as silent 'O' through his gaping mouth as he sunk insensible to the wet grass. Blinking to clear his vision of the incessant rain, Cornelius was surprised to find that the solider was none other than his old tent mate, Bassanius.

"Lucius!" he called above the din. "Thank the Lord of heaven you're safe!"

Bassanius grinned, his face smeared by mud and blood. "You know me, Cornelius," he shouted back with his old jauntiness, "Never was one to miss a good fight!"

Cornelius smiled through his fatigue. "This fight's getting too rough, my friend. I think we should move back and make our stand at the standards."

Bassanius snuck a furtive glance behind Cornelius before looking back. "What standards?"

Cornelius whirled around with a start. Varus was gone! And so were the eagles of the Seventeenth and Eighteenth legions along with their aquifilers. For a few moments, he stood frozen by the shock. Then the world about him suddenly exploded, sending him tumbling headlong into the dark chasm of a starless night.

XXIV

Varus had in fact not moved at all.

The friction of combat along the battle lines had forced his company out away from the governor general's position so that by the time Cornelius attempted to locate the standards, he was more than seventy-five yards away from them. Another knot of three hundred legionaries had taken their place and arrayed themselves around the commander-in chief and the battle standards of the legions. The epicenter of the struggle now centered completely upon Varus and his valiant guard as the Germans concentrated their attack against the heart of the Roman army with a ferocity that dismayed the worn out legionaries. The minds of the barbarians burned with a feverish desire that caused them to press forward with unrelenting fury. Each man fought, strained, bled and died for the privilege of being the first to put his hands on the legendary eagles of Rome. Each man knew what awaited the warrior who was first to lay hold of the prized emblems of the legions; the Druids had promised as much. A hero's welcome into the deathless halls of Odin the king of the gods where they would spend eternity quaffing ale from golden drinking horns all while enjoying the sensual delights provided from the virgin garden of the goddess Frig. Their battle rage thus stoked and fired by visions of a warrior's paradise, the Germans fought with a maniacal vigor.

And with the desperate strivings of the doomed, the Romans replied in kind.

As his legionaries prepared to make their last, heroic stand before their battered eagles, Varus prepared himself for death. He did not loose his sword from its scabbard. Nor did he shout commands or encouragement to his men whose lives would now be lost because of his incompetence. He sat stoically upon his horse, watching with a detached interest as the battle raged around his person. At that moment, Silvanius suddenly reappeared on the field with five battered and dazed horsemen, the last of his meager force. He tried to reach Varus by cutting through the pressing lines of barbarian warriors. It was a futile gesture. One by one, the cavalrymen were dragged from their mounts and torn apart by the frenzied hands of the Germans, their blood lust now at its peak. Silvanius tried urging his horse forward into the crush of men and weapons, hacking away the hands and swords that tried to reach for him from either side. But the situation was impossible. While Varus looked serenely on, the tribune was finally pulled from his saddle only to disappear under a quivering mass of flashing swords and pummeling fists.

The end followed swiftly after that.

When the defenders had dwindled to less than fifty, Varus swung silently down from his horse and stood swaying upon the bloody field. "I cannot allow myself to be captured," he said to no one in particular. "I have done my duty for Caesar and for Rome. There is only one more duty to perform."

Sliding his ivory-handled sword from its magnificent sheath, he held it up in front of his face. In this supreme moment of his life, Varus lost all contact with reality. He stared mesmerized by the spidery patterns and shapes created by the raindrops as they ran down the blade of his gladius. For a few minutes he remained swaying on his feet, unsure of where he was and oblivious to the storm raging about him. Suddenly, he felt moisture at the corners of his eyes. Reaching up with his hand, he was surprised to discover they were tears. Tears for the opportunities lost. Tears for the flower of a great army, lost. Tears for the lost glory that should have been his.

Whispering in the choking voice of a child, he said to his sword, "I did the best I could, mama. Forgive me." Unbuckling the straps of his beautiful black and silver cuirass, he let it fall to the ground. Placing the point of his sword on his inner tunic above his heart, Varus closed his eyes and cried out in a loud voice at the same instance he drove the weapon home. Publius Quinctilius Varus, Imperial Legate of Germania and commander of the Army of the Rhine was dead even before his lifeless corpse slumped to the blood-soaked grass.

XXV

From somewhere far above him, Cornelius could make out a light shining out of the inky blackness. As he watched, it seemed to grow larger and brighter, causing the envelope of night to fade as it floated down toward him. Taking the shape of a globe, it increased in size and luminosity until Cornelius had to shield his eyes from its intense approach. A rushing wind filled his ears and he felt a warm tingling pass through his body as the globe washed over him, delivering him into the opaque light of the real world.

Cornelius felt the warm oozing of blood trickle over his eyelid and down his cheek. He tried to move his hand to his face to wipe away the flow but found he was unable to do so. Turning his head slightly, he saw the reason why. All around him, a tangled mound of bodies were piled up around him in a grotesque wall of bruised and bloodied flesh. From various parts of the pile, he could see lifeless hands clutching the broken shafts of swords or spears, feet muddied and shorn of their heavy-soled sandals as well as the occasional glimpse of the matted gold tresses of their enemy. His own hand was caught underneath the corpse of a large German warrior, sprawled upon his back in the moment of death, his neck torn open by a deep, ugly wound. Stiffly, he pushed against the body with his free hand in an attempt to free his trapped appendage, an effort that sent a searing wave of pain through his head and a spurt of fresh blood down his face. When the pain had passed, he gingerly began to maneuver his hand free a little bit at a time. When it was finally clear, he brought it to his temple and began to probe the area where he felt the greatest pain. His fingers traced the outline of an angry gash that ran from the hairline at the ear to within a hair's width of the corner of his eye. He deduced it must have come from the blow that had driven him to unconsciousness. It had originated from somewhere behind him. The blow had struck him with such force that it tore the helmet from his head, no doubt convincing the German who delivered it that it had been to the death. He had not bothered to make sure of the finality of the stroke. Either he had been struck down himself or had moved off to another part of the battlefield in search of fresh victims.

Relieved that the wound was not life threatening, Cornelius for the first time noticed the guttural voices of the victorious barbarians echoing across the marshy plain. Raising himself on an elbow, he peered over top of the wall of corpses in the general direction of the sound and saw a huge mass of barbarian soldiery gathered around a hastily erected scaffold not more than two hundred yards away. Shrieking, yelling and gesturing with their weapons raised in triumph over their heads, the Germans were celebrating their victory over the might of Rome. Two men stood on the platform. One in particular, the man on whom most of the cheering fell, drew Cornelius' attention. He was tall and powerful, exuding an air of authority that seemed to encircle him like a wreath. His long blonde hair flowed down upon his broad shoulders, plastered to the surface of his handsome leather cuirass. His red and gold tunic and deerskin breeches molded pleasingly to the contours of his body, further enhancing the natural comeliness of the man. The face reflected a feral power that seemed to hold others in a grip of fearful respect. The steel-gray eyes glittered with satisfaction as it swept over the sea of delirious faces crowded against the scaffold. He could not be sure, but Cornelius suspected the man was probably Arminius, the barbarian leader. The man behind him was obviously his lieutenant Segimerus. They had undergone a strange metamorphous since the days of their residence at Castra Vetera when they had earned the hatred of the army by becoming the unlikely boon companions of the man whose death they now celebrated with such obscene delight.

Slowly, Arminius raised his arms aloft, demanding quiet. Immediately, the cheering faded and the last of the piercing battle cries died away as an expectant hush fell upon the field. The big warrior put his hands on his hips and shouted, "My brothers! Victory is ours! Those who sought to enslave us have been destroyed!"

The fens erupted again with a wave of shouting and clashing weapons. Over the heads of the cheering masses, the captured eagles of the annihilated legions were passed from the hand to hand until they reached the edge of the platform where they were drawn up and displayed for all to see. From somewhere in the crowd, a bundle wrapped in black cloth was produced and passed forward. It was thrown at the feet of Arminius with a heavy thump. As it landed, it spilled open, revealing the beautiful ebony cuirass and ostrich-plume helmet of the ex-legate of Germany.

Arminius reached down and picked up the helmet, holding it high over his head. "I see the general's clothes," he shouted gleefully, his face split by a wide grin, "But where is the man himself?"

Harsh, raucous laughter rang out in answer to Arminius' crude joke. A chant began, swelling to a strident crescendo as the tribesmen pumped their arms in the air and cried, "Varus! Varus! Varus!" Once again, an object was flung at the platform from the mob. No one could tell exactly what it was until it rolled and bounced across the platform, coming to rest at Arminius' feet. Looking down, the barbarian commander was met by the sight of General Varus' lifeless eyes staring back up at him. A voice boomed from the cackling rabble, "I want that back! I'm going to make a drinking cup from the general's skull!" More laughter, dark and mocking. Arminius picked up the grisly trophy by a tuft of lank hair and plopped it on the point of a proffered spearhead, raising it above his head like a battle standard. Thunderous cheering and jeering catcalls ensued from the display of Varus' disembodied remains. Concealed behind the wall of corpses, Cornelius was on his hands and knees retching from the hideous sight.

When they had finished making sport of Varus' severed head, Arminius placed it beside the three captured eagles as if it were just another prize of battle. "Where is the rest of the noble Varus?" he demanded from the mob. The headless trunk was soon produced and hauled upon the scaffolding where Arminius watched a number of frenzied warriors literally tear it apart, tossing the bloody limbs out into the waiting crowd. There innumerable hands pounced on them and tore them into smaller pieces until finally, there was nothing left of what had once been a human being except a ghastly, grinning death mask lodged on the point of a German spear.

With their blood lust temporarily abated by the desecration of Varus' remains, Arminius once again called for order. "Bring me the prisoners!" he cried, pointing to a knot of bareheaded, bound Romans kneeling together in a small, pathetic group off to one side of the platform. Guards roughly pulled up the first of the prisoners and drove him toward the platform with the butts of their spears. As he was pushed up on the scaffold, now slippery with Varus' blood, he was made to stand before the imperious Arminius. Cornelius was shocked to see that it was Tribune Silvanius. He offered a silent prayer of thanks for the deliverance of his friend from the worst of the barbarian excesses. A broad, angry abrasion down his right cheek and a large bump on his forehead was already showing signs of bruising. The Germans may have spared the tribune's life, but they had not been gentle doing it. For his part, Silvanius seemed oblivious to his hurts, setting his face into a grim mask of defiance. He was not about to give his barbarian captors the slightest satisfaction concerning his predicament.

Arminius, eyeing Silvanius intently, was the first to speak. "Well, tribune. We are well met, are we not? Tell me; did you ever think you would live to see your proud legions humbled so? And by those you arrogantly call 'barbarians'! Come now, tribune. Speak freely. We are all friends here!"

Silvanius kept his silence.

"So you refuse to speak to your new masters, do you?" continued Arminius pacing in front of the reticent Roman. "A good slave does not provoke his master. You must learn this if you are to go on living."

"Go to hell!"

Arminius struck Silvanius across the face with the flat of his hand, drawing a trickle of blood at the corner of the Roman's mouth. "Hold your tongue, dog! Don't you know it is up to me whether you live or die?"

Silvanius contemptuously licked the blood from his lips. "Enjoy your victory while you can, traitor. There will be ten legions on the Rhine within a month to avenge your treachery. Mark my words well; there will not be a single man here who will be able to escape Caesar's justice!"

The tribune's bold words rang hollow from the scaffold soliciting mocking laughter from the rabble. "Let them come!" jeered Arminius. "They will meet the same fate as Varus did. As long as I live, Rome will never rule over us. Never!" Loud cheers punctuated Arminius' declaration. But there were some in the crowd who did not cheer. The mysterious fate of the Bructerian contingent two nights previously was still fresh in their minds. There could be no doubt as to who was responsible for their elimination.

"You cannot defy Caesar forever," cried Silvanius above the shouting. "Many have tried but none have succeeded in resisting the will of Rome!"

"Then we shall be the first!" answered Arminius confidently. "But such things would not be my worry were I you, tribune. My primary concern would be for my life. And yours is hanging by the thinnest of threads."

"Death does not frighten me. It has been my constant companion since I became a solider."

"But I am sure life would be more preferable to you as it would any sane man. Believe me. If I could work my will concerning you, tribune, you would already be dead."

"Then why do I live?"

"Because of a promise."

"A promise?"

"Yes," affirmed Arminius, his manner suddenly subdued and reflective. "I have pledged my word to the one I love most in this world. It is for her sake that I am sparing your life."

"Thusnelda?"

"So you do remember? Yes, Thusnelda who is now my wife. She is the one who begged me for your life, tribune. And upon my love for her, I have granted it. Against my better judgement, you will be taken from this place and escorted to the borders of the Great Forest. After that, it will be up to the gods to preserve your life. Pray we do not meet again, tribune! For if we do, I will not be held by my oath and you will surely die! Unbind him!" The guards hacked off Silvanius bonds from his wrists and ankles with their swords and stood back. Rubbing his wrists, Silvanius glared at Arminius and said,

"Since I am indebted to the good lady who is your wife for my freedom, then please extend my compliments to her. Tell her I remember fondly the nights I spent beneath her father's roof and the joyous times of fellowship we enjoyed at his table. The Lady Thusnelda then, as now, possesses the nobility of her race in full measure. Unfortunately, the same cannot be said of her husband."

Arminius' eyes blazed with black anger. With jaw muscles throbbing and teeth clenched tight, his voice dropped into a rumbling whisper. "Go, you son of a Roman whore! Before I forget my pledge and kill you where you stand. You offend me with your words and by your presence. Go I say! And do not return!" Turning to the guards, he commanded them to take Silvanius from the platform.

"What of my officers?" demanded Silvanius, indicating toward the bound group of tribunes and centurions who stood waiting under guard.

"They need not concern you," snarled Arminius, "They are mine according to the rules of war, to do with as I please. Be thankful I have left you with your own worthless life. Now go!" But Silvanius was adamant.

"I will not leave here unless the men under my command go with me. We are no longer a threat to you, Arminius. If you lead these people as you claim, then show them you are capable of great clemency as well as great cruelty. Show them that you are a leader to be both feared and admired."

Arminius stroked his chin with the palm of his hand. The Roman part of him acknowledged the wisdom of such a demonstration, especially to the civilized peoples of the Roman Sea. Diplomacy was not always accomplished at the point of a sword. The German in him, however, knew that he could not offer mercy to his vanquished foe and hope to hold his position long as high chief. Many of the tribes had only agreed to bury their traditional animosities by the promise of plunder and captives in the wake of a successful campaign. To grant Silvanius' request would be to deny them the very thing they had come to fight for. Even if he wanted to exercise clemency, (and he was not at all sure he did), given the circumstances, it would be akin to slitting his own throat.

Choosing his words carefully, Arminius replied, "Are you saying that you would prefer to share the fate of your fellow soldiers, tribune? That you will not accept the pardon for your life?"

"I cannot," answered the Roman. "I am responsible for these men, responsible for seeing to it that they one day return again to their family and kin. But I do not expect you to understand this, Arminius, for such thinking is foreign to one as you. You do not possess the one quality that separates a civilized man from a savage: honor. Without it, a man's pledge means nothing. It makes him faithless to his family, his friends and to himself. Without it, a man is little better than an unthinking beast. No one can tell which way he will jump. His word holds no credit with those that hear it. He breaks his oaths and pledges as easily as he breaks a cup or plate and is heedless of the consequences of his actions. Beware of such men, Arminius, for their hearts are cold and loveless. The road they trod leads to disaster. They can never be trusted. To such men is not given the task of building a great nation."

Arminius trembled in a blustering rage, knowing full well to whom the rebuke was directed. Prodding his finger at Sylvanus he said, and cried, "By your own words you release me from my vow, Roman! And since you have expressed your desire to share the fate of your officers, I will now accommodate that wish." Looking over the tribune's shoulder, he nodded to one of the guards behind him. In one motion, the guard cocked his spear to his ear and let it fly. It struck Silvanius in the middle of his back with such force, that it literally lifted him from his feet and sent him sliding face first across the scaffold. He was dead by the time his body came to rest near the front of the platform. The horrified Cornelius had to bite his own hand to keep himself from screaming.

Striding to the corpse, Arminius flipped it on its back, its weight snapping off the ash shaft of the weapon near the spine. The bronze spearhead protruded gruesomely from Silvanius' chest, draped in bloodied bits of flesh and bone. Addressing the mob, Arminius cried, "And so shall all our enemies perish!" In response, the plain shook with the noise of war.

XXVI

And then began a progression of work of such monstrous evil, that the images of it haunted Cornelius for the rest of his life.

As he helplessly looked on, the captured officers whom Silvanius had tried in vain to save were brought one by one to platform. There the barbarians entertained themselves while at the same time undertaking to derive a modicum of revenge for past injuries by indulging in various acts of degradation. The poor, unfortunates were spat upon, insulted and struck with the butts of numerous weapons as well as enduring other less savory tortures. All of the surviving centurions were dragged off the scaffold and conveyed to the nearest tree where they were hung on stout ropes or placed in hanging wicker cages and slowly burned alive beneath stoking fires. The few tribunes and senatorial officers who remained were also subjected to the public abuse on the platform. But unlike the junior officers, their lives were valuable to the tribesmen for the rich ransoms they could expect for their return. So they were divided up amongst the strongest and most powerful of the chiefs and their warriors to whom they would serve as slaves until their ransoms were paid in full.

For the unsuspecting group of lawyers captured in the train of the beaten Roman army, the Germans reserved a special hatred. Too many of the tribesmen had experienced the heavy hand of Roman justice and authority through these mealy-mouthed practitioners of legal trickery. They had come to see them as the embodiment of everything they detested about Rome. Land, money and pride had all been lost to these men with their mouths crammed with endless and meaningless gibberish concerning witnesses, investigations and finer points of Roman law. Many had felt the sting of the rods of the lictors on their bare backs as they dispensed a code of justice they did not understand or respect. Now, the gods had delivered them into their hands. Now they would show these snakes and jackals the real meaning of justice!

The terrified lawyers were made to run a gauntlet of jeering barbarian soldiery who inflicted fearful wounds with well-aimed blows at the soft parts of the body. The victims emerged from the gauntlet dazed and reeling, stumbling about as if drunk, blood oozing from every orifice. Crude wooden chairs were brought out and placed in a line before the platform into which the lawyers were securely lashed. A group of tribesmen stripped to the waist and brandishing long, sharp daggers, stood before each chair. While others forced open the victim's mouths, they expertly grasped hold of each Roman's tongue and with a single, deft slash of the dagger, cut it from their throats. Yet even this mutilation was not enough to slake the thirst for vengeance in the German heart. As the lawyers lolled their heads in shock from side to side, expressing their pain in pitiful moans and strained screams, the torturers each produced a ball of coarse twine and a curved needle used for stitching animal hides together. Setting to their gruesome task, they proceeded to sew each victim's mouth shut by piercing their lips and pulling the twine taut around them. Soon, every lawyer's mouth was sewn shut by an ugly criss cross seam of twine and blood. Standing back to admire their ghastly handiwork, the Germans filled the ears of their dying victims with the same mocking taunt. "Hiss now, viper!"

The treatment meted out to the Roman lawyers was too much for Cornelius to stomach. He slumped upon his back and stared up into the rain-soaked heavens and wondered why he had watched as long as he did. What he had seen had not only sickened him but poisoned his soul. Never before in his young life had he witnessed the depths of depravity and brutality into which the human animal could descend. And yet he had seen it all played out before him in a theatre as macabre and surreal as any on earth. Cruel reality had interposed itself upon the tarnished dreams of glory that now seemed so naïve and impossible. The world was bigger and more deadly than he had ever imagined. What, he thought with bitterness of mind, had ever made him think he had a place in it? He found himself wishing he had died in battle with his friend Bassanius rather than survive to witness the horror of these last hours. A thought of suicide flitted across his thoughts as an honorable way out. Better to die by his own hand than suffer the fate of his fellow centurions.

Cornelius raised himself up again and cast around for a sword. As he did so, he caught something from the corner of his eye at the edge of the forest some fifty yards distant. What he saw caused him to rub his eyes in disbelief. There, standing serenely beneath the boughs of the overhanging trees, was the Man of Dreams! His appearance was exactly as he remembered except that he seemed more corporeal, without the opaque illumination that had characterized the manifestation of his dreams. The same beatific smile lit his striking features. Raising a hand to Cornelius, he called, "Come to me, Cornelius Strabo!" The mellifluous voice boomed and echoed across the plain like a peal of thunder. Cornelius looked wildly around him, certain that the barbarians could not have failed to hear it and rush with drawn swords to his hiding place. But to his amazement, they seemed utterly indifferent to the blast of the divine voice. They continued in their repulsive task without showing the slightest sign they had even heard it.

"Come to me, Cornelius Strabo!" boomed the voice again in Cornelius' ears. "Come and I will give you life!" Beside the Man of Dreams there suddenly appeared a tunnel cut into the forest wall, its interior illuminated with golden light. A stairway of dressed stones rose gently from the floor of the plain toward what Cornelius surmised to be the upper reaches of the far wood. But for all the long, dark days they had spent in the clammy bowels of the Teutoberg Forest, he could not remember seeing such an exquisite pathway.

Rising to his feet, Cornelius felt the wound at his temple begin to throb. A fresh trickle of blood warmed his cheek as he stood swaying on unsteady feet. He wondered why the God (for by this time he had come to accept the Man of Dreams as a divine being) did not heal him as he had in the surgeon's tent. But on the other hand, he had seen enough to know he could place his trust in this apparition. He had spoken of offering Cornelius life. He took it to mean deliverance from a hideous fate of torture and death. Cornelius steeled himself to sprint across the open field to where the forest door stood beckoning, his stiffening resolve lending strength to his body. Choosing his moment, Cornelius willed his muscles into action and bolted toward the edge of the wood.

The sudden motion of a figure splashing across the marshy fens caught the attention of several tribesmen. The alarm was raised and before Cornelius was half way to his goal, a snarling group of barbarians were in hot pursuit. Arminius' orders had been most explicit. Not one Roman was to escape his justice.

As he neared the Man of Dreams, Cornelius could hear the cries at his back growing closer and more shrill. Chancing a glance behind him, he could see his pursuers were quickly cutting the distance between them. When he turned again to increase his pace, he was startled to find the Man of Dreams had vanished. But the passageway still remained. Bowing his head, he ran as fast as he could to cover the final yards, his lungs burning fiercely with the effort. With one last leap, he gained the threshold of the tunnel just as a hail of aggesais and darts began falling around him. Scampering up the stairs, he could see that the passageway ascended slightly to the right allowing him to see only a few feet ahead of him at one time. Unwilling to chance another look behind him, Cornelius ran on, permitting the tunnel to lead where it would. A strange sound like the snapping and breaking of many branches seemed to fill the tunnel as he ran. Since he could still hear the braying voices of the barbarians from somewhere behind him, he assumed the noise was merely the result of their lumbering pursuit through the underbrush. Had he taken a moment to investigate the phenomenon, he would have been astounded to find the tree-hollowed tunnel collapsing by itself as if being pushed down by an invisible hand.

Cornelius could never say where he drew his strength that day to run so long or so hard. After what seemed like hours but was in reality barely a quarter of an hour, he ran out of the end of the passageway onto the heavily treed summit of the spine of the forest. Looking left and right, he was unsure which way to go. In which direction lay the fortress of Aliso? Something pricked at his awareness urging him to go left. Heeding the strange sensation, he set off along the spine in that direction and immediately found the way solid underfoot and devoid of any clinging undergrowth. The difficult pace began to slacken as the ground proved to be fairly even. The fact that he had not heard the strident voices of his pursuers for some time convinced him he had succeeded in eluding them at least for the present. His surmise was soon to prove wrong. Rounding a slight bend in the pathway, Cornelius came face to face with the largest German he had ever seen.

"Going somewhere?" he smirked in heavily-accented Latin, pounding the flat of his sword blade into a beefy palm. In German he shouted, "I've got the bastard!"

Cornelius looked furtively about him, knowing he must somehow get by the big barbarian before the arrival of his companions. But so quickly had he fled the battlefield that he did not have time to think about replacing his lost sword. It was a lapse that was about to prove fatal since he was now weaponless in the face of a superior foe. Casting about for anything he could employ as a weapon, his eyes fell on a stout, wooden staff, partially covered by a blanket of dead leaves and brush. Miraculously, it lay across the path between himself and the waiting barbarian. It was almost as if someone had foreseen its need and had hidden it there for him to find.

"It's the end of the road for you, pup!" grinned the German menacingly, "Maybe I won't wait for the rest of 'em to get here. Maybe I'll finish you off myself! Don't move and I promise I'll make this quick!" The giant moved a few steps toward Cornelius, dangerously minimizing his window of opportunity. A few more steps and the barbarian would be on top of the staff, putting it out of his reach and leaving him at the mercy of his steel. Instinctively, Cornelius somersaulted at the feet of his adversary, springing out of his crouch and onto his feet with the staff grasped firmly in both hands. The sudden move caused the German to halt in his tracks, stunned by the unexpected maneuver. Before he could recover from his bewilderment, Cornelius swung his weapon with all his might and caught the big tribesman flush on the cheek. The staff snapped in half with a loud crack. With flailing arms and legs, the man staggered backwards, his sword tumbling from his hand into the woods. Submitting to the effect of the blow, he thudded full on his back, lying still on the ground with eyes closed, a furious wound pouring blood from his ruined cheek.

Tossing away the broken half of his staff, Cornelius rushed from the path and retrieved the German's weapon from the underbrush. Hefting it in his hand, he realized it was much heavier than his own short gladus but was thankful for it nonetheless. Tucking it into his belt, he set off again along the pathway just as other voices became audible from somewhere off to his left. It would not be long before they stumbled upon their fallen companion and the chase would be taken up again. The fact that he had bested one of their fiercest warriors would no doubt serve to stoke their wrath. He chided himself for not pulling the unconscious barbarian into the forest. He would much rather the Germans waste their time searching for their lost giant then spending it looking for him.

Setting a steady pace that would ensure minimum fatigue, Cornelius ran on. The throbbing of his head had curiously subsided almost from the moment he had entered the forest tunnel. Touching the wound on his temple as he ran, he could feel that it was already dry and beginning to scab. Somehow, the fact was reassuring if only to remind him that his life was now being orchestrated through a divine agency. It bolstered his faith in his ability to survive his present circumstance. And so on he ran, his mind fixed with the assurance that the path on which he ran was the right one. His expectation was such that he expected the fortress of Aliso to come into view around the next bend or turn in the way.

After a while, the ground began to descend from the wooded heights of the Teutoberg's spine into rocky lowlands of coniferous trees, moss and lichen. The pathway once again rolled across rivulets and creeks as they meandered and picked their way through irregular outcrops of moss-covered rock. Cornelius splashed through many of these, grateful for the cooling water that splashed over his sweating calves and thighs. Once or twice he stopped to splash the cold, mountain-fed water over his face and arms, reviving and invigorating his tired muscles. Then he would move on, determined not to stop until he reached Aliso's safety. But the rains which had temporarily abated during the horror-filled aftermath of the defeat, returned with renewed vigor near sundown. Cornelius decided the wisest course was to seek shelter from the elements and the onset of night by finding a place to rest and recoup his strength. In the fading dusk he found what he sought, an abandoned animal's den set beneath an overhanging block of limestone camouflaged behind a copse of mulberry bushes. Crawling inside, he found the space could easily accommodate him. Stretching out on the warm remains of the den's bedding of dried leaves and moss he fell instantly asleep.

Cornelius awoke to a wash of sunlight on his eyelids. Blinking, he sat up and crawled out of his refuge into a warm, bright fall day. All around him, the leaves of every bush and tree were beginning to reveal the first blush of autumnal splendor beneath a coverlet of silver droplets. Taking a quick survey of his surroundings, Cornelius could see that he had almost reached the foot of the forest spine. Behind him, the landscape rose in tiers of bare, broken rock, scattered with pockets of narrow evergreens and covered in carpets of emerald moss, to the summit of the wooded heights from which he had emerged the day before. In front of him lay a flatland of dense mixed forest stretching into the west, its perfect roof marred by the deep gash of a forest river. That, he reasoned, must be the tributary of the Lippe for which Aliso derived its water. General Varus had tried in vain to reach it in his attempt to retrace his steps back to the fortress but Arminius had headed him off and led him instead to the ambush on the plain. Once he found its course, Cornelius reasoned he would do what Varus could not: follow its passage through the lower reaches of the forest until it flowed free of the Teutoberg and out onto the grassy upland on which Aliso was part. Offering a silent prayer of thanks for the unseen hand he knew was guiding him; he slipped the barbarian sword in his belt and started off to find the river.

Two thoughts concerned Cornelius as he moved down the forest path. The knot of hunger in his stomach reminded him that he had not eaten since the previous morning when they had broken their final camp. And that meal had not been substantial, consisting of only a crust of bread, a finger of old cheese and a cup of water. He would need to replenish himself soon or face the prospects of having his reserve of strength dwindle to the point where he would not be able to continue. A second thought crowded in on the first. What had happened to the barbarian party that had been tracking him? After his encounter with the giant tribesman on the path, he had heard nothing further of them. Had they given up the chase, believing Cornelius had eluded them in the night? Or perhaps they had gone a different route to another place in the forest? Whatever the reason, he knew he must remain vigilant and ready for anything. And above all, he would have to find food. Yet as it would turn out, both these concerns would soon be answered in a way Cornelius could not possibly have foreseen.

Reaching the start of the wooded plateau, the path proceeded to drift off to his right toward the sound of distant water. The forest was thicker here and in many places, the pathway had become overgrown with encroaching roots and branches. As the noise of moving water grew louder, so did another sound beneath it, the sound of human voices. At first, Cornelius thought it merely a trick of the heavy air about him that translated the rush of river water into snatches of conversation. Nearing the river itself he soon discovered they were definitely speaking voices. Unfortunately for him they were German.

His first instinct was to move off in the opposite direction to avoid any contact with his pursuers. But something else had caught his attention and was even now overriding his desire to flee. It was the mouth-watering smell of roasting meat cooking over a fire.

Sliding on to his belly, Cornelius silently eased his way through the underbrush until he came to a ring of trees hard by the banks of the river. Peering through a break in the tangled foliage, he saw a party of six barbarians sitting and standing around a stone-ringed campfire, the haunch of a freshly-killed deer turning tantalizingly on a spit of green wood.

Cornelius' hunger tightened its grip on his stomach as he watched the juices from the meat drip and sizzle into the flames. His mouth watered at the sweet, drifting odor of the deer meat as he pondered how he might avail himself of even a single slice. But to do that, he must somehow separate it from those for whom it was intended. And there were six of them.

As he considered how it might be accomplished, Cornelius' gaze fell on a heart-sinkingly familiar figure. The giant barbarian who had barred his way on the upper path, now sat on an old log, his bruised face cast into a glaring mask as he stared into the fire. The side of the face that had borne the brunt of Cornelius' blow was swollen into a yellowish purple mass twice its normal size, lending a demonic twist to the man's visage and making him even more fearsome, if such a thing were possible. Idly, he traced patterns in the dirt at his feet with a stick while holding the good side of his face in his hand. One of his companions hailed him and in the same oddly inflected Latin asked, "Why so glum, Gainas? Breakfast is almost ready. We will eat and then get back to work."

Gainas looked up at the speaker with disgust. "Just like you to think of your stomach, Osric. If you had not whined about how hungry you were we would not have had to stop. We would have caught up to that dog of a Roman by now."

Osric snorted through his nose. "Can I help it if breakfast came bounding through the woods? Would you deny us the chance to retrieve your sword on a full stomach? Besides, I still say we should have gone back with the others."

Now it was Gainas' turn to snort in derision. "Cowards!" he cried, "All cowards. And you too, Osric, with such talk! You would think that one Roman was too much for you. That he was some kind of bogeyman or evil spirit come to claim your soul. As if Hades himself would want it! Stop your complaining, Osric. If you want to go back, go back! But I won't rest until my sword is back in its scabbard with the bastard's blood dripping from it!"

Another of the Germans, clipping a piece of skin from the deer haunch with his sword and popping it in his mouth, suggested, "Yes, Gainas, we all understand you want vengeance for your pretty face and lost sword. After all, if it were me, I would not like to admit that I had been spanked by a puny Roman with a stick." The comment caused snickering around the fire.

"Hold your tongue, Ruric!" barked Gainas, "Or I'll tear it out of your stupid head!"

"Alright, alright," laughed Ruric good-naturedly. "I meant no harm. We all agreed to follow you into the forest to find this fellow. But don't you think it may be too late, Gainas? The trail is cold and he could have gone anywhere during the night."

Gainas wrinkled his nose like a hound on the scent of blood. "No. He is close by. I can smell him!"

Cornelius involuntarily shivered from his hiding place. For a brief moment, he wondered if the big man actually could smell him.

"That's just breakfast you smell," commented Ruric, "And it's ready!"

The barbarians except Gainas and Osric all rushed to cut themselves the first slice. "You not eating?" asked Ruric of Osric through a mouthful of tender deer meat.

Jerking his thumb over his shoulder, Osric replied, "I need to relieve myself first. I'll be back." Osric passed into the far side of the woods, moving noisily inside the heavy brush to find a convenient place to urinate. From where he watched, Cornelius suddenly hit upon a plan.

Edging himself back from the tree ring until he was sure he would not be seen, Cornelius stood up and circled around to where Osric was still stumbling around, filling the air with curses. Cornelius drew within ten paces of the barbarian before Osric found a place that satisfied him, a small open space before a huge oak tree. Sighing with contentment, he directed a golden stream onto the forest floor while turning his upraised face into the morning sunshine that streamed down through the spreading branches above him. The last thing he saw was the gentle waving of the oak tree's large, rounded leaves in the breeze as Cornelius stepped out from behind him and swung Gainas' sword. The blade bit through Osric's neck like butter, separating the head from the collapsing body and sending it rolling to the oak's massive trunk. Even though the attack had been quietly efficient, Cornelius looked back toward the tree ring, the bloodied sword at the ready for the possibility that someone had detected anything coming from the woods. When after a minute there was no reaction from the feasting Germans, Cornelius turned back and picked up Osric's severed head by the braided hair.

"The lives of many noble Romans will be avenged this day," he whispered into its ear. Putting it down for the moment, Cornelius dragged the lifeless trunk to the foot of the great tree and propped it up into a sitting position. A tell-tale swath of black blood marked the place where Osric had been slain to where it now rested. He removed the dead man's shoulder cloak and wrapping the severed head inside it. Then he made his way back to the unsuspecting tribesmen.

Taking his vigil outside the ring of trees once more, Cornelius saw that the Germans were busy cramming chunks of steaming meat into their mouths while Gainas continued to sit impatiently upon his log, scratching his stick in the earth. Carefully unwinding the blood-stained cloak, Cornelius removed Osric's head and set it down at his feet. He folded the cloak into a makeshift sling and placed the head inside it, hefting it on his forearm to check its weight. Then in slow circles, he began to swing it, increasing the speed with each revolution until finally, judging the velocity to be right, he let the ghastly projectile fly. It flew straight up in the air to clear the line of trees and in a majestic arc, sailed across the clearing to land with a soft thud close to the place where the rest of the body was hidden.

The reaction of the Germans was immediate.

Every man was on his feet. Drawing their swords they rushed to where the head lay, cursing and swearing in their rage. Rolling the head over with a booted toe, Gainas muttered, "It's Osric. I told you that dog of a Roman was still about. Quick, now! Fan out and find him before anyone else loses his

head. And yell out if you find the rest of poor Osric!"
The baying Teutons crashed into the woods,
hacking and slashing at the thick vegetation. It
wasn't long before someone shouted, "I've found
him! I found Osric! Come quickly!" Soon they were
all gathered around the trunk of the oak tree staring
down at the macabre sight of Osric's headless torso
in a sitting position.

"I swear by the infernal gods," rumbled Gainas,
absently rubbing his own wounded cheek, "that this
man will die a slave's death for this!"

While the barbarians were distracted by his
diversion, Cornelius crept into the empty clearing
and tiptoed to the campfire. Cutting a piece of meat
from the haunch, he tore into it with relish, his
starving palate salivating with delight. Fully aware
that it would not be long before the Germans
returned, he pulled another strip of flesh from the
roasting carcass and started back for the woods. But
it was too late.

"There he is!" shouted a horse voice at the far
end of the clearing. "It was a damn trick to steal our
meat!"

Cornelius bolted heedlessly into the forest,
branches lashing across his eyes and face like
whips, half blinding him in the process. The
succulent meat he had labored so hard to acquire
was now useless, cast aside as he fled for his life.
Behind him, the barbarians fell hard on his heels,
the instinct of the hunt coursing through their veins,
their voices raised in the joy of battle joined. The
fearful racket spurred Cornelius forward through the
unfamiliar ground, stumbling over unseen roots and
sustaining numerous stinging cuts on his hands and

feet from the jabbing of wild thorns and thistles that seemed to be everywhere. His lungs vainly tried to fill themselves with the dense air of the wood even as his legs became leaden beneath him with fatigue. With every stride he steeled himself for the blow he expected between the shoulder blades that would bring him down and finish the chase. He prayed the end would be swift and that his death would be one befitting a Roman officer.

"Fear not for the hand of the Almighty shall overshadow you and protect you and deliver you from the valley of death."

The promise of the Man of Dreams blazed like fire in his mind.

"....the hand of the Almighty shall overshadow and protect..."

Overshadow and protect?

".... And deliver you from the valley of death."

Where did he find himself at that moment if not in the valley of death? What choice did he have but to trust in the invisible hand that had delivered him from the destruction of the entire Roman army? Inexplicably, hope flooded his soul and strengthened his resolve. It was only many years later that Cornelius would come to regard those terror-filled moments during that deadly chase through the hellish confines of the Saltus Teutobergensis, as the first step taken on his journey to faith.

Strangely fortified and renewed, Cornelius ran on in a strength he knew he did not possess. Leaping and striding over the fallen debris of the forest floor, he began to distance himself from his pursuers. In front of a blind of leafy birch and elm, he vaulted over the decayed remains of an ancient trunk and found himself suspended in mid air. Pin wheeling his arms for balance, he fell some ten feet before his feet slammed into the steep edge of a ravine concealed by the line of trees above him. His momentum caused him to pitch forward and tumble awkwardly down the remainder of the ravine's face until he rolled and stopped on an old, dried up stream bed covered in a carpet of dead leaves. He lay panting, staring at the cobalt sky above him while waiting for the sound of the hunters' approach.

Minutes passed. Nothing happened. After a while, Cornelius raised himself on his elbows and looked about him. He could see that he had indeed fallen into a narrow ravine whose slopes rose fifty feet to the wooded heights on either side. The stream that had originally cut the gorge from the soft forest earth had long since dried up and ceased to run, leaving a serpentine trail to mark its course. Rising slowly to his feet, Cornelius brushed the leaves from his hair and arms, wondering why the barbarians had not followed him down into the ravine. It was inconceivable that they had not seen him disappear through the forest hedge and would more than likely have toppled down the slope after him. And yet there was no sign they had done so. He looked upstream and then downstream, before convincing himself that he had not been followed. Once again he had been the beneficiary of whatever supernatural agent had inexplicably chosen to preserve his life.

The pursuit through the forest, however, had left Cornelius hopelessly lost. He could not tell in which direction the river lay but reasoned that the old stream would have one time run into it. By following its course as it descended off to the right, he felt certain he would eventually reach the river again. And so he set off down the stream bed, scanning both sides of the ravine for any sign of the barbarians.

The world was quiet as Cornelius walked. Except for the rumbling of his complaining stomach and the muffled footfalls of his sandals on the bed of leaves, there was not another sound. Nor could he tell how far advanced the day was since the canopy of the forest roof hid the sun from view, casting the ravine in almost perpetual shadow. The farther he walked, the more clogged with dead branches and rotten, moss-covered trunks the river bed became, the flotsam of an ancient flood during the days when the stream coursed with water. Where the passage of the stream bed had previously been fairly straight and even, it now began to fall off sharply as it entered a series of meandering curves and twists through rocky and overgrown country. As he picked his way through the debris of the stream bed he was suddenly conscious of a new sound growing steadily louder with every step. It was the unmistakable gurgling of flowing water. Somewhere ahead of him, the river flowed unconcerned in its ancient course. Rounding a final turn and ducking beneath a natural archway created by the wedging of a pair of huge oaks that had fallen in against one another, Cornelius stood on the river bank once again.

XXVII

W*hich way to go?*

Cornelius watched the eddying of the brown river water below his feet and pondered his next move. He had no idea if Aliso lay upstream or downstream. He tried to recall to his memory the image of a roll of maps he had seen through the open flap of Varus' command tent during the chaos of their departure from the second night's camp. The maps had shown a spidery network of rivers and streams branching out from the root of the great Rhine, weaving in and out of the broad swaths of heavy forest that characterized the German bank. Varus had been using them in a desperate effort to pick out the best route back to the fortress of Aliso. Indeed, Cornelius remembered seeing the small symbol of a tower and gate labeled 'Aliso' drawn on one of the inky veins of the leather parchment. If this particular river was that one, he reasoned, then by following where it ran, he would, if his luck continued to hold, emerge from the Teutoberg Wood at some point near Aliso. But if were not, then the river would eventually lead him back to the Rhine itself and the welcome refuge Castra Vetera. Either way, he knew he must find safety in Roman territory somewhere along the river's length. With the comforting knowledge that his ordeal would soon be at an end, he set off downstream, confident he would find Aliso before another night fell.

The river bank was not much different than what Cornelius had already had to contend. The feet of the surrounding forest came almost to the water's edge, allowing only a narrow, slippery trail on which his feet found purchase. More than once did a sudden misstep threaten to send him tumbling into the swirling muddy water but he always managed to restore his balance by taking hold of the nearest overhanging branch. For an hour or two, he navigated the river bank in this manner until finally coming to a place where the forest widened out, providing a wide, comfortable shoulder of grass on which to pass. Fatigued by his labors and feeling thirsty, Cornelius removed the sword from his belt and laid it down beside him. Kneeling down by the bank, he scooped up a palm full of water and tossed it back into his dry mouth. The water was cold and refreshing even if possessing a slightly brackish aftertaste. Like all Roman soldiers, Cornelius wore a focale, a kind of rough linen scarf around his neck to be used as a general wash cloth and towel as well as protection from the rubbing of the collar of his cuirass. Untying it from around his neck, he dipped it into the water and washed the sweat and grime from his face and neck. On the far side of the river, a small family of mallards looked on unconcerned from the haven of a protected cove, only mildly curious at the stranger in their midst. Cornelius stared at them with acute interest, hungrily weighing the possibilities of catching one of them. Suddenly, the mallards were thrown into a flurry of flapping wings as they noisily took to the sky. Wondering what had startled them, Cornelius never saw the blow that sent him sprawling across the greensward.

"Roman bastard!"

Gainas stood snarling over him, his lost broadsword back in a beefy fist.

"You thought I'd given up the chase, didn't you? Thought you were pretty clever back at the river, killing poor Osric and giving me this!" Gainas ran his finger down the yellowish-purple mound of his broken cheek. "Well, my friend, it is time to repay the debt. With your life!" As he shouted the last word, he swung the broadsword in a deadly arc down at the prone figure of the young centurion. But Gainas had foolishly given Cornelius the time he needed to clear his head from the daze of the blow. He saw the blurred motion of the blade long before it reached him and easily rolled out of the way. The weapon drove down into the soft grass with a thump. Cornelius was on his feet ready for the next thrust even before the big barbarian could free his blade.

"There's no place to run this time, dog," growled Gainas, measuring the distance between himself and his quarry through narrowed eyes. "And there's no stick to save you, either. Why not give in to the inevitable and let me run you through, nice and quick like?"

"I'd sooner be a slave to a seller of horse dung then let someone as ugly as you kill me," Cornelius bantered back. He hoped the insult would anger the German into a rash decision. Gainas did not disappoint him. Trembling with rage, the giant tribesman let out a strangled cry and raising the point of his sword at Cornelius, proceeded to run straight at him. Cornelius timed his response perfectly. With his back to the river, he waited until the very last moment before Gainas was on him and then knelt on one knee, turning his hip into the side of the barbarian's leg. Gainas' forward momentum carried him up over Cornelius and pitched him head first into the cold waters with a huge splash. He came up out of the water, which turned out to be only waist high, bellowing like a wounded bear. Unfortunately for Cornelius, the broadsword did not sink into the river as he had hoped. It stood quivering in the muddy bank in front of Gainas. Grasping the hilt and clambering up onto the bank, the seething German cried, "You will die slowly and in pain for that, I promise you!" Again he came at Cornelius with his blade swirling about his head. Cornelius managed to step out of the way of the first swing but this time Gainas followed in behind the retreating Roman and caught him a glancing strike on the left bicep. The muscle in his arm burned as an ugly red gash a couple of inches long began to seep blood.

"That was only a down payment!" laughed Gainas maniacally. "You'll lose a lot more than blood before I'm done with you!" He waded in again, barely missing Cornelius' neck with a savage lunge of the broadsword. If he did not soon disarm his adversary or discover a route of escape, Cornelius knew that it was just a matter of time before Gainas would strike the mortal blow. Convinced he could not separate the big man from his weapon this time, Cornelius settled on the latter. As Gainas drew back his sword for another flurry, Cornelius turned and bolted down the greensward.

Roaring in fury, Gainas followed, swinging his sword in sweeping arcs as he went.

Cornelius ran toward the far end of the broad, grassy space where it narrowed once more into a winding path close by a bend in the river. If he could reach it, even with Gainas hot on his heels, the German would be hard pressed to use his sword in the constricting confines of the forest, effectively disarming him. Cornelius would then try to elude him by ducking into the dense cover of the underbrush. Putting his head down, he focused his energy for a final spurt to the place where the greensward ended and the path began. But abruptly the earth and sky changed places and before he realized what had happened, Cornelius was lying painfully on his back, gasping for air. His foot had caught a protruding edge of rock concealed in the grass and had tossed him in a complete somersault through the air. He slammed hard onto the ground, knocking all the wind out of his lungs.

Gainas ran up and stood over him, a triumphant smile twisting his features, the great broadsword drawn ready to strike above his head. "There's no escape for you this time, you Roman scum. You are going to pay for the trouble you've caused me. But before I kill you, I'm going to make you suffer. Before I send your shade to the underworld, you will have the agony of seeing your arms and legs piled up beside you like cord wood, you stinking heap of Roman dog shit." Gleaming in the soft sunlight, the barbarian's blade inched back for the first blow.

Phhhhhhhtttt.

The hiss of an arrow in flight whispered in the air. With a dull thud, the missile implanted itself in the middle of Gainas' back, smashing vertebrae and severing the spinal column in half. Like a puppet whose strings were suddenly cut, the big German lost all control over his body. He crumpled in awkward angles to the ground, paralyzed and unmoving as the last vestiges of life ebbed quickly away.

Cornelius sat up in alarm and saw the figure of another barbarian carrying an empty bow coming slowly toward him. He immediately recognized the man as the one called Ruric. Picking up Gainas' sword, he scrambled to his feet and readied himself for the expected attack. Ruric, however, was smiling. He held up an empty hand to show the young Roman he was not armed with another arrow.

"Peace to you, my friend," said Ruric in perfect Latin. "I mean you no harm. I am the Lord Segestes' man."

Although Cornelius had never met the Cherusci high chief, he had seen him often enough in the company of Varus and other staff officers around Castra Vetera. The story of what had occurred between Segestes and Arminius was well known amongst the legionaries, even before their ill-fated foray into the Teutoberg Forest.

Cornelius licked his parched lips and replied, "How do I know you are what you say?"

Ruric's tanned face broke into laughter. "I killed Gainas for you, did I not? I assume your life has some value to you."

"My question is 'why'?"

"Because not all Germans are oath-breakers or Roman haters. There are many of us who continue to honor our pledges we made to Rome. We remember with fondness the days of marching together under the eagles. We understand that the future of Germany lies with Rome and not with would-be kings."

Cornelius clucked his tongue with disdain. "You speak like a patriot," he offered, "but your hands are covered with the stench of Roman blood!"

"I have not killed a single Roman!" protested Ruric.

"Were you not with Arminius? If you stood on that field yesterday and watched the flower of the northern army succumb to treachery, than you share his guilt."

"Aye, I was with Arminius. I do not deny that. But it was by Segestes' order that I as well as a few others attach ourselves to the rebels in an attempt to save as many Roman lives as we could. I have been true to that charge today by preserving yours."

"Then why did you try and hunt me down with the others?"

"I will explain but first..." Leaving the sentence hanging, Ruric put his bow down and slipped a leather drinking horn tipped with brass from his shoulder. Holding it out to Cornelius, he said, "You must be thirsty. Here, drink." Tentatively, Cornelius reached out and took the horn from Ruric's grasp, careful to keep the point of his weapon between them. With one eye on the barbarian, he opened the horn and took a long, deep draught from the cold water, letting it soothe his parched throat. While he drank, Ruric reached inside a leather pouch on his hip and produced a crust of baked bread and a small chunk of white deer meat. This time there was no reservations as he eagerly snatched the proffered food from the barbarian's hand and ate it as only a ravenous man can. When he had finished, he wiped his lips and lowered his sword.

"My thanks," he said gratefully. If anything, the food and drink had done much to give credence to the barbarian's story. Ruric nodded and smiled.

"Now as for the rest of my story. When Arminius saw you running across the field, he called Gainas to him and commanded he bring your head back on a pole. He knew he could rely on Gainas to carry out his order to the letter."

"He seemed to have an unnatural hatred for Romans," interrupted Cornelius.

"He had reason. Gainas once had a wife and young child he loved very much. One day when he was out hunting, one of your Roman lawyers entered his village with an armed group of lictors, looking for a fugitive who had escaped from one of their tribunals. The lawyer was a particularly hard man who did not believe the villagers when they told him the fugitive was not there. For whatever reason, he decided to make the people an example of the futility of resistance against Roman authority. He herded them into the village common and ordered his lictors to execute all the elders and children while the horrified mothers looked on. Then this 'honored' bureaucrat of Rome allowed his men to rape all the young women and girls who were left. Gainas' wife was one of the first to suffer this indignity. But she refused to allow her spirit to be broken in her disgrace. She spit in the face of the lictor who attempted to ravage her. But she was after all just a woman. The Romans set on her and beat her mercilessly into unconsciousness. They raped her and then slit her throat. They did the same to the rest of the women until none remained. They then piled up the bodies and set fire to them before continuing on in their search for the fugitive. This was how Gainas and the other men of his village found their families when they returned from the hunt."

Cornelius' head bowed in quiet shame. Could such a thing be true? How could his countrymen behave is such a brutal manner? Was this the bright flame of civilization that Rome promised to illuminate Germany with? If the story were true, then who were the true barbarians?

"Bastards!" muttered Cornelius, not meaning the Germans.

"Yes. There are many such stories all over the north," continued Ruric soberly, "So as a Roman you should not wonder why it was relatively easy for Arminius to make common cause against you. There are many Germans like Gainas who have little reason to love Rome."

"Were these men ever brought to trial?" asked Cornelius.

Ruric offered a rueful smile. "If you mean a Roman trial, no. They came under German justice." Cornelius nodded. He knew what the reference meant.

"What happened," continued Ruric "Was that Gainas hunted down and killed with his own hand every man who was involved in the massacre of his village. And he saved the most brutal punishment for the lawyer who gave the orders. He caught up with him and his escort beside a river very much like this one. After killing the last of the lictors,

Gainas tortured the man for three whole days. Disemboweled him and burnt his entrails right before his eyes. Not a pleasant way to go, I'm afraid."

"Not anymore than the man deserved," replied Cornelius grimly. "I see now why this man Gainas acted as he did."

Ruric nodded. "After that, with no family to go back to, he wandered around Germany until he attached himself to Arminius as his bodyguard. It was Gainas whom Arminius turned to whenever he needed a bloody piece of work done. That is why he told him to track you down."

"So where do you come in? How did you come to join Gainas in this business?"

"As I have said, those of us who remain loyal to the Lord Segestes were sent to salvage what we could from the disaster that all but Varus saw was about to occur. I fell in with Gainas to ensure that nothing would happen to you."

Cornelius gave a wan smile. "My thanks to you again, friend. I am indebted to you for my life. But if you will forgive me, I must be going."

"Where are you going?" asked Ruric as he watched the Roman remove the scabbard of Gainas' sword from the body and strap it around his own waist. "The woods are still full of armed bands searching for survivors."

"I am making for Aliso," explained Cornelius, sliding the weapon into the scabbard. "We left a garrison there before we entered this damned forest."

Ruric nodded his acknowledgement. "I know it. It is a little more than a day's journey from here."

"I reckon if I follow this river, it will eventually lead me out into the plains somewhere near the fortress itself."

"True. But the journey from here will still be perilous. As I have told you, there are still many search parties scouring the woods. You will need someone who knows the way and will guide you safely there."

Cornelius looked into the blue eyes of the barbarian. "You?" he inquired. "You have already done enough for me. I couldn't ask you to risk your life further for my sake."

"I'm offering."

"Why?"

"Because like a lot of my countrymen, I prefer the devil I know to the one I don't. Many of us desire to place ourselves under the authority of Caesar rather than that of Arminius the Traitor."

"But he is a German like you!"

"He is a murderer and an oath breaker. Augustus will give us peace. Arminius will only bring war and destruction. Rome will make us prosperous and civilized. The promises of Arminius will leave us penniless savages. I will not bow my knee to a man whose rule will only destroy us in the end!"

Cornelius marveled at the depth of feeling Ruric possessed concerning the matter. Together, he mused, they were a people capable of crushing the best Rome had to send against them. But their penchant for petty quarreling and fighting condemned them to a stunted promise. Even when a leader as capable and bold as Arminius appeared to lead them, they preferred to work against him and make deals with the very enemy they had gathered to fight. The barbarian soul was like that of a rabid dog, frothing with madness while biting the hand of friend and foe alike. How could such a people ever be conquered, let alone governed?

Adjusting his cuirass to sit comfortably on his shoulders, Cornelius said, "Very well, my friend. Lead on. I would like to get to Aliso as soon as possible."

XXVIII

"**W**hose markings are these?"

Arminius clutched the broken shaft of Ruric's arrow in his fist, holding it over his head for the entire company of warriors to see. At his feet lay the crumpled corpse of his giant bodyguard, a twisted gray mound face down in the waving grass of the river greensward. It had been two days since they had lost contact with Gainas' war party after following with a larger force to sweep the forest behind him. Just as Ruric had told Cornelius, Gainas had been charged with seeing to it that the Roman officer who had fled the battlefield was apprehended, a command Arminius had reiterated when they had crossed paths two days earlier. Gainas had blustered and bellowed before his chief, offering to end his own life if he did not make good on his promise to return with the head of the Roman swinging from his belt. But it was Arminius who now stood tight-lipped with fury over his slain executioner.

"There is a stench of treachery in the air," spat Arminius with undisguised disgust. "This is a German bolt. And so I ask again: does anyone recognize these markings?" The hard eyes of men inured to the sight of death as common place, stared blankly ahead waiting for the other to give a response. Finally, a tribesman in the back of the group reluctantly raised his hand.

"You there!" cried Arminius, "Come forward." The man edged his way to the front of the company and stepped in front of the German chieftain. Thrusting the broken shaft into his face, Arminius demanded, "Do you know whose this is?"

The man looked intently at the arrow and then into Arminius' face. Turning around to where his companions waited, he glanced at them with askance as if unsure whether he should have been so rash.

"Well?" roared Arminius, his voice echoing in the open space of the greensward. "Do you know who this is or don't you? Speak up, man before I decide to cut the answer from your throat with my dagger!"

The tribesman swallowed hard. "It is true," he began slowly, "that I recognize the markings. They are used by the clan of Falkard, kinsmen to the House of Segestes the High Chief."

The mention of Segestes' name brought a murmur to the rest of the barbarians. Arminius silenced it by striking the man across the face with the back of his hand, drawing a trickle of blood at the corner of his mouth. Prodding an accusing finger into his bewildered expression, he threatened "The next man who calls Segestes 'high chief' will die by my hand. I am the High Chief of the Cherusci, not Segestes. It was I who drew the legions into the Teutoberg Wald. It was I who destroyed them while Segestes remained at home like an old woman. He has turned his back on every true German by remaining a slave to the Romans. He is not to be honored with the name of 'high chief' again. Do I make myself clear?" The dumbfounded nods assured Arminius he had made his point.

"Now then," he continued, glaring at the man whose words had provoked the outburst. "You say you know this clan?"

Wiping the blood from his mouth, the barbarian replied, "Yes. Some of them accompanied us from Rheinsdorf. They claimed they had had a falling out with Segestes when he forbade them to answer my lord's summons to fight the Romans. They asked if they could join us and we agreed. I got to know their leader quite well."

"Who is he?" demanded Arminius, "and how many men were with him?"

"His name is Ruric. He told me he was kin to Segestes through his mother's side. As to how many were with him, I would say no more than a century."

"Tell me," replied the German chieftain thoughtfully, balancing the shaft of the arrow in his raised palm. "How do you know this belongs to this Ruric you speak of?"

"As I have told my lord, I recognize the markings. I remember thinking at the time how striking they were and commented as much to Ruric. He told me with great pride that they were peculiar only to his father's clan, the Falkards. All of their weapons, shields and scabbards carry the same mark."

"Interesting." Arminius stroked his chin, carefully examining the beautiful scrollwork etched into the surface of the wood, his mind working. *So! There is a wolf amongst the sheep is there? Well whomever you might be, Ruric Falkard you will wish you had never come to the Teutoberg once I am finished with you!*

"Arnulf!"

"Here my lord!" A slightly hunchbacked individual with a pockmarked face framed in a cascade of long, stringy hair, shuffled to the front of the line of warriors. Despite his appearance, Arnulf enjoyed a well deserved reputation of being the best tracker between the Rhine and the Elbe, a talent that Arminius had come increasingly to rely on.

"What did you find?" asked Arminius curtly.

Pointing downstream to where the greensward narrowed into the pathway, Arnulf reported, "I found a set of tracks in the grass leading as the water runs. My guess is they are following the river."

"They? How many are there?"

"Two."

"Aliso?"

"That would be my guess."

"How long?"

"Two hours. Three at the most."

Arminius pursed his lips and nodded. "We have them!" Turning on his warriors, he cried, "Let's move out! These men must not be allowed to reach the Roman fortress alive. When we come upon them, you may kill the Roman as you find him but I want this Ruric Falkard brought to me alive. He will pay for his treason with more than his life! Now get going!"

XXVIX

To his mild surprise, Cornelius found himself enjoying Ruric's company despite his earlier misgivings. He was so unlike any barbarian he had yet seen or met. Far from being rough and uncouth, Ruric proved instead to be a garrulous traveling companion filled with stories and information about a wide variety of subjects, reflecting an intellect Cornelius would never have ascribed to a savage. This was particularly true concerning the thorny subject of Roman-German relations. It soon became apparent that Ruric had been privy to its sometimes-treacherous ebb and flow at the highest levels.

"I have had the opportunity to meet your General Varus on several occasions," he began one such discussion, hacking away at an offending branch that protruded across his path. "I will never understand the Roman propensity to appoint incompetents to ranks of high command in the legions."

The remark raised a welt of offence from Cornelius. The memories of the horror in the fens were still fresh in his mind. He stopped his own chopping and glared at the German. "General Varus was a great man from a noble family, one of the oldest in Rome. His death is a tragedy and blow to our cause in Germany."

Ruric ceased his hacking and grinned at Cornelius. "I am sorry, my friend but you have it backwards. His death is the only thing that has saved your cause in Germany. If you want my opinion, the true tragedy in all of this is the fact that Varus wasted the lives of three legions in making his funeral pyre. The gods work in strange ways when they demand such a price for the life of a fool. How much better would it have been if someone had stuck a dagger between Varus' ribs before he ever had the chance to cross the Rhine, hmmm?"

"How can you call yourself a friend of Rome," retorted Cornelius, his voice simmering with anger, "when you stand here and advocate the murder of one of her noblest sons?"

Ruric laughed and resumed his cutting. "Come now, my friend, surely you are not that naïve! Rome is just as capable of producing idiots as she is birthing genius. Will you stand there and compare Varus with a man like Julius Caesar or Augustus himself? The fortunes of one's birth do not dictate what a man will be in later life. Does not your own history prove that? Gaius Marius was a man of low birth and yet he managed to become master of Rome over the heads of a gaggle of well-bred Roman noblemen. And why? Because men like Marius rely on their talents and inner strengths to achieve what they want. Incompetents like Varus depend upon the birthing chamber to acquire what they do not merit by nature."

"For a barbarian you seem to know a lot about us."

"I like to read. Especially your histories. Ever read any of Titus Livius' books?"

"No."

"A pity. I think you'd find him quite stimulating."

"What does that have to do..."

"Livius is unusual as historians go because he views history from a moral point of view rather than a political one. He sees the strands of history weaving together through the efforts of great men and personalities, not from the whim of your stone gods."

"If I didn't know better I'd take you for an educated Roman rather than an uncivilized barbarian."

Ruric feigned hurt. "I? Uncivilized? You cut me to the quick, centurion. An accident of birth may have put me on the wrong side of the Rhine but in my heart I am pure Roman."

"I don't doubt you sound like one."

"Thank you, my friend. I take that as a compliment."

"Compliment or not, what does all this talk about Titus Livius have to do with getting to Aliso?"

"None at all."

"Well then?"

"I only mention it because when he comes to write about what happened in the Teutoberg Forest he will undoubtedly place the blame squarely where it belongs. On the shoulders of one man and one man only."

"Quinctillius Varus," offered Cornelius ruefully.

"Who else? Varus' behavior and character shaped the decisions that were made that ultimately led to disaster. Tell me, do you think things would have turned out as they did if Tiberius or Germanicus had been in command?"

At the mention of the stepson and great nephew of the Emperor, Cornelius blanched. Both men were without question the best generals in the Empire with a string of successful campaigns behind their names to prove it.

"Alright I agree with you. How does that change our current circumstances?"

Ruric grinned and returned to the task of clearing their path of choking underbrush. "It doesn't," he chuckled nonchalantly, his blade singing in the foliage. "I just thought I should put the whole matter in perspective for you in case you believed the notion that the circumstances of one's birth somehow leads to greatness. If that were the case than Arminius would have spent his life as a pig farmer. Better for poor Varus if he had I suppose."

"That's not funny."

"It wasn't meant to be. Now are you going to stand there all day arguing with me or are you going to help me cut through this mess?"

Together the two men worked in silence cutting away the scrub and underbrush from the path. So thick was the overgrowth in places however that Cornelius began to doubt that any track could possibly be anywhere near it. But Ruric pressed on with an enthusiasm that gave Cornelius enough comfort to assure him the German knew what he was doing. After three quarters of an hour, they broke through the last tangled hedge of hawthorn and wild mulberry out into an opening in the forest proper. Here the gloom of the wood lessened and dissipated due to dust-filled shafts of yellow sun that filtered down from openings in the canopy above. Thankfully for Cornelius, the path had miraculously reappeared under his feet again. He could see now where it emerged from the obstruction of heavy brushwood to run on ahead of them through a stand of widely spaced oak, spruce and elm.

Still panting from the exertion of his efforts, Cornelius asked, "Well, what now?"

Ruric, who did not appear winded at all much to Cornelius' annoyance, pointed to where the track disappeared into the dimness of the distant tree wall.

"We follow the path," he answered in a tone that suggested the response of an indulgent parent with a backward child. "Let's go."

As they walked, Cornelius picked up the thread of their earlier conversation.

"There is something I still don't understand, Ruric."

"What is that?"

"If you have thrown your lot in with Rome as you say, why participate in the slaughter of our troops in the marshes?"

"Did you see me killing Romans in the fens?"

"I didn't know you then!"

"True. But you know me now. Do you think me capable of such a thing?"

"Well no. But you were there."

"I admit it. And as I have explained, I had gone to the gathering of the tribes to keep an eye on Arminius for my Lord Segestes. As for participating in that nasty business back in the fens, you will have to take my word for it. Unless of course you think killing Gainas for you is not enough proof of my fidelity."

Cornelius was chagrinned by the rebuke. It was true of course. The man had saved his life. And now he was risking his own to ensure Cornelius reached Aliso safely. How could he have ever thought Ruric was playing him false? Cornelius' felt his face flush hot with guilt. "Forgive me, my friend," he said his voice restrained and quavering with emotion. "If I hadn't said it before I say it now. I am grateful for all your help. I was a fool to question your loyalty and your honesty. I am sorry."

Ruric stopped walking and put a friendly hand to the other's shoulder. "Think nothing of it, friend Cornelius. Given the circumstances, your suspicion is natural. I hope I have passed the test."

"With colors flying."

"Good. Then we trust one another. Believe me. We will need to if we are to get out of this place with our skins."

"What do you think will happen now?" asked Cornelius as they resumed their pace along the winding pathway.

Ruric grunted. "Rome is rarely shamed twice. For fifteen years Hannibal the Carthaginian defeated every army you sent against him. But in the end it was Hannibal who was ruined by the power of Rome. The next commander of the Rhine will not make the same mistakes as Varus. The gods have given the mastery of the world over to Rome and only a fool could think otherwise. Arminius believes that by destroying three legions he has destroyed the power of Rome. But he knows! He has seen the glory of Rome and in his heart he knows the only thing his victory has bought is time. Winter will come and his warriors will return to their homes. By next spring, when the snows return to the mountain tops and the rivers are freed from the choking ice flows, Augustus will have ten legions poised on the banks of the Rhine. And this time, it will not be Varus who commands them. What will Arminius do then? Does he think that those who heeded his call today will listen to his summons tomorrow? No. I know my people. They will cower in their villages and farms and leave Arminius to face the vengeance of Rome alone. After all, is it not better that one man should die rather than an entire nation?"

Cornelius could not argue the point. "Tell me then. What do you think your people will do now they have their great victory? Will they march on the Rhine frontier and seek to enter Gaul and Italy?"

"No doubt that was Arminius' plan all along," replied Ruric, "But it is late in the year and I doubt he will be able to convince many of those around him to embark on a long campaign in the south. They will be anxious to return to their wives and children before the first snows set in. That is why I believe Augustus will have more than enough time to shore up the frontier before Arminius can convince our people to breach it in the spring."

"Then someone must go to Rome and inform the Emperor of what has happened here."

Ruric stopped walking again and turned to Cornelius, his pleasant face split into a wide grin. "And who do you have in mind for this important task?" The question caused them both burst into laughter. The sound of it was immediately swallowed up by the heaviness of the forest air that hung between the cathedral columns of tree trunks like a damp curtain.

"Alright, alright," admitted Cornelius with a chuckle, "Guilty as charged! But in all seriousness, I feel I must go. Who else is able? What if I am the only survivor of the massacre? In that case, mine would be the only eyes through which Caesar might view the disaster. I would be the only one who could convince him of the gravity of the situation. And you must come with me, friend Ruric!"

"Oh, no!" cried Ruric, shaking his head. "I will take you to Aliso or even the Rhine frontier if necessary, but I am not going to Rome. I have promised Lord Segestes that I would return to his service when this business is finished and I intend to honor my word. Go if you feel you must but I shall remain here on the far side of the Rhine. Now what do we have here?"

So intent had their conversation been that they did not notice they had suddenly come out into a wide clearing atop a rounded hilltop where the trees fell away on all sides. Above them, a patch of blue sky opened revealing high wispy clouds like brush strokes on a cobalt canvas. Tipping their heads back, their eyes inured to the dimness of the inner wood, drank in the brilliance of open sky over the heads. Squinting against the brightness of the glen, Ruric pointed to the line of jutting treetops behind them. "What do you make of that?" he asked.

Cornelius turned and saw a trio of dark specks circling above what he assumed to be the tree lined course of the river some distance behind them.

"It would seem," commented Ruric soberly, "that the carrion have discovered our handiwork back on the river bank. Rest assured, it will not be long before Arminius does the same. We had better get moving. Come on."

Their conversation at an end, they hurried across the last yards of open ground before plunging again into the forest beyond. Cornelius was sorry to leave the bright openness of the glade behind him after days spent wandering the sunless paths of the gloomy wood. Now the sunlight penetrated only a little with half its normal intensity and warmth. It was as if the massive boles of the ancient trees were drawing the very life around them into their great roots dispelling a gloaming dimness in its place. Judging from the slanting beams of weak sunlight splayed here and there on the forest floor, Cornelius surmised that it was close to the third watch of the afternoon. If Ruric was correct in his estimate of the distance to Aliso, then they would not make the fortress before nightfall. The possibility of another night in the forest began to loom as an unpleasant reality. Food and shelter would be a priority once again. They had eaten the last of Ruric's meat and bread some hours before and now his stomach ached with hunger. His legs were like wood beneath him and his arms pained from the exertion of hacking through the hours of dense bush. He wished he possessed some of the Northman's inexhaustible energy. Ruric seemed to be able to travel endlessly without food or rest. When at last he felt he could not proceed further without rest, he cried out to his guide, "For pity's sake, Ruric, wait! I must insist we halt and rest. I feel like I shall soon die if we do not get something to eat."

Ruric stood with his hands on his hips plainly enjoying the Roman's distress. "Where is that famous Roman pluck I've heard so much about, hmmm?" he teased.

Untying the stained focale from his neck, Cornelius used it to wipe the sweat from his damp brow. "What has happened to good German common sense? A man needs food to feed the body and sufficient rest to restore the strength of his limbs. Why are you any different than me?"

"Rest assured I am not," replied Ruric, "but if it makes you feel any better, I too am hungry. But I was hoping to find the first bridge before we thought about supper."

"First bridge?" echoed Cornelius as he took off his hobnailed sandal and rubbed the ball of an aching foot.

"Yes, perhaps I should explain. Look at this." Ruric took a stick and drew a large semi-circle in the soft dirt of the forest floor. At both ends of the circle he drew a pair of parallel lines and then a box a few inches past the last set of lines. Pointing with the end of the stick to the circle he said, "This is the river we are following at the present. We Germans call it the Glorendel while you know it as the Lippe. It is one of the numerous branches that flow out of Father Rhine. At the western flanks of the Teutoberg Wald, it bows much as I have shown it here. When Tiberius was here last he had two bridges constructed to cross it, here and here." He pointed to the twin sets of parallel lines. "As you can see, the bridges eliminate the need to follow the course of the river. The journey is longer that way. It also passes through as wild a country as we have had to endure thus far. From this first bridge, which is the one I am looking for, it is a straight line to the next one from where the fortress of Aliso is only four miles distant. Otherwise, it would take us two to three days to make Aliso from where we stand."

"If as you say, these bridges are here and we built them, how is it we did not use this route to enter the forest from Aliso?"

"Arminius knew well the existence of the bridges as readily as the Roman high command. But it was essential for Arminius to draw Varus down the path of his choosing in order to maneuver him into the position for the ambush on the plain. If there is one thing that Arminius learned from his time under the Roman colors, it is the importance of discovering and exploiting the weaknesses of his adversary. In Varus' case, he knew that by waving the savage murders of soldiers under his command in his face, the lawyer in Varus would not be able to help himself. He hoped Varus' misplaced sense of justice would move him to indiscretion. Arminius was counting on Varus to heedlessly plunge into obvious danger where a more prudent commander would not allow such sensibilities to intrude upon the general welfare of his army. And as things turned out, Arminius was right."

Cornelius nodded absently, already becoming numb to the ongoing revelations about the incompetent leadership to which the doomed Rhine legions had been entrusted.

"And besides," added Ruric pointedly, "remember the birds. I don't want to be on this side of the river as long as there are patrols about scouring the woods. The sooner we can put the river between us and our pursuers, the better. So come. You've rested long enough. The bridge cannot be far and then we will see to supper, eh?"

Wearily, Cornelius retied his sandal and rose to his feet. Much to his relief, the bridge that Ruric spoke of was nearer than they thought. After five minutes of walking, they rounded a small bend in the trail and bumped straight into the bridge itself. Cornelius could see it was typical of the type constructed by the corps of engineers, the cohortis fabrum. Logs, planed to a square of four inches a side, were fit into a frame based upon a larger square and joined at the corners by a crisscross of spars, all held together by metal fasteners and nails. A parallel line of large tree trunks was driven into the rock bed of the river upon which the frame was assembled in the shape of an arc spanning the distance from bank to bank. Once the superstructure was in place, heavy wooden planks were laid across it, providing a stout roadway easily capable of accommodating four legionaries marching shield to shield at one time.

"Thank the gods we got here before Arminius," commented Ruric briskly. "I don't mind telling you I was afraid he may have already been here ahead of us and destroyed the bridge. Come on, let's cross." Once safely on the other side, Ruric put his hand to Cornelius' shoulder, telling him to stop. Slipping his dagger from its sheath, Ruric began to cut the large rope that was knotted to a great oak, providing an anchor for the bridge.

"What are you doing?" yelped Cornelius, pulling the German's arm away from the tree. "You can't do that! This is a Roman bridge!"

Ruric stood up and eyed the Roman sternly. "Cornelius, think! If we destroy the bridge, the only way they can follow is to go around the river, which I have told you will take at least three days. If we destroy it, we rob Arminius of the ability of throwing the bulk of his forces at Aliso and against the Rhine defenses any time soon. It will give Rome the time she needs to stabilize the frontier. Now, if you wish to serve your country, you will go and cut the other side while I cut this one."

Again, Cornelius found himself marveling at the Roman sensibility of Ruric's mind. The thought of thousands of defenseless citizens and allies alike in the huge province of Gaul at the mercy of an invasion of bloodthirsty barbarians streaming unopposed over the frontier caused him to visibly pale. For if Gaul were to succumb to the hand of the German conqueror, than Rome's greatest fear would be realized. For the first time in four hundred years, a northern army would once again be encamped upon the Campus Martius. The City, the People, the Empire. All would be lost. He closed his eyes and shuttered at the thought.

"Cornelius! Stop daydreaming and come and help!"

Cornelius' eyes snapped open. "Yes, yes, you're right, of course. I'll get the other anchor." Together the two men set about their task and before long, the ropes were severed. The bridge began to creak and groan as its loosened timbers struggled against gravity and the stiff current of the water below. For a few unsure minutes, they watched as the bridge shifted and shivered but refused to buckle.

"Damn you Romans!" swore Ruric, wiping his mouth with the back of his hand. "Why do you have to build things so well?" Yet even as the words left his lips, the bridge gave a final loud, grating cry before collapsing, sending broken planks and timbers crashing into the moving water.

"Now," said Cornelius as he replaced his sword in its scabbard. "Where is that supper?"

⌘ ⌘ ⌘

"Well? What did you find?"

Arnulf the tracker bowed obsequiously before the impatient Arminius. "Alas, lord," he whined, "It is as you feared. The Roman bridge has been destroyed."

"I expected no less. Did the traitor pull it down or has it been destroyed for some time?"

"The damage is recent, lord. There can be little doubt it was the work of our quarry."

"It will take too long to rebuild it and even longer to go around the river," mused Arminius, not caring to hide the disgust in his voice. "We must find another way across and quickly. Arnulf, you had better pray your skill warrants your reputation. Your life just may depend on it. I can't allow a single word of what happened in these forests to be breathed into Caesar's ear before I am ready to move. It is absolutely essential that we keep these men from leaving Germany. Understand? Find a way across this river! Now!"

Arnulf saluted and scampered away into the underbrush, yelping like a wounded puppy.

XXX

The sparks from the fire flitted toward the ember silhouettes of the treetops, mingling in a luminescent dance with the night stars above. Cornelius watched from his perch against an ancient trunk with a lazy contentment; a by-product from one of the most satisfying meals he had ever enjoyed. Picking his teeth with a splinter of bone, he observed Ruric from the other side of the fire, as he busied himself carving the remainder of their feast into manageable portions for the next day's travel. How they had come by such a bounty was, in Cornelius' mind, nothing more than divine providence.

Once the bridge had been destroyed, they were freed to concentrate on their more immediate concerns, which for Cornelius meant answering the groaning of his stomach. Ruric advised moving on since there were still some hours of daylight left for which they should make the best use. Cornelius was pessimistic as only a starving man can be.

"We've nearly marched an entire day and I haven't seen as much as a mole!" he complained. "Are you proposing we strip the bark from the tree and eat it?"

"If we have to," replied Ruric in all seriousness. "But I have a feeling our luck is about to improve on this side of the river."

"We should have gone back and gotten more of that meat you were preparing when I found you," grumbled the Roman.

"Be at peace, my young friend," chided Ruric good-naturedly. "There is more than one deer in a great forest like this one."

Even as he spoke the words, the wood ahead of them bristled with the sound of cracking branches and rustling leaves. As they stood and listened, the sound became louder and more insistent; indicating that whoever or whatever was responsible for the racket was heading in their direction. Instinctively, both men readied themselves for battle. Cornelius eased the long barbarian sword from its scabbard while Ruric soundlessly fitted an arrow from the quiver into his bow of bone white ash. Muscles taut and ready, they waited with quiet expectation as the din drew nearer.

"What is it?" whispered Cornelius out of the side of his mouth.

"I don't know," whispered Ruric over his outstretched arm, "A bear, perhaps. Maybe a wild boar. Be ready to strike when it clears the trees."

Suddenly, the forest seemed to part of its own accord. Out of the underbrush bounded the largest stag Cornelius had ever seen. Stretched to its full length, the animal sought to clear the open space before the two hunters in a single, powerful leap. The rays of the dying afternoon sun had the effect of transforming the stag's brown pelt into a sheen of dull gold. Eyes of dark musk blazed out of an exquisitely sculptured skull, crowned by a cluster of antlers like that of a spreading oak. So breath taking was the sight that Cornelius was momentarily frozen with wonder. It was as if one of fanciful creatures portrayed in the mosaics of his father's house in far off Rhegium had actually sprung to life before his very eyes. Ruric, however, steeped in the hunting ways of his people, reacted with the swiftness of instinct. His bow sang sharply; the arrow flew swift and true to the target. Before the hooves of the stag could set down upon the ground again, the arrow found its mark in the mass of muscle clustered around the shoulder joint. With bone, muscle and sinew shattered and torn by the effects of the arrowhead, the animal crashed crippled to the forest floor. As it struggled to rise to its feet, Ruric yelled, "Quickly, finish it off with your sword!" Cornelius moved toward the injured beast seeking to plunge his sword into its throat but was nearly impaled himself on the points of its antlers as the maddened stag attempted to drive its attacker away with a sweep of its massive head.

Fitting another arrow into his bow, Ruric cried, "You fool, you could have been killed! Go around and come at him from behind so he can't use his antlers. Drive your blade into the back of the neck. Hurry now before he can recover!"

This time, Cornelius circled around the struggling creature and did as Ruric instructed. Stepping lightly so as to not startle his quarry, he managed to creep in close enough to deliver the required blow. Putting all his weight behind the pommel of the sword, he drove it into the neck of the stag. But even in the throes of death, the mighty animal possessed an unsuspected strength. To his surprise and horror, the stag thrust his head back with a force that threw Cornelius from his grip on the sword, still embedded in the animal's neck. He sailed through the air and landed hard on his back, knocking the wind from him temporarily. Ruric let a second arrow fly but it was unnecessary. By the time the projectile found its mark, the great stag was dead.

"May the great Hunter be praised!" exclaimed Ruric as he helped Cornelius to his feet. "See what a magnificent meal the Lord of the Forest has provided, eh my friend? Never have I seen such an animal! It could feed an entire village for a week! "

Cornelius grimaced as he walked off his injury. Talk of a 'great Hunter' and "Lord of the Forest' left him acutely aware of just who was responsible for their good fortune. Rubbing the back of his neck, he offered a wan smile. "If we stand here any longer, I think I shall faint from starvation! Let's eat!"

Ruric laughed and slapped him on the back. "You Romans! Always thinking about your stomachs! Very well. I'll prepare the meat while you build the fire. Come on, then."

Two hours later as dusk deepened into a depthless purple shadow, Cornelius enjoyed a feast he would long remember. Ruric proved to be an expert when it came to preparing and cooking game meat, using a variety of herbs and leaves from the surrounding wood to bring out the meat's succulent flavour. Cornelius hungrily gorged on the tenderly roasted flesh until he felt he had devoured half the stag himself. With a full belly, he sat against the tree and watched in fascination as Ruric packed the next day's provisions inside a wrapping of tender green leaves before placing them in his leather pouch.

"How far to Aliso from here?" he asked idly as Ruric packed the last of the provisions.

"It is ten miles between the bridges," explained the German. "If the weather holds and there are no other distractions, we should reach it just after midday."

"I for one shall be glad to see the last of this wretched forest," said Cornelius, tossing away the bone he was using to pick his teeth. "It will be good to sleep in a decent bed again, to enjoy the pleasures of the Roman table and hear the voices of home in my ears. All I want to do is to forget what I have seen and drown my nightmares in a cask of Falnarian wine."

"Do you still intend to go to Rome?" asked Ruric.

"Of course. Someone must impress upon the Emperor the seriousness of the situation here. Why do you ask? Have you reconsidered coming with me?"

Ruric shook his head. "Like you, I have a duty to attend. We both have masters who are awaiting our return. But it is time to sleep now. Take your rest and I will stand the first watch."

"Is that necessary?" queried Cornelius with a yawn. "I thought you said we were safe on this side of the river."

The German shrugged his shoulders. "At times such as this, I prefer to follow the Greek maxim: if you must error, error on the side of caution. Besides, not all the predators in this wood are human."

⌘   ⌘   ⌘

The dreamless sleep under which Cornelius had fallen was shattered by a commotion nearby. Struggling to gain his wits, the first thing Cornelius noticed was that the fire had dimmed to glowing embers. Its feeble light could no longer hold back the night's relentless gloom. Off to his left, he could hear the sound of scuffling and muffled groans and as his eyes grew more accustomed to the dark, he began to make out a pair of shadowy shapes wrestling near the fire. Reaching for his sword, Cornelius called out, "Ruric, where are you?"

From the direction of the struggle, a high-pitched voice protested in pain before it was abruptly cut off by sound of a dull thud. Immediately, the fight ended, as one figure grew limp and sank slowly to the ground.

"Bring a light!"

The voice was Ruric's, hoarse and breathless from the struggle. Cornelius retrieved a half burned tree branch from the fire and by blowing on the coals, managed to set it alight. Holding it over his head, he saw Ruric standing over the semi-conscious form of another barbarian. The man was slightly shorter than Ruric, his thin face spattered with dirt and sweat, an ugly goose egg already swelling on his right temple. Cornelius also noticed that the man was slightly hunchbacked.

"What happened?" asked Cornelius, staring at the dazed barbarian as Ruric held him up by the shoulders of his torn tunic. "Who is he? Where did he come from?"

In the flickering shadows of the makeshift torch, Ruric's features appeared harsh and malevolent. "About half an hour ago, I thought I heard a noise in the forest. I decided to investigate but at first saw nothing. I was just about to come back and wake you, convinced it was merely a night creature that happened to be passing close by when I saw a shadow near the edge of the trees. As I circled around, I suddenly came upon this fellow trying to creep towards the fire. I dare say he was just as surprised as I was. We struggled together and that was how you found us."

"Do you know him?" asked Cornelius again.

"His name is Arnulf. He has a reputation as one of the best trackers in Germany. He is so good, in fact, that even you Romans have employed him from time to time as a scout for the legions. I have no doubt he was responsible for leading Varus into the ambush in the first place. The fact that he is here now tells me he is presently in the pay of new master. A German master."

"Arminius?"

Ruric nodded. "Undoubtedly. And if our friend Arnulf here has found his way to this side of the Glorendel, then you can be sure Arminius is not far behind."

"But how did they get on this side of the river if we destroyed the bridge?"

Arnulf began to moan softly as consciousness returned to his scattered senses.

"I don't know," commented Ruric grimly, "but we're about to find out. On your feet, dog!"

Ruric pulled Arnulf roughly to a standing position where the bleary eyed tracker stood weaving on unsteady feet. Blinking his eyes to focus, his vision fell on Cornelius holding the torch above his head. The light of recognition immediately returned to his eyes.

"You!" he rasped, "You're the one we've been looking for."

From behind him, Ruric pulled one of Arnulf's arms behind his back and began applying a steady pressure. Barking in his ear, Ruric charged, "Curb your tongue, you moronic pig. We've a few questions to ask you! Tell us! Where is your master?"

Arnulf's face grimaced with discomfort. Between clenched teeth he answered, "Dead. He died fighting the Romans in the Teutoberg."

"Liar!"

Ruric pressed his weight down on the other's arm, bending it further from its socket. Arnulf howled in pain.

"If you don't want me to break it the next time, you will tell us the truth. Where is Arminius?"

"Ow, ow! All right! All right! He is camped an hour's distance from you, waiting for me to report back to him. I was instructed to pick up your trail if I could..."

"How did you get across the river after we destroyed the bridge?"

"Less than a mile downstream there was a large tree lying across the water. It must have been stuck by lightning during the summer. I couldn't believe our luck. We used that to get across."

Cornelius peered at Ruric through the gloom. "Then we haven't lost the barbarians at all."

"It would appear so."

"If that is so we'd better get going. We can't afford to wait for daylight."

"Agreed. But just to be sure our friend here doesn't bring our enemies down around our ears; I'm not going to let him out of my sight. He might prove useful if we run into trouble."

Arnulf attempted to struggle free from Ruric's grasp but his efforts were roughly stifled by a judicious twist of his already aching arm. "Ow, damn you! You're going to break my arm!" he wailed.

"I'll do more than that if you don't cooperate," threatened Ruric.

Arnulf ceased his resistance and spat with disgust at Cornelius' feet.

"You are a traitor if you help this man escape. Arminius has promised a hundred gold pieces for the warrior who brings the Roman to him alive. Think of it! A hundred pieces of gold! And all we have to do is bring him to Lord Arminius. We can share the reward. Fifty a piece. What do you say?"

Now it was Ruric's turn to be disgusted. Tightening his grip on Arnulf's bent arm, he said evenly, "I am neither a traitor nor an oath breaker like your master, you stupid son of a simpleton! Arminius has opened a box he can never close and I for one do not wish to have my fingers crushed when the lid is slammed shut again. What good would a hundred pieces of gold be to me if I'm dangling from a Roman cross? Now, get moving! Cornelius! Douse the fire and let's go before I change my mind and slit this snake's throat while I have the chance!"

⌘   ⌘   ⌘

"They were here!"

Arminius did not need the tracking skills of Arnulf to know that was true. The old campsite was ablaze with many torches carried by the company of men who attended Arminius as his personal guard. The barbarian leader stood beside the blackened remains of a fire as well as the scattered bones of a recent kill. He looked up into the sable night sky where a patchwork of autumn stars burned with cold luminosity. It was still a few hours before dawn.

Something had spooked his enemies to suddenly break camp in the middle of the night. His guess was that Arnulf had somehow blundered into their midst, warning them of their presence on this side of the river. Judging from the marks of a struggle near the fire, the fool had not only cast away Arminius' best chance for surprise but had also gotten himself captured in the process. No matter. Arnulf had outlived his usefulness at any rate. He already knew where the fugitives were heading. There was only one place they could go: the second bridge near the front gate of the Teutoberg Wood. Arminius was determined that they would not get there alive.

⌘ ⌘ ⌘

In the dead of night, the dark malevolence of the forest seemed to be magnified into a living thing. The natural ambience of woodland life, while hardly noticeable during the daylight hours, had now, in the dark, become harsh and shrill to the ears. With every snap of a twig underfoot or the ghostly hooting of an unseen owl, Cornelius felt themselves betrayed. Even the rhythm of their own heavy breathing sounded like the pounding of distant drums. The night air was so still, he thought the sounds of their passage must be audible for miles. It would not be long, he thought miserably, before their pursuers would catch up to them. Ruric on the other hand seemed oblivious to such worries. He had somehow managed in the darkness to find and cut a length of green vine, which he fashioned into a halter for his prisoner. Looping it around Arnulf's neck, he bound his hands at the wrists in front of him and wound the free end of the vine leash around his own wrist. As they began to walk, Arnulf complained loudly of the tightness of his bonds. Ruric tugged on vine, causing it to bite into flesh as well as tighten around his throat. "Shut up, toad," he threatened, "Or I'll pull so tight on this rein that your eyes will pop out of your head!" After that, Arnulf kept his peace.

Cornelius marveled how Ruric could hold their direction in the dark without the aid any recognizable landmarks. The blackness was so thick in fact, that Cornelius was unable to see any of the surrounding vegetation until lashed in the face by unseen branches. Uncannily, Ruric's course remained steady and unwavering; his pace focused and relentless. At one point, Arnulf's foot caught a root and caused him to tumble forward onto the ground, which in turn, pulled his bonds taut around his neck to the point of strangulation. Alerted to what was happening by the choking sounds being made by the struggling Arnulf, Ruric reached down and pulled him to his feet. Quickly he eased the noose around the tracker's neck so he could breathe once again.

"Are you mad?" gasped Arnulf finally when his breath returned. "Why not just strangle me and get it over with? What are you trying to do, run me to death? I need to rest!"

"I agree," interjected Cornelius. "I could use the rest myself."

"You can rest when we get on the other side of the river," growled Ruric impatiently. "Unless you prefer being caught here in the open ground?"

Pausing only long enough to drink from Ruric's water skin, they started off again. Before long, the gray light of dawn crept into the eastern sky, revealing a patchwork of shredded clouds. Still Ruric drove them on as the forest around them became visible once more under the light of the new day. Despite the weariness of his bones and his earlier fears of detection, Cornelius was thankful they had passed through the darkest hours of the night watch without incident. Wherever Arminius was, it appeared unlikely he was anywhere close by.

About an hour after sunrise, before the disk of the sun had begun to clear the eastern fence of the tree line, the sounds of the waking forest gave way to a new sound. It was the sound of murmuring water. Breaking through a screen of pine and tamarack, the weary trio found themselves standing on the empty riverbank. There was no sign of the expected bridge.

"Where is it?" asked Cornelius plaintively.

Ruric pulled the corner of his mouth back in a gesture of perplexity. "We must have strayed from our original line. We've come to the river alright but I can't tell if we're above or below the bridge."

"Can't you tell from the current?"

"No. Without another point of reference, I would just be guessing."

"Well, what should we do?"

"Let me think."

"I know which way it is."

Arnulf, who had taken advantage of the conversation by sitting down to rest on the bank, smiled smugly up at his captors. Annoyed at the man's conceit, Ruric angrily yanked on the vine causing Arnulf to howl in pain.

Cornelius put his hand out to stay Ruric's anger. "Easy, my friend. Let's hear him out."

"Don't be a fool, Cornelius," shot back Ruric. "He would sooner lead us straight to Arminius if we gave him the chance. And I for one, am not about to give him that chance."

The Roman shrugged. "What other choice do we have? If we guess wrong, we are just as liable to stumble into Arminius ourselves. I am willing to take the chance."

"Well I'm not!"

For a few moments, the two men eyed one another, as if testing the strength of the other's resolve expecting the other to back down. Ruric, however, was the first to break. The familiar grin reappeared, wiping away the harsh lines of anger from his features.

"Very well, my stubborn Roman friend. Have it your way. We shall see what this dog can do for us. But in the mean time, I plan to keep him on a short leash." He held the vine up to emphasis his point.

Turning on Arnulf, he threatened, "All right you puss-filled maggot. Which way do we go?"

Arnulf pursed his lips and shook his greasy hair. "Not so fast. My help comes with a price."

Ruric's anger flared again. "Gutless dog! You will be fortunate if I let you keep your life, you spawn of Hectate!"

This time Arnulf was uncowed by his captor's bullying. He knew full well who had the upper hand. "That's part of it," he replied airily. "When I bring you to the bridge, you spare my life and let me go."

"So you can warn Arminius?"

"You'll be across the bridge before I can sound one blast of the horn."

"But you will tell him where we have gone. It would not be long before he had ten thousand men before the walls of Aliso."

"Not Arminius. He has no siege equipment. None of his troops are schooled in the Roman methods of a siege. My Lord Arminius is smart enough not to get bogged down in a siege operation he can't finish. It would give the enemy more than enough time to get his reserves back onto the frontier."

"You sound more like a general than a tracker," commented Cornelius.

Arnulf shrugged. "I hear things. My Lord Arminius sometimes takes me into his confidence."

"Lying dog!" spat Ruric. "You are no more privy to what Arminius is planning than I am to what Caesar is thinking. I've heard enough of this foolishness!"

"Patience, Ruric, patience. I would like to hear more. You say you know of Arminius' plans? How does he plan to exploit his destruction of the Rhine army?"

"Are my terms accepted?" asked Arnulf warily.

"Yes, yes," replied Cornelius with a wave of his hand. "I promise on my honor as a Roman officer to let you go if you bring us safely to the bridge. Does that satisfy you?"

"What about him?" retorted Arnulf, nodding his head toward Ruric.

"The Roman speaks for both of us."

"Well?"

Arnulf unfolded his crossed legs and rose stiffly to his feet. "I'm satisfied. Come. I will show you the way."

Cornelius placed his hand on Arnulf's shoulder. "You still have not answered my question. What is Arminius planning to do?"

The barbarian stared hard at Cornelius, unsure of what to say. "If I tell you, will you free me from my bonds and let me walk freely? I promise I will not escape. I have pledged to show you the way to the bridge."

"No!" cried Ruric.

"Yes!" countered Cornelius, "But only if you answer my question."

"Cornelius!"

"Answer me!"

Arnulf put his bound hands out in front of him. Cornelius took his sword and slit the vines from his wrists. "One last time. What is your master up to?"

Rubbing the red bands of raw flesh across his wrists, Arnulf replied, "My Lord Arminius is planning to cross the Rhine frontier with his army and enter the province of Gaul. There he plans to rouse the enslaved tribes of the Gauls to rise up against Rome and take back their ancient homeland. Once the Gauls have been added to our numbers, my Lord Arminius plans to march on Rome and destroy the empire."

"After which he will proclaim himself king of all the territory north of the Alps, I've no doubt," said Cornelius, thoughtfully pondering the implications of Arminius' audacious designs. It was now even more important to reach Rome as quickly as possible in order to forestall a threat worse than that of the barbarian invasions of Gaius Marius' day.

Prodding the point of his dagger in Arnulf's ribs, Ruric said, "Now you can show us where the bridge is."

With the hunched tracker leading the way, the party followed the course of the river as it flowed due east. Unlike their earlier excursion along the overgrown pathway to the south, here the bank was wide and clear, making their progress much easier with less effort. When about a half hour had passed, the ground, which had been fairly level to that point, began to dip down under their feet. It was also the point at which the forest intruded again upon the riverbank, causing them to push their way through numerous overhanging branches. Ruric was careful to stay within a dagger thrust of his prisoner, aware that Arnulf might try to make a break for freedom in the bush. But the tracker seemed oblivious to the danger behind him. His attention was seemingly bent on following a trail only he could see. Abruptly, he stopped and put up his hand for silence. Ruric and Cornelius obeyed, straining to hear for anything out of the ordinary above the ceaseless murmur of moving river water. Turning slowly around, Arnulf cupped a hand to his mouth and whispered, "The bridge is just ahead. But I fear someone has gotten there ahead of us."

"How do you know that?" demanded Ruric in a scornful whisper.

"I know my business," replied Arnulf with professional confidence. "Follow me. Quietly. I will let you see it for yourself. Come on."

"Just a minute," said Cornelius. "Who is at the bridge?"

Arnulf shrugged. "Traveling merchants from the south perhaps. They often use the bridges to trade with our people. It might even be a detachment of soldiers from the fort. They have been sending patrols to the area of late."

"Or it could be your master," suggested Cornelius, sliding his sword from the scabbard and forcing the tip under Arnulf's chin. "And we are betrayed."

"I told you not to trust this weasel!" growled Ruric, sticking his own blade into Arnulf's side.

"Gentlemen," chided the barbarian nervously. "We made a bargain. I am an honorable man."

"Hah!" spat Ruric.

"Why would I do such a thing? It would mean my life. I promised to bring you to the bridge and I have done so. Why am I being treated so shabbily?"

"Because you're a liar and a murderer just like your master," replied Cornelius. "I fully expected treachery on your part. Ruric, hold him here. I'll scout ahead and see if what our friend here says is true or not. You'd better hope for your sake, Arnulf, that it is a cohort from Aliso and not a trap."

With as much stealth as he could muster, Cornelius edged his way toward a hedge of tangled evergreens. Sliding onto his belly, he crawled through the damp-smelling earth beneath the low-slung boughs of the trees until he came to a break in the undergrowth. Easing aside a leafy stem, Cornelius looked out and saw the bridge. It was a hundred yards distant and several feet below his vantage point which he could now see was the crest of the long incline they had been following. The evergreens seemed to mark the end of the trail. From their line the ground began to slope steeply down into a wide clearing encompassing both sides of the river. The bridge held the middle ground of the clearing. But it was not the welcome sight of the wooden span that caught Cornelius' attention. It was the company of tall barbarians who held the bridgehead, pacing back and forth with sword and axe in hand, their faces set in stony vigilance. He counted at least ten, guessing there were probably more scouring the surrounding forest.

Carefully he retraced his way back to where Ruric waited with Arnulf.

"Well?" whispered Ruric when Cornelius had sidled up beside him.

"It appears our friend Arminius has somehow managed to gain the bridge before us," replied Cornelius. "I counted ten at the river but there are probably more in the woods. Fortunately they have not destroyed the bridge yet."

"No doubt hoping to use it to march on Aliso and Castra Vetara."

"I swear I had no idea," said Arnulf trying to clear himself.

"Shut up!" hissed Ruric, slapping the tracker's ear with the back of his hand. "Who's the bastard who brought them here in the first place, hmmm?"

"Enough, Ruric. This is getting us nowhere. We've got to think of a way to get across that bridge."

"Well, for a start we can lighten the load," shot back Ruric, pressing his blade further into Arnulf's side to emphasis the point.

Cornelius shook his head. "He may still be of some use to us. What we need is a diversion to draw them away from the bridge. Any suggestions?"

"I can go and talk to them," offered Arnulf timidly. "Tell them I lost your trail somewhere back in the forest. I can convince them you're heading in the opposite direction."

Cornelius raised his hand to stifle Ruric's reaction. "Why would you do a thing like that?"

Trying to muster as much dignity as he could, Arnulf replied, "I meant what I said earlier. I am a man of honor. I did not bring you here to fall into a trap. I did it to buy my freedom. I am still willing to fulfill my part of the bargain."

Cornelius pretended to think over the offer, prompting Ruric to exclaim, "I can't believe you're even considering this! It's madness!"

"Nonetheless it's the only chance we've got. I am willing to risk it."

"Well, I'm not! Cornelius, the minute he gets to those guards down there they'll be on us before we have the chance to draw a sword. If you let this weasel go you will be signing our death warrants!"

Cornelius placed a gentle hand on his friend's shoulder. "Ruric, I respect your counsel. You have proven to be a true friend, not only to me but to Rome as well. But I am a Roman and I am bound by a code of honor respected throughout the civilized world. Forgetting the circumstances, I gave my pledge freely and I intend to keep it, even if it should mean death. You have been among us for so long and yet you still don't know us. If I should break my promise, how then am I any better than Arminius? You see now why I am willing to accept the barbarian's offer of help?"

Ruric shook his head in doubt. "Madness," was all he could manage to mutter.

Turning to Arnulf, Cornelius said, "Very well. I will rely on your honor, Arnulf. Go and see if you can move the obstacle from our way."

Looking from Cornelius to Ruric, Arnulf looked like a man who could not believe his sudden good fortune. Unable to suppress the grin on his face, he offered a mock bow. "I will not fail you, gentlemen. You may rely on me." Then he quickly scampered down to the line of evergreens where he turned a final time as if to see whether they were following him or not. Satisfied he was a free man, he disappeared through the trees.

Ruric faced his Roman companion with his hands on his hips. "Cornelius, I...." Cornelius cut him off.

Grabbing the German's arm, he pulled him toward the forest. "Quickly!" he urged, "It won't be long before they charge up here looking for us. When they do, the bridge will be left unguarded, but only for a moment. We will have only one chance to cross it."

"Brilliant!" exclaimed Ruric, laughing and slapping Cornelius on the shoulder. "I should have thought of it myself! Using Arnulf as a diversion to create a diversion. A pity you were not the one in command of the legions! Arminius would now be the rabbit and we would be the hounds!"

Keeping low to the ground to hide their movements, the two men crouched through the undergrowth tracing a semi-circular line parallel with the river itself. The success of Cornelius' plan rested on how the barbarians would react. He was counting on Arnulf being convincing enough to send the tribesmen clamoring up the bank to where they believed their quarry would be obligingly waiting. Meanwhile, he and Ruric would come out into the clearing at a point opposite the bridge where the ground was flat and the trees less confining. They would then sprint the last thirty or so yards to the bridge and freedom, hopefully before their pursuers even realized they had done so. As they neared the spot where they planned to make their break, they were startled by the sudden piercing wail of the barritus. The tracker had apparently not disappointed them. The warriors were even now in full cry, brandishing their weapons and running for the far embankment with Arnulf close on their heels, intent on betrayal. And just as Cornelius had hoped, the bridge was left open.

"It's now or never!" cried Ruric. "See you on the other side!"

The German bolted into the clearing and headed straight for the bridge. Cornelius was three strides behind, his pace slowed by the added weight of his cuirass and balteus. Nearing the bridge, Cornelius could see that it was positioned between two large oaks acting like natural columns to which the support ropes and beams of the structure were attached. Ruric was a step away from mounting the threshold when a figure stepped out from behind one of the oaks and struck him in the side. The blow sent him tumbling through the air, his body like a rag doll, turning a complete summersault before crashing motionless to the ground. His heavy breathing was proof that the blow was not mortal.

Stunned by the sudden attack, Cornelius stopped dead in his tracks and gaped at the perpetrator. Arminius stood between the Roman and the bridge, his handsome face twisted by a wicked grin of triumph, a great broadsword tracing the air in small circles in front of him.

"So you thought you could escape my justice, eh my Roman friend? I knew I could trust that fool Arnulf to bring you to me eventually. Well, before I'm through, you and this traitor will wish you had died with the others. Who shall be first, hmmm? The traitor or the coward?"

Cornelius peered into the boiling eyes of his adversary and saw no mercy reflected there. For a moment his eyes flickered over Arminius' shoulder to the bridge now so tantalizingly close.

"You'll never make it," chuckled Arminius softly. "You will have to get by me first and even if you do, it will not be long before my men return. Face it, my friend; your fate is sealed. Just like that fool Varus. And I will have just as much pleasure dispatching you as I did him!" Arminius suddenly lunged to the attack, aiming a thrust toward Cornelius' throat. Without thinking, the soldier's instinct responded in Cornelius. Swiftly he parried Arminius' attack with his own blade, deflecting it harmlessly out of the way. The German leader recovered his momentum by pivoting around on the balls of his feet and arcing his blade in the opposite direction towards Cornelius' open side. Nimbly, Cornelius bent at the knees and hopped back out of Arminius' range. As he did so, he could hear the metallic whisper of the sword pass over his head. Anger welled up in his breast as the realization dawned on him that here was the man responsible for the destruction of all he had held so dear; the men who had shared his tent and fatigues as family, the officers whose experience and bravery were likely irreplaceable to the Roman cause in Germany, barbarians like Ruric who were determined to remain loyal to Rome despite the cost. But most of all, the face of Gaius Silvanius, a man who had become as close as a brother, swam before his eyes. It was for him that the fire of revenge was now kindled full blown in his heart. Here was the enemy who was responsible for all his grief!

Cornelius gritted his teeth and swung his barbarian sword with all his might. Seeing the danger, Arminius brought his own blade up to block it. The two swords met with a jarring clash that threw off sparks at the point of contact. Arminius stumbled backwards a few steps before regaining his balance. Raising his weapon to counterattack, he stared at it with eyes widened with astonishment. His blade had been broken in half.

Tossing the damaged weapon away, Arminius pulled his dagger from its sheath and then cupped his hand to his mouth, emitting a shrill, piercing cry. Looking back at Cornelius who stood panting waiting to renew the attack, he said, "A broken sword won't get you across the bridge. My men are on their way. There's no escape, Roman. None."

A strangled cry of rage and frustration rose out of Cornelius' soul as he came at the barbarian chieftain with his sword poised above his head. Arminius stood his ground coolly allowing the Roman to get within an arm's length. Then in one swift move, he sidestepped Cornelius' assault, grabbing him by the arm and flipping him over his hip to the ground. The maneuver dislodged the sword from Cornelius' hand, disarming him and leaving him pinned beneath Arminius' knees, the German's dagger at his throat.

"Did I not tell you escape was useless?" he clucked, his tone low and menacing. "Yet because of you, I will need a new sword. No matter. I will take yours. It was poor Gainas' after all. But enough talk. We must finish our business; you and I. Greet that stupid old man Varus when you reach the underworld and tell him who it was that sent you there. He will know only too well. Farewell, centurion."

Cornelius squeezed his eyes shut, steeling himself for the sting of the dagger and the blackness of death that would surely follow. Instead, he felt the weight on his shoulders and chest suddenly lift. Opening his eyes he saw Ruric and Arminius rolling and struggling on the grass. Ruric had recovered his wits in time to save Cornelius' life.

"Hurry, Cornelius!" he heard Ruric rasp as Arminius' hand clawed at the side of his face. "Get across, now!"

Cornelius leapt to his feet and picked up his sword, fully prepared to return the favor and kill the German chieftain as he wrestled with his friend. The warbling of the barrutus, however, caused him to stop and look back to the embankment where a knot of warriors was running to reach them. If he chose to save his companion, then the charging barbarians would waste no time in avenging their leader's death. If he ran for the bridge, Ruric was a dead man. Hesitation either way would spell disaster for both of them.

"For God's sake, go!"

Ruric's anguished cry settled the matter for Cornelius. Putting his head down, he raced toward the bridge. Bounding across the creaking timbers, he reached the far side and turned around. What he saw sickened him. Arminius had gained his feet and together with a circle of tribesmen was savagely slashing at the prone figure of his friend with flashing swords. Twice Ruric tried to rise and twice he was mercilessly beaten down under a rain of blows. Tears burned in Cornelius' eyes as he watched the last of his friends being murdered in front of him. Moved by an irrational urge to go back and join the fight, he took a step onto the bridge and stopped. Ruric had rendered an incalculable service to Rome with his life. If his friend's sacrifice was to have any real meaning, then Cornelius must carry out his original intent. He must go to Rome.

The bridge supports on this side of the river were similar to those on the opposite side inasmuch as they were tied with thick rope to the trunks of large trees acting as anchors. Cornelius was thankful to see that unlike the first bridge they had destroyed, this one had no columns supporting it from the riverbed. Its sole support came from the fist-sized cables secured to the great trees, suspending the wooden span ten feet above the water's surface. Cornelius set about to sever the first of these massive ropes with feverish effort, hacking at the fraying strands of hemp as chips of tree wood flew in all directions. He was almost through the first rope when Arminius roused himself from his blood lust long enough to notice what was happening.

"The bridge!" he managed to yell, pointing toward Cornelius as he worked. "He's trying to destroy the bridge!" At that moment, the last strand of the support cable split under a final blow of Cornelius' sword, causing the bridge to list crazily toward the water. Immediately, Cornelius moved to cut the remaining cable even as the barbarians made a mad dash to the riverbank. He prayed to the Unseen God to grant him the time and the strength he needed to complete his task. His muscles ached and burned from the constant motion of chopping at the rope, his sword growing heavier in his hand after each blow. As he worked, he heard the sound of barbarian feet stepping onto the creaking timber of the bridge's roadbed. His pursuers filled the air with curses as they found their footing treacherous on the swaying span. Grasping the very rope support that Cornelius was endeavoring to cut, they began to edge their way along the precarious angle of the twisting timbers. From his vantage point on the riverbank, Arminius shrieked for his warriors to close in on their quarry.

"Two hundred gold pieces to the man who kills the Roman!"

The promise of gold dissipated the fears of the clinging barbarians on the bridge. They abandoned their previous caution and began to leap across the sagging spaces of the bridge in an effort to be the first to claim the prize. Cornelius knew that unless his next blow severed the cable, the first barbarian would be on him before he would be able to send a second. Summoning the last reserve of his strength, he reared back and flung the sword into the center of the fraying gap of thick rope. Fatigue and haste combined to skew his aim. The blade nicked a piece of the rope before biting into the trunk of the tree where it stuck fast. To his horror, Cornelius realized that the cable had remained intact.

Frantically, he pulled at the hilt of the weapon but it would not budge. The lead warrior was now only three steps away. Behind him followed a line of eight others hanging from the support, their eyes filled with the lust for gold and blood. Cornelius whirled around to find himself staring into the fierce glare of a leering tribesman. His square face was split by an idiotic grin, the handle of a great battle-axe ready in his hand.

Suddenly, the groaning sound of splintering wood erupted from the center of the straining cable supports causing the barbarian to look back with alarm. The bridge lurched abruptly toward the water, increasing the angle of the timbers and throwing three of the tribesmen into the swift current below. The barbarian in front of Cornelius lost his balance in the shifting of the dying bridge and fell onto his back. Twisting to his stomach, he desperately tried to find a handhold on the slick timbers of the bridge deck but could not. With a cry of panic mixed with frustration at seeing two hundred pieces of gold slip so easily through his clutching fingers, the tribesman slid feet first into the river water. The rest of the barbarians hung on to the tottering trestle to avoid the fate of their foundering companions. Their weight on the severed ropes had accomplished what Cornelius' sword could not. As they clung to their precarious perches, the thin strand that had refused to be cut snapped with a loud crack. Bellowing in fear, the remaining warriors splashed down into the current of the river amidst the bobbing wreckage of the last bridge to the Roman frontier. Screaming for help from their companions on the far bank, they began to be carried downstream toward the heart of the Teutoberg. In an uncontrollable rage, Arminius struck Arnulf a vicious blow, sending the hunchbacked tracker sprawling senseless to the ground.

"Roman!" he shouted with seething fury, "Tell Augustus that I am coming for him! Tell him that I will not stop until I have burned Rome to the ground and wiped its memory from the minds of men! Tell him to be afraid, Roman! Tell your precious Emperor that Arminius king of the Germans is coming for him!"

Cornelius stood blinking in the bright sunlight unaware of either his surroundings or the bellicose threats directed at him from the other side of the river. From somewhere off in the distance, he heard a roll of low thunder. It was only after a few moments that he was shocked to discover that it wasn't thunder at all but the roaring of his own heart in his ears. Every muscle in his body ached to the rhythm of the pounding in his chest. Pain crowded in behind his eyes searing them to the texture of old leather. His legs and feet were leaden refusing any command to move. His arms sporting a patchwork of cuts and bruises courtesy of the last wild dash to the bridge hung like dead weights at his sides. He had reached the end of himself both physically and emotionally. Despite his tender age, Cornelius felt desperately old. The last desperate bid to escape had not only sapped him of the last reservoir of bodily strength but had unleashed a blinding sorrow upon his heart. The spectral faces of his friends and companions lying dead upon the killing field of three legions floated up before his mind's eye. One by one, they shuffled past Cornelius bent under the weight of unseen shackles, whispering in cold fell voices. *Why have you broken faith with us, O son of Strabo? Were you not one of us? Did we not call you 'brother'? Why then did you not follow us down into the pit? To what pitiless god do you owe your salvation even as our very souls are condemned to death?* As the ghostly cacophony began to fade, a surge of guilt rose burning in Cornelius' throat. Dropping on all fours, he retched out the meager contents of his stomach onto the hard ground.

After a few minutes, the wave of vomiting mercifully receded and stopped. Rising unsteadily to his feet, Cornelius turned and was startled to see a frowning soldier standing only a few paces from him, watching his discomfort without comment. Behind the man stood a company of armed legionaries all gawking at the ruined bridge and the sight of the enraged barbarians shouting and gesturing from the far bank.

The soldier took one look at Cornelius' wounds and his filthy uniform and then back at the shattered wreck of the bridge.

"What the hell is going on here?" he demanded.

Cornelius made no reply. Without warning, his knees buckled beneath him pitching him forward onto his face. The smell of earth filled his nostrils, the taste of dirt like iron settled on his parched tongue. A wrenching sob rose up from the depths of his soul sending a spasm shuddering though his weakened frame. Before long the sobbing gave way to a flood of bitter tears.

End of Book One

NEXT:

Book Two: Rome

Coming in June, 2004

About the Author:

Richard C. Peele was born in Hamilton, Ontario, Canada. He attended McMaster University in Hamilton where he studied ancient and medieval history along with religious studies concentrating on Judeo-Christian civilization. After graduating *summa cum laude* in 1978 with an Honors degree in History, he spent a number of years as a full time musician before settling down to raise a family of four. He is currently married to his second wife Anne, a singer/songwriter and between them have eight children. They continue to reside with their children in Hamilton.

Printed in the United States
16579LVS00001B/169-186

9 781414 005546